Readers love
AMANDA MEUWISSEN

Coming Up For Air

"*Coming Up For Air* by Amanda Meuwissen is the first book that I've read by this author, but it won't be the last."

—OptimuMM

Interpretive Hearts

"This is my second book by the author and I've got to say I'm turning into a real fan."

—OMGReads

"I truly enjoyed this book and read it in one sitting."

—Paranormal Romance Guild

By AMANDA MEUWISSEN

Coming Up for Air
Their Dark Reflections

DREAMSPUN DESIRES
#77 – A Model Escort
#94 – Interpretive Hearts

DSP Publications
After Vertigo

Published by DREAMSPINNER PRESS
www.dreampsinnerpress.com

THEIR DARK
Reflections

AMANDA
MEUWISSEN

DREAMSPINNER
PRESS

Published by
DREAMSPINNER PRESS

5032 Capital Circle SW, Suite 2, PMB# 279, Tallahassee, FL 32305-7886 USA
www.dreamspinnerpress.com

Their Dark Reflections
© 2020 Amanda Meuwissen

Cover Art
© 2020 Tiferet Design
http://www.tiferetdesign.com/
Cover content is for illustrative purposes only and any person depicted on the cover is a model.

Trade Paperback ISBN: 978-1-64405-863-3
Digital ISBN: 978-1-64405-862-6
Library of Congress Control Number: 2020940964
Trade Paperback published November 2020
First Edition
v. 1.0

Printed in the United States of America

This paper meets the requirements of
ANSI/NISO Z39.48-1992 (Permanence of Paper).

To Meagan Hedin, who I will always share my deepest hopes and dreams with, and who understands how well a good horror story can still work in a romance.

CHAPTER 1

SAM KNOCKED on the paneling of the wrought-iron doors, trying to peer through the glass. It was frosted, offering no insight into what lay inside. Mr. Simons's instructions were for him to

let himself in, but he still wanted to announce himself.

Hearing no response, Sam tried one of the handles, and it gave way with ease.

"Mr. Si—" He cut off with a gape as he entered. He'd known the house would be impressive from the outside, but this was *Real Housewives* kind of ostentatious, opening into a huge two-story entryway with a grand staircase leading to the second floor.

The décor was antique and modern mixed, with standing radios from the '20s or '30s on either side of the doors, resting atop trendy black-and-white tiles. Two matching art deco tables bookended the staircase in similar fashion, sporting their own vintage radios. This guy must be a collector.

Good. That meant there would be even more worthwhile prizes than what Sam planned to steal.

"Please close the doors behind you, Mr. Coleman," a voice called from the second floor.

Sam obeyed, noticing how the opaqueness of the glass kept out any natural light. The nearby curtains were closed as well, making it harder to blink upward through the dimness and see his host.

Sam had ridden there on his motorcycle to throw off his new "client." Any other professional with his resume would drive something more practical. The bike added a distinctive edge, so that when his skills proved worthy, Mr. Simons would be that much more intrigued by him—and easier to con.

Little good that did when the man couldn't see outside. Sam openly gawking around the foyer like an amateur didn't help either. He was twenty-three, not a child. He needed to act like it.

"Mr. Simons," he said, clearing his throat to start over, "a pleasure to finally meet you in person. I hope you don't mind me parking my motorcycle in the driveway."

"Not at all." He must have seen the bike after all or wasn't that easily surprised. At first, he made a somewhat hazy figure descending the stairs until he was close enough for Sam to see him clearly. "And call me Ed."

Sam nearly gaped again, because *Ed* was not the old rich guy he'd expected.

First, he couldn't have been older than thirty, with well-coifed strawberry-blond hair, green eyes, and a tall, slender frame dressed primly—and maybe a little ridiculously with a sweater vest and bow tie—which all amounted to a nerdy boy-next-door who didn't seem to realize he'd grown up hotter than his wardrobe.

"It's a pleasure to meet you too." Ed smiled warmly and extended his hand.

Hot *and* nice. This wasn't turning out like Sam had planned at all.

"If I can call you Ed, then please, call me Sam."

Attractive *and* well-mannered. This wasn't turning out like Ed had planned at all.

Sam's skills and experience had been listed as housework, groundskeeping, scheduling, even personal finance—everything Ed needed in a temporary assistant. He hadn't expected someone so young, though, or with such a roguish smile.

Ed never realized how much he'd enjoy curls on a man, either, rich black with a few unruly ones falling into eyes that were almost black themselves and easy to get lost in.

Ed had to focus.

"It's cozy in here," Sam said.

"Yes, I keep the house fairly warm, since I tend to run cold. I'm sure you noticed." Ed waved his hand.

"Cold hands, warm heart, right?" Sam flashed a smile again. "Are you an antiquities collector? I couldn't help noticing the radios."

"A little," Ed admitted. "I love theater, but there's something special about purely spoken stories."

"A radio drama fan? That's rare. I enjoy the old oral traditions too." He cocked his head with a stretch to his grin that made Ed forget himself for a moment.

"I-I, um…. W-we should…." He paused to collect himself. "How about I give you a tour, and then we can discuss your schedule?"

"Sounds perfect."

Ed led Sam into the living room that spanned almost one whole side of the house and connected to the back patio that opened to the fenced-in backyard and pool. "I know it's a lot for one man, but I like my space, and I have numerous possessions I don't want to part with."

"I can imagine," Sam said, looking at Ed's framed photographs on the wall. Ed's three favorites were prominent: The Grand Canyon just after sunset, Times Square in 1957, and one of Big Ben first being built, two-thirds to completion. "This last one must be over a hundred years old."

"A hundred and sixty, give or take."

"Famous photographer?"

"Just a family heirloom."

"Must have been a cool family. I take it groundskeeping will include cleaning the pool?" Sam moved to the patio doors and pulled aside the fitted curtains.

"I like to swim at night under the stars," Ed said, holding back in the shadows, "so it can be your last duty of the day."

"You only swim at night?"

"I have photodermatitis and light sensitivity, so the sunlight can be dangerous. That's why I keep the curtains closed."

"I'm sorry." Sam let them fall back into place.

"The tools you'll need are in the pool house, but let me know if anything is missing."

"Stargazer too?" Sam indicated the telescope near the doors.

"Yes, I bring that outside on clear nights. I'm a Pisces myself."

Sam looked at him as if in surprise.

"Not that I take astrology seriously! I just think it's fun. Besides, the stars have their own stories to tell, and how people choose to interpret them can be fascinating, don't you think?"

With his grin creeping up again, Sam sauntered closer to Ed. "Pisces, huh? No wonder you like to swim. I'm a Gemini. What's that say about me?"

Ed felt his face flush as Sam drew closer. "Th-that you're adaptable, curious, witty. You can be the exact person someone needs you to be."

"Lucky you," Sam said. Then, when Ed stood staring like an idiot, he followed with, "For the job."

"Right! You're quite the Renaissance man from your credentials."

"I hope I live up to what you expect of me, Eddie. Can I call you Eddie, or is that too informal?"

Ed could usually read people well, but he didn't often have them in his home for very long. He must be imagining that Sam was flirting. "I don't mind." Although no one *ever* called him Eddie. "Shall we?" Turning swiftly, he continued toward the dining room and kitchen around the other side of the house.

Sam followed. "This Renaissance man can also cook. Did you want—"

"No need," Ed broke in. "I order in all my food and don't eat much. It'd be a waste to have you cook for me. You're welcome to help yourself to anything in the pantry or fridge, though, and since you'll be staying over lunchtime, feel free to make requests."

"I'll take you up on that."

They came around to the staircase again and headed up to the parlor, which Ed considered to be the best place in the house to read, since it looked out over the high ceiling down to the foyer. He still had a book resting beside the armchair where he'd been awaiting Sam's arrival.

"*The Tempest*?" Sam read the title.

"We are such stuff as dreams are made on, and our little life is rounded with a sleep," Ed recited, and then chuckled bashfully when Sam grinned at him. "I, uhh... like to reread classics between new titles."

"Impressive library," Sam said, scanning the bookshelf behind the armchair.

"That's just for what I'm currently reading or about to start. The rest are in the *real* library." Ed motioned for Sam to continue down the hall, enjoying the shock that briefly filled his features.

They passed a bathroom, the office, a guest room, and entered the second guest room that Ed had turned into his library. He'd not only covered every spare inch of wall space with ceiling-high bookshelves, but had placed standing bookshelves in rows like a true library in order to hold everything he owned. He rarely got rid of books and kept adding to his collection.

"*Harry Potter* next to a first edition of *The Canterbury Tales*." Sam sputtered a giddy laugh as he looked around, but then the humor seemed to leave him, and he frowned as he continued scanning.

"What's wrong?"

"There's no order to any of this. Not by title, author, genre."

"I was more concerned with getting them on the shelves."

"Is that how all your organizational attempts pan out?" Sam looked at him with something akin to pity.

"I just don't like the tedium of it," Ed defended.

"I meant no offense." Sam held up a hand and gave a short laugh—hypnotic really, or magical, because it loosened Ed right up again. "Luckily for you, I live for tedious planning. Shall we move to the master bedroom?"

Ed was close to reprimanding Sam for such cheekiness when he realized he meant the *tour*. "Yes! Last stop." He moved swiftly once more to prevent Sam from seeing how red his face had become. He'd avoided real interaction with people for so long, he'd forgotten how to act normally.

Or Sam was just that charming.

The master bedroom was large, with its own bathroom, and housed a four-poster bed and matching dresser, along with a shelf for Ed's cameras—some modern, some antique—but he spent the least of his time in that room. It was mostly only for his safe, set into the wall by the closet.

"You know, people usually put paintings over those," Sam said.

"I will eventually. I just haven't decided which one yet. Besides, I wanted you to see it since you'll be helping me with my finances. It mostly only holds cash and the logins to my offshore accounts on a flash drive. I can't let you have access to any of that or the safe, but you can see printouts of my holdings once we get to that part."

"No problem. That's all I'll need. Do you only collect cameras and photographs or take your own?"

"I take some. Whenever something beautiful catches my attention."

Eager to be out of the bedroom given Sam's effect on him, Ed started to lead them downstairs, but Sam pointed to the pull ladder at the end of the hall.

"That's to the widow's walk."

"May I?"

"Be my guest."

Sam pulled the string to bring the ladder down. The sun spilled into a little pool at the base, which Ed sidestepped with a simple pivot. Once Sam was almost to the top, he turned back.

"I suppose you can't join me, huh?"

"Still a little too bright for me. Go ahead."

Sam nodded and finished the climb. He disappeared for a spell, but then his voice filtered down. "You should bring your telescope up here!"

"I'm not a fan of heights either!" Ed called back. He could never quite get over that sudden feeling of vertigo when he was high up.

Sam returned and carefully replaced the ladder. "No basement?" he asked as they headed to the main level.

"No." At least, not that Sam needed to know about.

"Are you sure you only need me for two weeks?"

"We can play it by ear," Ed said, but he had no intention of extending the contract. Any longer would be too risky. "Shall we plan out your first few days?"

"Absolutely. I'm all yours, Eddie."

Definitely only two weeks.

DEFINITELY NO more than two weeks.

Ed wasn't like the others Sam had conned. Sam considered himself a Robin-Hood-for-hire, targeting rich assholes who had it coming. Granted, he kept all the money for himself, his crew, and his employers, but at least he only stole from bad people.

Until Ed, who didn't seem to have an ounce of badness in him and had no idea who he'd just let into his home.

Sam *Goldman*, not Coleman, who was currently scamming him for every cent in his offshore accounts.

"You got a full tour of the house, know exactly where the safe is and what's in it, and he's lax on security?"

"I even know the model number to the safe."

"Then all you have to do is play it cool for two weeks, and we can make a clean getaway."

"Yep."

"He probably won't even realize he's been robbed for months, with how much he has."

"Yep."

"It'll be the easiest job we've ever pulled off."

"Yeah...."

"You like him, don't you?"

Sam stared at Mim beside him at the table, his best friend and confidant, practically family, who knew him better than anyone—save maybe Gerry, the other member of their "family," who knew him even better from sheer force of will and prying.

Mim was tiny, blond, gorgeous, but packed a mean punch when she wanted to. She was playing with a knife, twirling it around her fingers while they talked, the complete opposite of Gerry.

"Do either of you know what this cord is for?" Gerry called from across the room.

He would have been an imposing man if he wasn't tall, dark, and bumbling more than any other adjectives, a cream puff in the body of a bouncer.

"I mean, it's HDMI to HDMI, which is always useful, but I already packed the other adapters except for what I need for my laptop. Although, since I have the others, I can probably get rid of this one."

"Gerry—"

"Only the moment I do, I just know I'm going to find whatever this goes to and wish I still had it. I better keep it."

"Gerr—"

"Of course, if I do realize I need it later, it's not like it's hard to replace—"

"*Gerry*, will you shut up?" Mim snapped, pulling him into their close-quartered conversation.

They shared the one-room loft. Logan, who owned Lucifer's Rest downstairs, had a soft spot for them, offering free room and board for doing odd jobs and occasionally bartending or waiting tables.

It was meant to only be temporary, but two years ago Sam had finished his twenty-first birthday passed out on that floor.

"There might not even be a payday," Mim said.

"What?" Gerry lumbered over to them, still carrying the cord. "What are you talking about?"

"Sammy's smitten with the target."

"I'm not—"

"Ew." Gerry stopped with a grimace.

"It's not like that. And he isn't some aging sleazeball. This one's different. He's young and handsome and… kind of stutters when he gets flustered."

"He's smitten with you too?" Mim groaned.

"Took to my flirting like he is."

"*Sam.*"

"What? I've flirted to finish a job before."

"Not with someone you like."

Sam fell silent. That was their one rule.

Assholes only.

The three of them had no one else in the world, only each other, grifters since they could fit a hand in someone's pocket. Well, Sam did the pickpocketing, Mim handled muscle, and Gerry was in charge of the technical side. They were criminals, and they enjoyed being criminals, but that didn't mean they hurt good people.

"So that's it?" Gerry said, sinking into the chair at Sam's right. "No big score?"

"I don't know, but I'm not telling the Cramers we're backing out of a retirement-sized payday after only one meeting with this guy. Someone this rich has to have skeletons in his closet. Even if it's also filled with sweater vests and bow ties."

Brock and Celia Cramer, an up-and-coming power couple who'd just moved to Riverside, had come to them with this job. It had seemed like a dream come true when they told them of another transplant, a full-blown whale coming to town and bringing a fortune with him. Sam had never done a job *in* Riverside before—he wasn't an idiot—but this time, they'd be leaving afterward, so it didn't matter. Finally, all the scraping by he and his crew had done over the years would pay off, and they'd never need to con again, at least not to survive.

He couldn't call it quits after one day.

"Aw," Gerry said, bumping Sam's shoulder. "You do like him."

"That isn't a good thing, Gerry. The Cramers are expecting us to finish this job."

"We could always do it anyway, even if Simons is a nice guy," Mim said, picking at her nails with her knife.

Sam and Gerry glared at her.

"Can't blame a gal for trying." She shrugged.

"If Simons is on the level, we'll bow out, but the Cramers swore he was a worthwhile target, so keep packing," Sam told Gerry, "and start working on how to crack that safe. Simons has to be hiding something."

ED WAS hiding behind the curtains beside the front doors, watching his neighbors walk up the drive to greet Sam as he arrived on his motorcycle. They'd been trying to "welcome Ed to the neighborhood" ever since he arrived.

They were a young couple, the wife beautiful, with dark hair and skin to contrast her blond, blue-eyed husband. They must be professionals of some sort, always smartly dressed in a pencil skirt and three-piece suit respectively.

Today, they had children with them, twins, he'd guess, about five years old. Ed didn't immediately hear what the couple said to Sam, but as everyone was smiling and starting to chat, he grew curious and opened the window to listen in.

"I have my own key," Sam was saying. "He's probably not in, though. Busy guy. Said he'd almost never be home, which was why he needs my help. I'm sure you'll get the chance to meet him eventually, though."

He was covering for Ed, even though he knew Ed was home.

"He'll be relieved to know there's law-enforcement so close by."

What?

Ed peered harder around the curtain and saw a badge on the husband's belt.

"*Detective* Neu-Ryan, is it?"

"Just Daniel is fine. And Marie works for Channel Five. There isn't much that goes on in this city that we don't know about."

Ed's realtor hadn't mentioned any of *that*, though he had been more adamant about not having neighbors too close, not what they did for a living.

"It's not as glamorous as it sounds," Marie said. "I'm a producer more than in front of the camera. But you have to tell us. We've been so excited about someone finally moving into this house, and he's been a complete ghost." She stepped closer as if to share a scandalous secret. "What's Simons like? Cranky old millionaire?"

Sam laughed. "You know, that's what I thought he'd be like when we first met, but he's young, interesting, charming. Seems like a really nice guy, just private."

Ed wondered if Sam meant all that.

"Dawn! Joey!" Marie chastised her children as they chased each other down the drive and onto Ed's grass. "This is not our yard. What would Nana Ryan think if you stomped across her lawn like that?"

"It's okay," Sam said. "I need to mow anyway. How about we agree to not tell Mr. Simons, and I'll give you two a treat?" He retrieved a pack of gum from his pocket, eyeing the parents for permission.

They nodded, and Sam crouched to the kids' level as they approached him.

"Ah, shoot, I only have one left, and I was saving it for myself. I know!" He pulled the lone stick from the pack, made to unwrap it, and then—it disappeared with a flick of his wrist and he began to chew. "You don't mind getting it slightly used, do you?"

Dawn and Joey shared a curious glance.

"You do? Well don't worry, I can fix it." Sam brought his hands to his mouth as if to spit the gum back into the wrapper, then with another flourish of his fingers, the untouched stick reappeared in his grasp.

Ed smiled at the simple sleight of hand that left the children looking enchanted.

"Brand new. But you'll have to share it." Sam tore the stick in two and handed half to each twin, who eagerly accepted their treat.

"Not bad," Daniel said, while Marie helped the twins with their wrappers.

"Comes in handy sometimes." Sam grinned. "It was nice to meet you, but I better get to work. I'll tell Mr. Simons you stopped by."

"It was nice to meet you too, Sam," Marie said. "Kids, what do you say for the gum?"

"Thanks, Mr. Sam!" they said in unison.

"Any time." He waved goodbye as the family headed down the drive, and then turned to approach the front doors.

Where Ed was still hiding!

Like a shot, he raced for the living room and turned on the radio. It was another standing model, but the inside had been replaced with a digital jukebox. Last Ed had used it, he'd been listening to '70s music, and "Crocodile Rock" blared just as Sam announced himself.

"Eddie? Clocking in for the day."

"Oh, Sam." Ed feigned surprise when Sam appeared at the entry into the living room. "I didn't hear you drive up."

"Wow, you're a bad liar," Sam said, setting his bag against the wall and moving to join Ed. "You're welcome, by the way. I got the impression you weren't the 'play nice with the neighbors' type."

So much for performing his own misdirection. "Like you said, I prefer my privacy."

"That wouldn't have anything to do with them being a detective and a reporter, would it?" Sam draped an arm casually atop the radio.

"Would you want that pairing as your neighbors?"

"Not really," Sam said with a laugh.

"You're very good with children."

"It's easy to be good with them when you can give them back to their parents."

Now Ed laughed, completely disarmed around Sam, which was a rare experience.

"You might not be a good liar, Eddie, but you do have good taste in music," Sam said, tapping his fingers to the beat of Elton John giving way to the Beatles. "Since we won't be taking a stroll with the Neu-Ryans any time soon, shall we talk taxes?"

TAXES, NUMBERS, probability, and projections—that Sam found easy.

People were complicated.

Planning a heist with a detective and a reporter next door was insane.

Funny how the Cramers never mentioned that. Maybe they didn't know, or maybe they had known and threw Sam into the lion's den anyway.

He tried not to let it get to him, especially not in front of Ed, who he was desperately trying to read for signs that he was not what he seemed. Sam hadn't actually noticed him listening in to his conversation outside, but he'd heard the way the music blasted suddenly in the living room and took a guess.

Ed was avoiding his neighbors. There had to be a reason besides sensitivity to the sun—if that was even true—or being antisocial. He was friendly enough with Sam.

Diving into his second day of work, however, turned up nothing. Ed had an obscene amount of money, but it was all inherited or growing interest. He had no need to acquire his possessions illegally. Sam wanted to believe there might be mafia ties or drugs involved, but Ed's only source of income was investments. Nothing shady, other than poor record keeping, which only hurt Ed, not the banks.

The only other possibility, if the Cramers' intel was to be believed, was some sort of John Wick scenario, but Ed was so not the type. His inability to take care of his affairs properly kept coming across as endearing. The only bad things about him were his disorganization and terrible sense of fashion.

Today it was a suit vest over a button-down shirt, like he should have been wearing a blazer and working in an office, but instead, he was reading in the upstairs parlor with his feet up, which were currently encased in bunny slippers.

"Please tell me those were gifts," Sam said, emerging from the library.

"No. Why? They're comfortable!"

"I'm sure they are."

Ed grew flustered and dropped his feet to the floor. "What are you holding?"

"I was cleaning the library and found this with the nonfiction." Sam held out *Dante's Inferno*, which had definitely been entertaining to find in nonfiction.

"I was going to properly reshelve it later."

"Eddie," Sam scolded, reminding himself of his strictest teachers—before he dropped out—"we went over this. Keep doing that and you'll be back to square one the moment my contract is over. Now, come with me." He grabbed Ed's hand, pulling him out of the chair to wobble after him.

"Where are we going?"

"Teach a man to fish," Sam said and dragged Ed to the library. "Now, put it where it belongs."

"I'm not a child," Ed huffed, wrenching his arm from Sam's grasp.

"And yet."

A moment of tense electricity passed between them, but Sam had been warring against Mim and Gerry's stubbornness for years. Just because this was a con didn't mean he didn't take his job seriously.

Finally, with another huff, Ed snatched the book from Sam's hands and shelved it in the fiction section under *D*, since they'd agreed that titles made more sense than authors.

After a pause, Sam plucked the book off the shelf to reshelve it over a spot. Maybe because he was still grinning, Ed started grinning too, and the next thing Sam knew, they were laughing.

"What about this one?" Ed accused, picking up a book Sam had set aside. "It's out of place too."

"That's because I was going to ask you if I could borrow it."

"You like Greek mythology?"

"There's something about the fantastical that grabs my attention." It was one of the few subjects in school Sam had enjoyed besides math, and math he'd improved upon after dropping out, though his credentials alluded to a college education rather than his GED.

"What's your favorite myth?"

"Hades and Persephone, no contest."

"Kidnapping and forced marriage?" Ed scoffed.

"I prefer the modern retelling, where it's a love story about two very different people striving against all odds to be together."

Ed blinked, like he wasn't sure how to respond to that. "Can you… tell it to me?"

"Aren't you afraid of my darkness, dear?" Sam quoted, watching Ed's eyes widen. "And Persephone said, 'No. You haven't seen mine yet.'"

The library was a whole guest bedroom in size, but it felt like a closet suddenly, as if all the shelves were closing in to push them together.

Sam stepped back. He had to be more careful. Flirtations were one thing, but he couldn't allow more. "A full retelling would take time. I should get back to work."

"O-of course. Maybe as a celebration someday, after your two weeks are up. I was always partial to Psyche and Eros myself."

Oh, he did not make this easy.

"In the meantime, take it." He handed Sam the book.

"Thanks. I'll bring it right back. I just want to page through it off the clock."

"No. *Take* it. Keep it. I prefer celestial bodies over godly ones. Call it a gift."

He made this impossible.

"There really isn't anything indecent about you, is there?"

"I-I-I… w-well…." Ed startled, and no wonder, because Sam hadn't meant to say that.

"Thanks for the book, Eddie."

"Yes. My pleasure."

Sam couldn't do this. He had to see Brock and Celia Cramer.

Tonight.

THAT NIGHT there was a clear sky, truly breathtaking, prompting Ed to bring his telescope onto the patio as soon as the sun set—and after Sam had left for the evening.

Ed was used to being alone, but as he found his favorite constellations in the sky, he kept turning his attention toward Gemini, wondering if the stars would be lovelier with company.

Sam had only been on his payroll for two days, and already Ed was getting used to having him around. Loneliness was like that, like hunger: easy to ignore when he had nothing, but getting a taste made his appetite snap its jaws like a ravenous wolf. And Ed gave in to his wolf enough already.

Still, the solace of the backyard seemed less satisfying.

"It's mine!"

"Now it's gonna be *mine*. Hand it over!"

"No!"

"I said, *hand it over!*"

There was silence, then a whimper, a sniffle, and finally, the sound of rushing feet. The owner of the first voice was running away, leaving the other behind.

Slowly, not wanting to make any noise himself, Ed put thoughts of Sam aside as he stepped away from his telescope to approach the right gate. The left side opened onto his driveway, the right toward the wood.

He opened it, his eyes piercing the darkness. The running feet were moving north, back toward the city, but beyond the tree line was a shadow, moving slowly east, away from Ed's neighbors and their young children.

Ed gave chase, brisk but quiet, keeping track of the shadow. Even as he moved farther from the lights of his house and backyard, he zeroed in on the figure that took clearer shape in front of him.

A man, haggard and bent, dressed in rags, carrying a knapsack that had recently belonged to someone else. He also carried a knife. He was a vagabond and a thief, willing to kill to take what little someone else had for his own. And now he was completely alone.

Perfect.

SAM HIT the ground hard, the left side of his face exploding in pain after the brutal punch he'd just received.

Perfect. That was going to leave a mark.

Alverez, the Cramers' top enforcer, reached down to grab him by the scruff of his jacket and hoisted him to his feet. Their other muscle, Fitz and Shaw, looked on ominously, while the Cramers stood farther back wearing cold, satisfied smiles.

"Wait!" Sam cried when Alverez readied for another punch. "Rough me up too badly and Simons is going to get suspicious."

"He has a point," Celia said, beautiful in a vicious way, like the prettiest of vipers, next to Brock, her equally vicious husband. Sam hadn't seen it before. He hadn't wanted to. He'd been too focused on the potential payoff. "Now that you're talking sense again, Sammy, I trust you won't say anything else as foolish as wanting to get out of our deal?"

Sam staggered as Alverez released him with a shove.

"She asked you a question, Goldman," Brock pressed. "Do we have a problem?"

Sam had gone to see them at one of the clubs they frequented. He'd expected they'd bring one of their bodyguards along, but he should have rethought his words as soon as all three followed them into the back.

"You said Simons was bad news," Sam challenged anyway. "When I agreed to this and told you my crew and I only steal from people who deserve it, you said Simons was the perfect target, but I haven't seen anything to prove that's true."

"So?" Celia sneered. "This is the type of score underlings like you can only dream about, and you're moping about morals?"

"Our intel says he's dirty," Brock said in a bored tone. "That's all you need to know."

"In what ways? How do you know? Who—"

"You're asking too many questions," Fitz snarled, the least threatening physically, but also the most unpredictable, with his eyes always bloodshot.

"Simons—"

"Won't notice the bruises on your friends if we take your insolence out on them," Shaw warned with a menacing tilt of her head.

Sam shut up.

They'd been so stupid to get into bed with these people without realizing that the real bad news was them. Maybe Sam was blind to Ed's true nature too. He couldn't be sure, but he also couldn't risk his friends.

"Are we going to have any more problems?" Brock pressed.

"No."

"Good." Brock nodded at Alverez, who moved too fast for Sam to backpedal, and a fresh punch struck him in the stomach, nearly dropping him to his knees.

"Bet Simons won't notice that either," he jeered, and gave Sam's cheek a pat.

Sam recoiled, slinking away slowly at first, then hurrying out of the room when they made no move to stop him. He beelined through the club for the street, fighting the bile that threatened to escape after that last punch.

He couldn't deal with Mim and Gerry's reactions, not tonight. He hadn't told them he was going to see the Cramers. He'd have to stay out, go for a walk, tell them to not wait up, and sneak inside after the lights were out. If he was lucky, he'd wake before them too.

Sam had to finish the job, sooner than two weeks if he could.

Even if Ed was hiding something, Sam didn't want to con him any longer than he had to.

ED DIDN'T want to con Sam any longer than he had to.

Sam was a good man. Thoughtful. Personable.

Attractive....

Which was why Ed noticed immediately when Sam strolled into the kitchen the next morning wearing a pair of sunglasses, as if trying to hide his face.

"Brought in your paper. Shall we see what the stars have in store for Pisces today?" Sam grinned as if nothing was amiss. "Here we are. 'The moon meets Pluto and opposes Mercury, stirring up intense emotions you want to get off your chest.' Well—" He glanced playfully over the top of the paper. "—I'm all ears."

"Your eyes."

"I said ears." Sam grimaced.

"Sam...."

"What?"

"What's going on?"

"Nothing."

"Are you drunk?"

"Of course not."

"Then why are you wearing those indoors?"

"It's nothing. You don't have to worry—"

Ed snatched the sunglasses from Sam's face, adamant because he knew Sam was lying. He could practically smell that something was wrong, like a tinge of copper close to the surface. Then he saw why as the light caught the fine contours of Sam's face.

Dark bruises were forming around his left eye and cheekbone.

"What happened? It looks like you got into a fistfight."

"You wouldn't believe I'm the type to do that, would you?"

"Then why hide it?"

"Because it's embarrassing. I took a tumble off my bike, but I'm fine. Luckily, I was wearing my helmet."

"Who's the bad liar now?" Ed said, and Sam sighed, looking utterly defeated, but he still didn't explain himself. "At least put ice on it."

"I did that last night."

"You should do it again. It's still swelling."

"I need to get to work. The schedule—"

"Can be adjusted. Now, stop stalling." Ed forced Sam onto one of the stools, and Sam didn't fight him.

He gathered ice into a dish towel, twisted the end of it to hold it in place, and returned to rest the cloth over Sam's bruises. Sam reached up to take it from him, and there was a spark, like a shock of electricity where their skin touched.

"Must be those cold hands," Sam said with a shudder. "Or your electric personality."

Ed snorted and sat on the stool beside him. "Are you okay?"

"I'm fine."

"But you don't want to talk about it?"

"I really don't." Sam closed his eyes, relaxing into the ice.

"Okay." Ed had no right to pry, but he couldn't help the worry he felt. The thought of someone hurting Sam made him want to hunt that person down and....

Well, best not to allow any more unplanned detours.

"You're wearing a bow tie again," Sam said after a few quiet moments, fighting what finally looked like a genuine smile.

"Yes. Is there something wrong with it?"

"No. It's fine, just a little... dated."

"You mean old-fashioned." Ed frowned.

"Well, unless it's black and accompanied by a tux, yeah."

"I've seen plenty of fashionable young men wearing bow ties."

"They're not fashionable, they're hipsters."

Ed gave way to a chuckle, unable to maintain his frown when Sam had so much warmth in his eyes. "Is it really so awful?"

"No. Some people can make it work. I just think you'd look better without it." Sam reached up, hesitated a moment, but finished the trek to tug on the end of Ed's tie. He had very deft fingers, even when only being able to use the one hand, and had it undone in no time.

Ed's eyes never once left Sam's.

"Magic," Sam said, pulling the tie from Ed's neck, rolling it in his hand, and then—poof—it was gone.

"Better?" Ed nodded at his attire.

"You could stand to lose the sweater vest too."

"Now you're just trying to undress me." Ed laughed. Then he realized what he'd said. "I-I mean...."

"It's okay," Sam saved him, smiling softly as he pulled the tie from his lap to set it on the counter. "Technically, I was."

Ed glanced down at the tie between them, if only to get the heat in his cheeks under control. "Shall we see what it says for Gemini?" he said, reaching for the paper. "'Break out of any restrictions that might be keeping you from doing what you want. Things should naturally flow your way, and you should be in a good mood for most of your waking hours.'

"What do you think?" Ed risked a glance up again, finding Sam's expression stoic. "Sam?"

"Sorry. It's just hard to believe you're for real sometimes."

"I'm hardly a saint."

"You sure about that?"

"You don't believe me?"

"At this point, I'm having trouble finding evidence to the contrary."

Ed felt his cheeks redden again. "Well, while you try to find my faults, why don't I make you some coffee, and we can multitask by going over those itemizations you wanted to start today."

"Deal," Sam said, smiling again, if a little somberly.

"And I'm sorry if I was a little rough earlier." Ed nudged Sam's sunglasses across the counter.

"Why don't you keep those for when the light bothers you? I don't really need them."

"Really?" Ed had never owned sunglasses and was charmed by the thought, picking them up to try them on. "What do you think?"

"You could still stand to lose the sweater vest."

Ed laughed and swatted Sam's shoulder. He supposed it had been a while since he'd rethought his wardrobe. As they chuckled, he set the sunglasses down again and started to fuss about the kitchen to make coffee.

Ed liked the way Sam watched him, the way he always looked at him with tenderness, even if Ed wasn't what Sam thought he was.

At some point, they discussed Ed's holdings and property ownership like the schedule dictated, but he wouldn't have been able to say at what time they left the kitchen.

EVERYTHING REVOLVED around Sam's kitchen—or Ed's lately.

Sam would rather be in Ed's right now.

"You idiot! Why the hell didn't you take me with you?" Mim griped, having finally heard the news about last night and getting a look at Sam's bruises. The ice had helped the swelling but not the ugly colors.

"It was a show of faith. I showed faith, and they showed me what a dumbass I am."

Gerry snickered, handing Sam a glass of water and some painkillers. They were gathered around the table again, since there weren't many other options in the loft. They rotated between sleeping on the bed, the pullout, and the recliner.

"Company wouldn't have changed anything," Sam continued. "There were three of them. Five counting the Cramers. I'm lucky I only got their fists, but I'm not taking any more chances. I don't need you two looking this pretty." He sneered as he swallowed down the pills.

"We could split town," Mim said. "Or take the money and then run."

"I'm not looking over my shoulder the rest of my life."

"And we're supposed to only steal from the awful rich," Gerry protested, "not sweet, blushing, perfectly nice—"

"I did not say blushing," Sam broke in.

"Swooning?"

"I said stuttering."

"So, he's not blushing or swooning?"

"He's... both. A little."

"Great," Mim groused. "Maybe try not making him stutter and blush and swoon, because odds are, you're still going to have to rob him or we're all dead. Even before we knew about your brilliant house call last night, we were already worried about the Cramers when Gerry overheard a little rumor from the new waitress."

"What rumor?" Sam asked.

"Lara," Gerry said dreamily, and then snapped back to attention. "Um... remember how the Cramers only just moved to Riverside?"

"Yeah."

"Well, Lara said she heard that in the last couple weeks, basically around the same time they moved here, there have been increasing missing persons reports and a mutilated body found last night."

"*What?*" Sam paled.

"It's pretty gruesome." Gerry had his laptop on the table and turned it toward Sam. "Someone got pictures and posted it all over online."

The images on the screen made Sam's stomach churn. He couldn't even tell that it used to be human. "Shit."

"Lara didn't mention the Cramers outright, but the timing's a little too perfect."

"We're not only dealing with scumbags," Mim said, "we're dealing with murderers."

"Is this a bad time to mention I'm pretty sure I know how to crack the safe?" Gerry said.

Sam scowled at him.

"It, uhh… has an electronic lock, so all you'll need is a specific kind of magnet. I already ordered one."

"Peachy."

"Anything else you haven't told us yet, Sammy?" Mim asked.

Sam bit his lip.

"*Sam*."

"His neighbors are a cop and a reporter."

"Fuck!" Mim cried. "We are so crashing and burning."

"No, we're not. I'll get us through this. I'll finish the job."

"But you're going to give yourself away if you keep falling for this guy."

"I'm not falling for him, he's just… easy to like. It has to be a lie, though. The Cramers still said they'd heard he was dirty. There has to be something I'm missing. Maybe he's just a talented actor."

"Sure, buddy, maybe," Gerry said.

But Mim shook her head. "I wish you sounded like you believed that."

"Forget the Cramers," Sam said plainly. "Start looking into Ed. Find me something. Anything. He can't be as innocent as he seems."

ED WAS not as innocent as he pretended. He should have let Sam go after two weeks. He should have let him go sooner. But they were halfway into week three, and he still didn't want him to leave.

It couldn't be his imagination that Sam seemed relieved every time he asked for another extension.

"Comic books?"

"Yes."

"You've invested $20,000 in comic books?"

"They're collectibles!"

Sam blinked rapidly, as if to avoid rolling his eyes.

"Is it that bad?" Ed deflated in his seat.

They were in the upstairs office at Ed's hand-carved desk, Sam in the roller chair, while Ed sat in the antique straight-back he'd pulled over from beside the large globe that opened into a hidden liquor cabinet. Most of Ed's possessions weren't from extravagant spending, though, just treasured favorites he'd had for years.

The comics, on the other hand….

"If you invested for enjoyment and like every single issue you own, that's your prerogative. If you invested for future gains, most of these are worth pennies now." Sam gestured at the computer screen listing Ed's impressive collection, which he currently had in storage but was hoping to move into the library soon.

"They're all really good!" Ed said. "Most of them."

Sam stared at him patiently.

"Some of them? What's so terrible about comics, anyway? You're young. You still like them, don't you?"

"You're not that much older than me, Eddie."

"I'm… older than I look," Ed said, averting his gaze to the floor. He forgot sometimes how young Sam was, given how good he was at his job.

"I like comics fine, but they're not a sound investment. You hired me to help organize your life. That includes investments, and comics are speculative at best, tricky to manage, far from liquid, and rife with fraud."

"Sorry. I'll stop buying so many." He just had a habit of clinging to the rare occasion when something modern struck his fancy instead of something from the past.

"It's your money. You don't have to apologize."

"But I'm giving you so much work to do!"

"That's what you pay me for, remember? But no more binging."

"I promise. I just wish I wasn't so bad at this."

"You'll learn. Or keep making excuses to keep me longer."

Ed looked at Sam with a start. He was grinning, only joking, but he didn't realize how right he was.

A chime at the door interrupted anything else they might have said.

"I'll get it," Sam offered, like he always did, rising from the desk to head downstairs.

Ed followed a moment later, swift and stealthy so Sam wouldn't notice him, and hid in the dining room to watch.

"Mr. and Mrs. Neu-Ryan," Sam greeted at the door. "Always a pleasure."

Them again. They never took the hint.

"Hi, Sam." Marie smiled.

"We're so glad we caught you," Daniel said, all smiles and friendliness too. "Is Mr. Simons in?"

"Just missed him. Maybe next time."

Sam never said otherwise, even though Ed hadn't asked him to lie.

Daniel held a nondescript box and lifted the lid to show off a pie—coconut cream, Ed would guess. "We made one too many for the station's potluck today. It's meant for both of you, if you'll take it."

"Thanks. I'm sure Ed will appreciate the gesture once he gets home." Doubtful.

"We also wanted to drop off your invitations," Marie said.

"For what?"

"Our annual barbecue." She handed him two handsomely scripted envelopes. "One for each of you."

"I'll pass on the message, but with Ed's condition, he might not go for it."

"The sun sensitivity, sure, but we hope he'll make an exception," Daniel said. "There'll be plenty to do indoors too. I can't believe we still haven't met him yet. We know you're scheduled to end your time here soon, but you're more than welcome to come to the barbecue even if your contract's over by then."

"It definitely will be. I'm already overstaying my welcome."

"Nonsense," Marie said. "Mr. Simons clearly doesn't think so if he keeps requesting you longer. Maybe this could turn into a full-time position."

"I don't think that's possible. I have another contract starting soon. I really can't stay after this week."

Sam had been saying that since last Friday, that he couldn't extend his time too many more days or his other employers might give him the ax, but Ed was still torn. He knew the danger increased every day Sam was with him, being in his home, a part of his life, but the unique hunger Ed felt around him wasn't going away.

He couldn't remember the last time he'd been so drawn to someone.

"Seriously, Sam, think about it," Daniel said, stepping up to the threshold to speak more hushed, even though, as far as they knew, there was no one to overhear them. "With all the missing persons lately, we worry Mr. Simons might become a target, living out here alone in such a nice house with so much… stuff." He eyed the lavish antiques visible from the foyer. "It's not quite public yet, but… we found another body."

Having a homicide detective next door was troublesome, but it was sweet that he seemed genuinely concerned for Ed, even if that concern was misplaced.

"I appreciate the warning, but you can relax," Sam said. "The security around here has been one of my top priorities. Thanks for the pie and invites. I'm sure we'll see each other soon."

Daniel nodded, but then scrunched his brow before stepping back as he looked once more around the foyer. "He really keeps it dark in there, doesn't he?"

"You get used to it."

"The Neu-Ryans again?" Ed said as soon as Sam closed the door, stepping from the dining room.

"They brought pie this time. Dastardly of them, wasn't it?" Sam said, taking the box past Ed into the kitchen with the invitations balanced on top.

"You can go if you like. To the barbecue."

"With you? Maybe you'll luck out and it'll be a cloudy day."

"No, thank you."

"It wouldn't kill you to invite them over for dinner." Sam opened the box on the kitchen island and moved to grab a knife—then grabbed a fork instead. "Or even a conversation."

"What are you doing?" Ed ignored his comments as Sam bent over the box.

"Are you going to have any?"

"No."

"All right, then." Sam dug in, taking a large bite with his fork and licking away the cream that caught on his lips. "Delicious."

He really would be....

"May I ask a question?"

"Huh?" Ed straightened, torn from his staring. "Certainly."

"Agoraphobic?"

"No," Ed said with a laugh. "I love open spaces. I go for walks all the time."

"I'll have to take your word for it. So, you only avoid people?"

"I avoid the sun."

"Then invite your neighbors over for dinner."

"I'm... not good at connecting."

"You connect fine with me."

"It's harder when there are more."

"You mean crowds?"

"Why so many questions all of a sudden?" Ed groused. He kept eyeing Sam's renewed forkfuls with envy, but pie wasn't what he wanted.

Sam didn't answer him but took another generous bite, chasing every morsel of custard and cream and holding Ed's gaze as if daring him to drop his eyes to his lips.

Ed dropped them to the counter. "I move so frequently, it gets harder as I get older to say goodbye."

"No family or friends and no desire to make any. Sounds lonely," Sam said, foregoing his fork finally and taking a large swipe at the top of the pie with his finger, drawing Ed's attention again as he brought it to his mouth.

"Sometimes...."

"Maybe some unexpected connections could be good for you."

"Yes... maybe."

"Like dinner." Sam took another swipe and popped it into his mouth.

"Or that finger."

Sam froze, eyes snapping up, finger still caught between his lips.

"Sorry!" Ed jerked upright, having sunk to his elbows while watching Sam. "I am so sorry. I can't believe I said that. You should go," he rushed on when Sam opened his mouth to speak. "It's been a long day. But you'll... come back tomorrow, won't you?"

Sam huffed a shaky chuckle. "I can, but we have to wrap up. I'm committed to that other offer, and I've already been postponing—"

"I know. End of the week? Through Friday? Please, we still have so much to cover."

"Okay. I can make that work." Sam closed the pie box, taking the fork and one of the invitations. After setting the fork in the dishwasher, he made a show of sticking the invitation to the fridge.

"Point taken," Ed said, not that he had any intention of making nice with the Neu-Ryans once Sam was gone.

Gone....

"And Sam," Ed added when Sam made to leave. "If Friday's going to be your last day, maybe you can finally tell me your version of Hades and Persephone."

"Sure," Sam said with a soft smile. "Why not? See you tomorrow?"

"Tomorrow," Ed said, wishing he could hold off the end of the week for as long as possible.

END OF the week. Final warning.

Sam noticed the text message as soon as he pulled up to Lucifer's Rest. He knew he'd been stalling, hoping to stumble across some vice or evil deed to justify robbing Ed, but they'd found nothing. At first it had been easy to make excuses, because Ed was the one requesting an extension, but the Cramers wouldn't wait much longer.

Worse was that it was only getting harder to be around Ed, their flirting becoming more blatant even without trying. Sam certainly hadn't meant to be so obscene with that pie, just like he didn't think Ed had meant to imply he'd enjoy licking it off him.

Sam shouldn't be pushing Ed toward a friendship with a detective and a reporter, though. They were nice, wholesome even, but not stupid. They might figure things out before Sam made his getaway. He just hated the thought of Ed being out there all alone after he left.

Especially with murderers in their midst.

Shaking his head, Sam shoved his phone back into his pocket without answering. He'd deal with them later.

The pie probably hadn't fared too well in the compartment of his bike seat, but it would still taste good, he figured, as he retrieved it and headed into the bar. Mim and Gerry were in their usual booth, waiting for him. Lara was at the table, a pretty little thing with dark hair. Gerry was smiling dopily at her while she took their order.

She had remarkable patience, since Gerry tended to fawn without ever making a move. She always made a point to be their server, though.

Sam started toward them but hadn't taken more than two steps before a pair of rough hands seized him by the shoulders, and the next thing he knew, he was being shoved into the men's room. The pie thudded to the floor as he was slammed up against the wall.

"Hey there, Sammy. Having trouble getting your text messages?" Alverez yanked him forward to slam him back again, turning his vision spotty when his head made impact.

"I-I got the message!"

"You didn't answer, and that got us all concerned."

"I was driving!"

"Excuses, excuses."

Alverez made to yank Sam forward again, but Shaw and Fitz came up on either side of him like a silent warning to hold back—Good Cop, Bad Cop, *Worse* Cop, only Sam didn't know which was which.

"Next time you get a message, answer," Alverez said, making a show of smoothing out Sam's shirt for him.

"I thought compliance was implied."

"Or you're chickening out," Shaw said. "With the way you've been stalling—"

"That's Simons's fault. I can't let him grow suspicious. Timing is everything. The neighbors—"

"We don't care about the neighbors," Fitz barked. "You knew there'd be risks. You agreed to this job as soon as you heard the price tag."

"Because I didn't know who I was working for!" Sam growled.

Alverez made to grab him again, but Shaw moved in faster, suddenly going from being at Sam's side to in his face with her forearm pressed to his windpipe.

He wanted to thrash back, ram his head into hers, and fight like hell, but that momentary surge of panic and rage was squelched by common sense. The missing persons reports kept getting worse, a new body found each week, and it would be too easy for him to become the next one.

"Now, now, Sammy boy," Shaw warned, "I thought we were friends."

She laughed, and the others joined her.

"Do your job and we won't have to get friendly again," Alverez said through dwindling chuckles, while Sam fought to take a deep breath with Shaw's arm still pressing on his throat. "You'll get your cut. Five percent."

Sam coughed and wheezed when Shaw released him. "It was… supposed to be ten."

"Consider it an inconvenience fee," Fitz said. "Take any longer and the next thing we'll be cutting into will be more personal." He pulled a switchblade with a jarring snap.

They laughed again and moved for the door, Alverez making a point to step on the pie box along the way. Fitz left last, barely bothering to hide his knife before passing a bystander in the hall.

Mim. *Shit*.

If Sam hadn't locked eyes with her, he would have stayed in the men's room longer.

"Five percent?" she said once they were alone, Sam having kicked the pie box into the hallway, too upset to pick it up.

"Five of what Ed has is still retirement money."

"Sam—"

"I'll handle it."

"You keep saying that, but then why do you look like you're still having doubts?"

Because he'd just been threatened by a knife, and Ed would have no idea how to handle people like that. Sam wasn't filled with doubt; he was filled with resolve. If he didn't finish the job, the Cramers might send those three.

Besides, Sam used to think he'd do anything to get out of Riverside and live easy, but he'd do worse to keep his life, even if it meant betraying a good man.

"He's decent. Sweet. Just isolated. I can't help feeling bad for him."

"You be sure and tell that to Bonnie and Clyde's cronies when they're breaking Gerry's legs."

Sam winced.

Then sighed.

"Sammy, you can't."

"I know. I just wish things were different." He finally bent to pick up the pie box. "Guess I should throw this away."

"What is it?"

"Coconut cream from the oblivious neighbors."

"Gerry will eat it." She offered a wry grin, and Sam chuckled despite himself.

"Come on. Instead of the quiet evening I promised him, I have two days to convince the world's biggest homebody that he needs to go out Friday night."

"OUT? WITH you?" Ed blinked at Sam, forgetting tact or subtlety whenever Sam flirted with him—which was often—but especially when he stood close, eyes flicking down and up his body with promise.

"We can still talk myths when we get back."

"I-I...."

"Please?"

Oh, that word was unfair coming from Sam. "I suppose I do need to get out more."

"Really? I mean, great! I thought I'd have to drag you kicking and screaming."

"It's not that I don't enjoy going out, I just… feel safer at home."

"Don't worry, I'll protect you." Sam grinned at him.

Ed blushed at the promise, though needing protection wasn't the problem.

"We'll do something simple with minimal forced mingling, I promise," Sam said, holding Ed's tablet with his calendar open.

They were in their chosen chairs in the office again, where Sam had been helping Ed move his entire datebook to digital.

"How about a movie or a show? We can get cocktails first, with a late dinner afterward. I'll keep my own drinking to a minimum and even DD."

"You mean drive us? On your bike?" Ed leaned back, torn between excitement and concern at the thought of holding on to Sam during the trip, feeling his pulse thrum beneath his hands and through their connected bodies.

"You'll love it."

"I… guess that could be fun. Okay. It's a date."

Sam startled, and Ed worried he'd said the wrong thing. He knew they couldn't be more than what they were, that he couldn't give in to their flirtations beyond a night out, but was it so wrong to want to pretend for a while?

"I-I'm sorry. I meant—"

"A date," Sam said. "Definitely."

Sam handled everything. Cocktails planned at a bar near the theater, *A Midsummer Night's Dream* playing, which was one of Ed's favorite plays, then dinner at a nice restaurant down the block, all close together downtown so they could walk between locations and easily escape when they were ready to go home.

Sam even chose something for Ed to wear.

"Are you sure I don't need a tie? It's the theater!" Ed said when he came out of the bathroom the next evening dressed in black slacks, a green button-down, and a charcoal gray sweater. With the black-and-gray peacoat, it was all very fashionable but still seemed too casual for a night out.

"No tie," Sam assured him. He looked sharp as well, in dark jeans, a blue sweater, and a heather-gray blazer.

For their date.

"I can't believe I'm finally going to see you eat," Sam said.

"I… eat."

"Never in front of me."

"Well… tonight will be a first for many things, then."

Sam gazed at Ed like he was trying to memorize how he looked. "Come here, Eddie. We have time yet, but there's something I've been wanting to do."

He grasped Ed's hand, and for a moment, Ed thought he was going to kiss him right there in the bedroom, but then he pulled him into the hallway and tugged on the cord for the ladder up to the widow's walk.

"Sam…."

"Here. I grabbed these from your dresser." Sam handed him the sunglasses he'd given him. "The sun should be mostly set by now anyway."

"It's not only that. I really don't—"

"Just this once. I promise I won't let you fall." Sam grinned, and Ed scowled at him for the jab but allowed himself to be led up to the roof.

The light was still a little much, making him grateful for the sunglasses, but the sun had dipped low enough below the horizon that it cast beautiful colors across the sky. Since they stayed near the hatch, he didn't have to look out over the side but simply watched the sunset.

"Once upon a time," Sam began, making Ed's chest grow warm as he realized what was about to happen, "Hades was on Mount Olympus for a yearly council with his brothers. On his way home, he took the long route along a winding path down the mountain. He liked the gardens there, mostly because no one else ever frequented them, so he could enjoy their color and beauty without anyone gawking at him.

"No bloom he'd ever seen, however, was as beautiful as the goddess he found there that day.

"'What are you staring at?' she asked, completely unafraid of him, but also unaware of who she was speaking to. Persephone was in a foul mood after having a fight with her mother, who'd forbidden her to leave home. Willful and proud, she'd snuck out to the gardens anyway. She was all grown up and wanted freedom, but her mother still treated her like a child. She wanted to run away for good but had nowhere to go. She told Hades all this, still not knowing his name, just needing someone to listen to her.

"'You can come with me,' he offered, utterly captivated by this fiery flower he'd found. 'It's not beautiful where I live, but your mother could never reach you there.'

"Persephone, finally and truly looking at Hades, realized how beautiful *he* was and couldn't imagine such a handsome god living anywhere that wasn't remarkable, so she agreed. She got so lost in talking with him during the long trek down the mountain that she didn't realize they were descending all the way into the Underworld until they came to the river Styx.

"'You're him. You're Hades,' she said. 'Yes,' he answered, assuming their time together would end now that she knew the truth. 'Would you like to go home?' But she surprised him. 'Why would I want that?' 'Aren't you afraid of my darkness, dear?' he asked. And Persephone said, 'No. You haven't seen mine yet.'"

Sam's smile was soft, maybe even sad, as he returned to the quote he'd first told Ed from that story. The space between them kept shrinking, Ed drawn in as Sam looked at him, certain that Sam began to tilt his head closer too....

Sam's phone erupted, causing Ed to snap back.

"What is it?" Sam answered sharply, his smile gone now, and his expression only dropped further. "Tonight? I was on my way out.... No, I understand. You're right, I did promise. I'll see you in twenty."

"Something wrong?" Ed asked.

"I've been helping some friends with moving plans, and I guess this is the only night they can pack up the heavier stuff. I promised to help and—"

"Oh," Ed said before Sam could finish.

"I'm really sorry, Eddie. You should still go. Enjoy the evening. I'll reimburse you for my ticket—"

"Don't be silly. I'm sure I can find someone to take it at will call. I wouldn't want all your hard work getting me out of the house to go to waste."

"I'll make it up to you," Sam said, seeming more upset than Ed was, which he decided to take as a compliment. "I'll call a Lyft so you can still have as many drinks as you want and make sure you're safely on your way before I head out, okay?"

They left the roof and waited in the foyer for the car to arrive.

When it did, Sam opened the front doors for Ed and joked, "Are you sure you're not a ghost haunting this place and you can't actually cross the threshold?"

Ed smirked at him and made a grand show of walking out of the house.

"I stand corrected," Sam said, locking up behind them. The driver was waiting. Sam's bike that Ed wouldn't get to ride on after all was also waiting. "Goodbye, Eddie," he said.

Ed wished that didn't sound so final. "Promise me, before you start your other job, you'll come back sometime and finish telling me that story?"

"I promise."

I PROMISE.

It wasn't the first time Sam had lied to Ed, but it hurt the most.

He took a different route than the Lyft, making sure it was well out of view before he parked his bike away from the house in a place he'd chosen earlier. He walked back by cover of nightfall, so there was no chance of the Neu-Ryans seeing him.

He'd stashed the needed supplies in the foyer closet, in a backpack he'd told Ed was his change of clothes. It had been, but it also contained the tools he needed to complete the job.

Sam had hours to get everything done now that Ed was out of the house, but he planned to be swift, if also careful. He'd leave no trace of the theft or his presence there once he was gone, and maybe Ed wouldn't ever find out. He'd wonder, though, what became of Sam Coleman when he never heard from him again.

Sam ditched his blazer and took the gloves from his bag. He'd memorized everything he'd touched, so he knew exactly what needed to be wiped down before his escape.

With the curtains drawn, he hardly had to be careful with his flashlight as he moved through the house. First, he'd remove his prints, since that would take the longest, and as he did, he also claimed several priceless trinkets Ed had forgotten he even owned until Sam cataloged them.

Once that was done, barely an hour having passed, all that remained was the safe. The only thing Ed hadn't entrusted to Sam was the combination, but he'd given his whole life over to him otherwise, never once doubting that he could trust him.

Gerry was right; the magnet opened the safe in seconds. There was hardly any challenge to it, no obstacles, just the ever-widening chasm in the pit of Sam's stomach that worsened when he found an unexpected item among the others.

There was a photograph, beautifully shot in black and white, of *Sam* on the back patio looking out beyond the fence. Sam had no idea when Ed had taken it, though he had to have done so from one of the windows. He must have been embarrassed and stashed it as a memento.

Whenever something beautiful catches my attention, he'd said.

Sam felt two inches tall, but he had to push past it.

He put the picture back and grabbed the flash drive. All he needed to do now was copy it onto his laptop and he could put it back, so that if Ed looked in the safe anytime soon, he wouldn't notice anything amiss.

Sam also took one of the stacks of cash. There were so many in the safe, Ed wouldn't notice that either.

He opened his laptop on the bedroom floor to start the transfer, but just as he slid the flash drive into place—a car pulled into the driveway!

Sam stiffened. The lights were off inside the house; it couldn't be Marie or Daniel checking up on Ed when it looked like no one was home.

After snapping the laptop shut, Sam shoved it into his backpack along with the cash, but he put the flash drive in his pocket, not wanting to risk it getting smashed. There was no time to replace it now; he'd have to bring it with him.

He closed the safe and then hefted the backpack over one shoulder, padding quickly from the bedroom across the upper floor. Below, in the foyer, the front doors opened. It had to be Ed, but it had only been an hour.

Sam heard Ed's voice, followed by a second voice just as he reached the parlor.

"This place is amazing."

"Thank you. I'm very happy here. How about we have that drink on the patio, and I can give you a tour later."

"You mean of the bedroom?"

"Wherever you want," Ed answered tellingly.

Ed, who'd brought a man home and was getting him a drink, inviting him upstairs, only an hour after he and Sam almost....

Sam shook his head. He had no right to be upset. He'd ditched Ed. He was betraying him right now. But it still hurt that Ed could move on to someone else that same night.

Their voices drifted from the foyer into the living room, and Sam hovered near the stairs. Once they were outside, he could leave right through the front door.

"I'm glad you came out tonight," the other man said.

"So am I. I had other plans, but once those changed, there was only one thing on my mind."

"Using me to get back at someone who stood you up?"

"Oh no. Trust me, I would never have done with him what I'm about to do to you."

Sam was halfway down the stairs when Ed's voice trailed off. Ed didn't even sound like himself. Had Sam read him wrong? Was this the real Ed Simons he'd been waiting to find to make robbing him easier?

It didn't feel easier….

Sam kept going. He could still hear them out on the patio, the doors left open, but they were definitely outside. He should go. The front doors were right there. But as he stood before them, his feet turned toward the living room instead.

He passed the radios, the old photographs he loved, even one of Ed's horrible cardigans draped over a chair.

No, that was the sweater Ed had been wearing tonight.

Nearing the patio, Sam could see them through the open door. Ed was missing his sweater all right, and starting to pull the tails of his shirt from his slacks as he crawled into the lap of the man sitting in one of the patio chairs.

Ed prowled. Sam had never seen him prowl. Or kiss someone. Or touch anyone but him, yet now he was allowing this stranger to get very handsy on his ass and up the back of his shirt. The way Ed writhed into those touches caused spike after spike of ugly jealousy to tear through Sam.

It shouldn't matter. He was always going to leave. Nothing could have happened between them, and if he'd let something happen, he'd still be leaving. He couldn't change that.

But he also couldn't stand the sight of Ed kissing another man, in his lap like that, tipping his head back to lick up his neck, and then—

Tearing into his throat with his teeth.

Sam froze. There was so much *blood* suddenly, but Ed was quick to lap it up and not let any go to waste as the man tried to struggle, tried to push him off, but Ed held him down with no effort at all and drank until the man's eyes glazed over and he grew still.

The horror that churned inside Sam made him feel like he was going to throw up.

The missing persons, the bodies found, it wasn't the Cramers.

It was Ed.

Sam backpedaled into an end table in his haste to get away, and Ed's head snapped around, catching him standing there. His face was entirely different, twisted into an animal snarl with yellow eyes that glowed and fangs dripping blood onto his chin.

Two terrifying seconds passed with their eyes locked, and then Sam bolted for the front doors.

CHAPTER 2

ED WAS a vampire.

Ed was a *vampire*.

But that was insane—vampires didn't exist!

Sam still had his backpack, the flash drive in his pocket, heart hammering thunderously as he ran and ran and finally saw salvation—only to be seized two feet from the front doors and whirled around so fast, he thought a tornado caught him. He was up against the wall in seconds, being held by his throat, feet dangling.

Then the backpack fell with a thud, and the stack of cash he'd taken spilled out onto the tiles.

"You were *stealing* from me?" Ed roared, yellow eyes blazing in the dark of the foyer.

They couldn't be contacts, and those razor-sharp teeth didn't look like plastic, but vampires were not real! If anything, Ed was a serial killer, and Sam was losing his mind after witnessing a murder.

"I-I'm sorry… I'm sorry!"

"It was all a lie?"

"You were going to kill me!" Sam defended. The blood still stained Ed's fangs and mouth and shirt….

"Not you," Ed said—soft, as if he meant it, hurt that Sam would ever think such a thing, even enough that his eyes dimmed and changed back to green like some movie special effect, but right in front of Sam. "Never you."

"You killed *him*," Sam said lamely, noting that while his feet touched the floor again, Ed didn't release his neck.

"I had to. I *have* to. When the hunger gets too bad, I…. But not you. I wouldn't have ever hurt you."

"Wouldn't have…," Sam repeated. "But I stole, and I saw you, so… now?"

Ed's eyes flashed yellow again, and Sam shook so hard he almost vibrated.

"N-no…. You can't be a vampire! Vampires aren't real!"

"Do I look like something else?" Ed growled, his eyes and fangs too plain before Sam to be smoke and mirrors or his imagination. "Tell me *why*."

"I-i-it was a job! What I was hired to do. Before I met you. Before I knew you! Please…."

"Before you knew me…," Ed repeated, soft again. "Then why did you still do it?"

"I had to," Sam echoed Ed's words. "They would have killed me and my friends."

"Friends?" Ed spat in distaste.

"I won't give them up. I don't care what you are or what you do to me!"

The silence that followed was worse than Ed's snarling. He just stared at Sam—with those eyes, those fangs, the blood. Sam could see it dripping onto the black-and-white tiles, making especially prominent splashes on the white.

But just when he thought his number was up, Ed's eyes turned green again, and his fangs retreated, vanishing like a magic trick.

"What will you give up?"

"What?"

"Will you give up your employers?"

Sam blinked at him mutely.

"You said they would have killed you if you refused them. So tell me, who—"

"Brock and Celia Cramer," Sam said in a rush.

Now Ed blinked mutely.

"I can give you the names of the others who work for them. I don't owe any of them anything. They haven't been friendly since I tried to back out."

"You…." Ed's grip loosened. "Your eye. That was them?"

"And a few bruises you didn't see."

Ed's expression softened like his tone, and slowly, his hand fell away.

Sam turned his head toward the doors. "Does that mean—"

"No. You don't get to just leave. Not after what you saw. Not after what you did."

Fighting down the tremors that caused, Sam looked back slowly, trying and failing to rationalize away what had to be true—that real monsters existed as much as the human version. "What do you want, then?"

"You're my assistant, aren't you?" Ed said with a cold stillness overtaking the softness. "Add *groceries* to your duties. Starting with the people who hired you."

Sam didn't know what to say. He had no loyalty to the Cramers, but being part of what Ed would do to them…. Did he hate them that much?

"Well?"

"What about my friends? They wanted out too."

"Tell me about them."

"I won't—"

"Not their names, but how many? Who are they to you?"

"There's just three of us. I grew up with them, conned with them my whole life, they're… family."

That seemed to appease Ed, and he softened again. "I won't touch them, but you tell them nothing about me."

"What am I supposed to say? I'm meant to deliver everything tonight. Are you just going to tear through whatever club the Cramers are at and—"

"No. We'll think of something else. But later."

"What—"

"Bring everything into the living room," Ed ordered, nodding down at the backpack and the stack of cash. "And don't try to run again. I'm not done eating."

SAM LOOKED like he might run anyway, battling that age-old fight or flight, but he finally chose submission. He steeled his expression impressively, given his shivering, and gave a short, affirming nod.

Ed turned to head back into the living room, trusting Sam would follow. Of course he would. He was terrified. Ed could have asked him to do anything right then. If he wasn't still so hungry, that would have made him feel sick.

That Sam had lied from the beginning, only there to steal from him, stung deeply, but not as badly as having Sam look at him like *that*. Ed had known the illusion couldn't last, but he hadn't expected things to end this way.

Glancing back when he reached the patio doors, he watched Sam set the backpack on the sofa, very obviously trying not to look at the body.

"Empty it. I want to see what you took," Ed said.

Sam did so. Besides the cash were various tools, Sam's blazer from earlier, his laptop, a flashlight, and a collection of items from around the house that Ed knew were his—and valuable thanks to Sam's cataloging—but none of them were pieces he would have missed. Miraculously, nothing had broken when the bag fell, since Sam had carefully wrapped all the delicate pieces.

It seemed so meager and pointless, though, to take so little when there had been far more at stake than Sam realized.

"Go get one of the washcloths and a towel from the master bathroom. You'll know which ones. Wet the cloth, please."

"O-okay." Sam turned swiftly to carry out the task, no doubt relieved to be sent away.

Ed should kill him. If it had been anyone else, Sam would be dead already. But it wasn't only sentiment that stayed Ed's hand; he didn't know what was going on. He had to learn more.

And he would, after he finished his meal. So much blood had already been wasted, spilling out onto the patio.

He picked up the man from where he'd fallen, deathly pale now but still clinging to life. At least there was that; blood tasted better when it was fresh.

Bringing the still spurting artery to his mouth, Ed drank greedily, trying to ease his mind and aching heart with the glorious sensation the blood gave him. He barely remembered the man's name anymore, but feeding from him was like experiencing every intense emotion the man had ever had, every wonderful meal he'd ever tasted, every writhing body he'd ever been in rapture with. Taking someone's life truly meant taking their whole life into him, and he never tired of how that felt.

The man's pulse continued to slow, beat by beat, barely there finally, just as Ed heard Sam return.

Opening his eyes, he watched Sam while he finished eating, holding the man with ease and letting every last gushing drop fall into his waiting mouth until it was merely dribbles.

Sam had the dampened cloth and a towel—both red—and was trying not to watch or meet Ed's stare. Ed had never let someone he didn't plan to kill see him like this. It didn't fill him with shame; he accepted what he was, but there was still regret.

Finished now, having taken as much remaining blood as he could, Ed let the man drop, and Sam flinched when the dead weight of the skull hitting the ground made an audible crack.

"If it helps," Ed said, "he wasn't a nice man."

"I'm... sure he wasn't."

"*Sam.*"

At the more obvious command, Sam glanced up, and Ed took the cloth from him to clean his face, remaining just outside the patio doors to keep from tracking in any more blood. He began to wipe his mouth and as much of the rest of him as he could.

"I decided to skip the show. Didn't sound as fun without you," he said wryly. "Drinks don't affect me, and dinner isn't necessary, so I took a walk. I waited, watched, and made a careful selection. He was dragging a very young man, who obviously wasn't in any condition to say no to him, into his car. I gave him a more willing option."

Sam visibly relaxed at the explanation, at least a little, but while that had been Ed's intention, he didn't want to lie to him anymore.

"Don't misunderstand. If I'm forced to choose between killing someone wicked or someone who's a threat to me, I won't hesitate. I've been around a long time for a reason."

"How long?" Sam asked tentatively.

"Long enough to know the tricks. I do like swimming at night, but the extra drains are useful." Ed gestured behind him to where the blood that had spilled, smeared on the glass doors and the chair, was mostly disappearing down the long strip drains around the pool that prevented excess water from leaking into the house. "And chlorine kills just about anything. But tonight, you made me stain the rug."

Another tremor tore through Sam. "I-I'm sorry. I'll help you clean it."

"I'd appreciate that. I expect you to be my employee again until this is over."

"And... when the Cramers and their crew are dead... it'll be over?"

He was smart to be afraid, to expect that Ed would tie up loose ends afterward, but even if it was foolish to show mercy, Ed truly didn't want to kill him. "I won't hurt you. Or your friends. I promise. Unless you give me a reason."

Sam nodded hastily.

"I'm a mess," Ed said with a grimace at his ruined shirt and slacks, taking the towel from Sam now, not that it would help much other than to dry his face. "I'm not always so wasteful, but I was in a bad mood."

That caused Sam to glance away again, even as he gestured weakly at the patio. "What, um...."

"I'll take care of the body. And his car. I know what I'm doing."

"Not very well," Sam muttered.

"Excuse me?"

Sam's eyes widened; he hadn't meant to say that apparently, but now he couldn't take it back. "They've been finding your bodies for weeks."

"Those aren't my bodies."

"What?" Sam's eyes flew back to him.

"You think the bodies the police keep finding are from me? Some of the missing persons maybe, but I don't get caught."

"Then who...?"

"I don't know. You thought it was me?"

"Before tonight, I thought it was the Cramers. Maybe it still is." He looked off distantly, but more in thought than in fear.

"Who are these people?" Ed asked. "What do they know about me?"

"I thought they were just typical gangsters, but I don't know how they heard about you or how much they know. They wouldn't tell me their source."

"Someone else told them about me?"

"I guess so. Yes," Sam said more certainly.

"Then we'll have to play this smart. Get to work on the carpet. I need to take a shower." Ed started to fold the cloth and towel, but then decided to only take the cloth and draped the towel over the body for Sam's benefit. "When you're done, find me upstairs."

WHEN HE was done. When he was done....

Cleaning up the blood.

Sam knew a few secrets for getting out blood. Never this much, but the principle was the same. Steel brush, dishwashing detergent in the water. Ammonia. He attended to all the spots he could find on the carpet, then took a few minutes to clean the sliding glass doors and the tiles in the foyer.

There was blood on him too, on his shirt from Ed's hands, that he scrubbed off in the kitchen sink. He was glad he had his gloves on, but when he was finished, he threw them away.

All that remained was the body.

The numbness and shock were starting to fade, leaving Sam shivering again. He could still run, but Ed would only catch him. And he wouldn't spare him again.

He couldn't be a vampire, he couldn't be, but no other answer made sense.

Now Sam was his… what? Servant? Minion? He'd said "employee," but it didn't feel like that anymore, not when the threat of death was glaringly present on the patio.

At least Ed had covered the body. The man's throat had become a mangled mess by the end. A normal human couldn't have done that.

But now Sam knew what Ed had been hiding. Why he didn't go out during the day, "sensitive to the sun." Why he didn't make friends. Why he didn't eat. Why he had so much money and possessions, a mix of old and new, like a collector over many decades.

Or was it centuries? Ed hadn't answered the question of how old he was.

Sam couldn't risk dawdling for too long, but he felt an awful dread wash over him with every step up the stairs toward the bedroom. The door to the master bath was open when he arrived, Ed just getting out of the shower and moving to find a towel—naked.

Sam had never seen him shirtless, let alone undressed, but Ed was as beautiful as ever, with flawless skin, long white limbs, a lean chest, and a toned backside. Despite everything, the same desire Sam had always felt for Ed stirred in him, and he stopped in the middle of the bedroom, unable to tear his eyes away.

"Have some decency!" Ed spotted him with a yelp and flung the door shut.

"You… left the door open."

"Only so I could hear if you tried to run again!"

"Then why didn't you hear me coming?"

The door swung back open, Ed now in a fluffy white robe, flushed—no, *blushing*, with a peek of skin in the parting of the robe that proved the scarlet went all the way down. "I was listening for the front doors, not you skulking about!"

Sam smiled. He couldn't help it. There was no coldness or real anger, just Ed's usual flustered self. "You were getting pretty hot and bothered with a stranger a few minutes ago." *Before you tore his throat out*, Sam didn't say aloud. "But indecency from me makes you blush?"

"I didn't like *him*."

"But you like me?"

Ed averted his gaze, hands fidgeting, like any other day when their flirting surpassed his comfort level. "I thought that was obvious."

Oh. Then not everything had been a lie.

Just that Ed was human.

"You're really a vampire?"

Ed raised his eyes. "You still doubt?"

"Well...."

In a blink, Ed was gone, and when Sam whirled around, he saw something like a blur moving about the room. Before he could question what was happening, a firm presence was at his back, and a quiet voice whispered beside his ear, "Yes, I really am."

Sam gasped, and the next second, Ed was back where he'd started.

"Are you finished downstairs?" Ed straightened, back to serious.

"Y-yes. Everything but the patio."

"Then—"

Sam's phone vibrated, startling them both. As he pulled it out to check the message, he remembered the flash drive in his other pocket.

"What is it?" Ed asked, moving toward him.

"Uh...." Sam stared down at his phone. "My friends, checking in on me. I told them I'd message them when I was on my way to see the Cramers."

"It seems like quite the long con for so few spoils."

Sam hesitated, but then, after putting his phone away, he took out the flash drive and held it out to Ed. "That's because the real prize was this."

"You were in my *safe*?" Ed snatched it from him, shocked and angry again but quickly becoming flustered like before. "Then you saw...."

"Your picture of me? Yeah."

Ed turned even redder. Did he blush easier because he'd so recently...?

Sam didn't want to think about that.

"I just...." Ed closed his eyes and took a breath, wrapping his fingers around the flash drive. "I wanted something to remember you by."

"You took all the photos downstairs, didn't you?"

"Yes."

"If you're afraid of heights, how did you get the one of the Grand Canyon?"

"I didn't take it from the *edge*," Ed blurted, looking up with a start.

Sam laughed so suddenly, it caught him off guard. "S-sorry."

"No, I… suppose I am pretty ridiculous sometimes," Ed said with a soft smile.

Soft. He could be soft, truly, despite his terrifying power.

"Thank you for being honest about the safe," he said.

"That's how I got the cash. The type of lock on your safe can be hacked pretty easily."

"You'll have to help me find a new one, then. Here." Ed handed the drive back to him. "Use it how you planned. Tell them you're on your way, that everything went fine. You're going to give your employers exactly what they asked for. I'll get it all back eventually."

"But what—"

"Do that much for now. I'm going to get dressed."

ED HAD to get dressed. He didn't want to be naked around Sam when he already felt so exposed.

Having Sam's eyes on him had reminded him of when they first met and Sam had him tripping over his tongue. Maybe Sam's advances hadn't all been a lie. Not that it mattered anymore.

Ed grabbed a change of clothes and shut himself in the bathroom, leaving the door cracked enough to hear Sam, who left the room for a while. There was no sound at any of the doors, and he soon returned. Ed had already deposited his bloody clothes and the towels in the basement. His secret staircase connected to the second floor, so Sam hadn't seen him descend. The towels Ed would wash in the extra machines he had down there, the slacks might be salvageable too—he'd at least try—but the shirt he'd incinerate.

He wasn't always good at his finances or organizing his possessions—or schedule or *life*—but he was an expert at covering his tracks.

Once he'd changed into a fresh pair of slacks and a simple long-sleeved shirt, he hung his robe behind the bathroom door and exited to find Sam sitting on the bed beside the refilled backpack with his laptop out.

"The information is copying," Sam said, not quite as timid, but there was wariness in his eyes when Ed sat next to him. "I was going to put the drive back after so you'd be less likely to notice anything right away."

"But I surprised you and upset your plans?"

"Yeah."

Ed wanted to ask if Sam would have just left then, never to return. Likely, yes. That would have been the smart play.

Which meant his "Goodbye, Eddie" *had* been final.

"I need to find out what these people know and who gave them the information." Ed focused on the matter at hand. "I also prefer to only kill when I need to feed, but I don't require blood more than once a week."

"Once a week?" Sam blinked rapidly, but it was difficult to tell if that meant he'd expected it to be less frequent or more.

"I can go longer, two weeks, even a month if I have to, but it's dangerous if I get too hungry."

"What happens?"

"I become less discerning," Ed said shortly, not wanting to discuss that right now, since Sam's spine had grown so rigid.

He just wished they could go back to the banter, the subtle flirting, the easy smiles and furtive touches, and pretend none of this happened, living blissfully ignorant in the past few weeks, but that wasn't possible now.

"We're going to take our time and pick off your employers one by one," Ed continued. At least then he'd get to see Sam for a while longer.

"But they know my friends and I were planning to leave town after we got our share."

"Tell them you want to keep the con going, see if you can get even more out of me. Make them think you want to win their favor, that you'll give them that much more of the final payoff. Sell it however you like, but from their perspective, you're the one taking the risk. They'll go for it, if this really is all about money.

"As for your friends, tell them the truth. That I caught you, and we're working together now to take out your employers. They can know I'm dangerous as long as they think I'm human. When this is over, I'll pay you handsomely, and you won't owe me anything."

"You'll pay me?"

"You work for me, don't you?"

Sam blinked again, like he wasn't sure how to respond to that.

The copying finished, and Sam handed the flash drive back to Ed. "You're going to need the information for the accounts they transfer everything to if you plan to get it all back."

"I'll get what I need." Ed could stand right over one of the thieves' shoulders while they logged into their accounts, and they wouldn't notice him if he didn't want them to.

"Also, you can have this back." Sam pulled the cash from the backpack. "It's not part of what the Cramers are expecting. I just took it for travel money."

"Then keep it." Ed waved it away. "Tell your friends it's an advance from our new deal."

"Are you sure—"

"Keep it."

"Okay."

"I'm going to let you go now, but I will be right behind you."

WHAT DID Ed mean—he'd be right behind him? How? On foot? Could he turn into a bat and fly?

Sam hurried through the dark to where he'd parked his bike, constantly looking over his shoulder but not seeing anything. Some of the blushing nerd he'd come to care about was still in Ed, but he couldn't shake that lurking sense of dread.

He needed to focus on following Ed's orders. And he had to up his acting game, because if he stuttered or faltered around the Cramers, they'd never buy this.

He'd texted Mim earlier that everything was fine, that he'd be leaving soon. Now, as he reached his bike, he messaged Alverez for where to meet and make the exchange. The address Sam received back wasn't for a club but a building in the warehouse district. A safe house. Somewhere secluded.

"What if they just kill me?" he wondered aloud.

"I won't let that happen."

He spun around at the sound of Ed's voice. He hadn't heard any extra rustling or a single stick crack underfoot during the walk from the house, yet there Ed was, materializing out of the darkness like a phantom.

"I'll keep you safe," Ed said earnestly. "I promise. Now go. I'll be watching."

There was still dread and fear, but something thrilling tingled at the base of Sam's spine at having such a powerful being as his dark guardian angel.

That thought assuaged his nerves during the ride into town, knowing that if anything got out of hand, Ed would be there to save him. Though he tried not to imagine the type of carnage that might leave.

The warehouse was indeed secluded. Sam didn't see any people on the streets nearby, and barely any vehicles. His shirt had dried by now from rinsing out the blood, but he still put on his blazer before heading inside with the backpack.

"Look at you," Shaw said with a whistle, lounging on a sofa. Alverez and Fitz were shooting pool in the back, and the Cramers sat at a table. All of them had drinks nearby or in hand, and there was cash out like they'd been counting it from another score.

"Everything as agreed," Sam said, setting the backpack on the coffee table in front of the sofa.

Shaw righted herself with a greedy grin, and the others crowded in. Sam retrieved his laptop and tried to hand it to Brock, but Fitz snagged it first and rushed over to a computer desk against the wall.

"Careful," Sam warned Shaw when she almost tipped the backpack upside down to get at the rest. "Some of what's in there is breakable."

"This junk is worth something?" Alverez scoffed once they'd removed it all and unwrapped the more fragile items.

A Baccarat crystal clock, antique gold Cartier pocket watch, and hand-painted porcelain vase from Germany were the highest-ticket items.

"I did the research," Sam said. "Go to your fences; you won't be disappointed. And Simons won't miss any of it."

"This is legit!" Fitz called from his computer. "It's all right here. And holy shit, this guy's loaded. It's even more than we were told."

"You did good," Brock said with a smirk.

"What about my cut?" Sam asked.

"You'll get your five percent."

"Make it ten again."

"You having a laugh?" Alverez threw down the pocket watch with a snort.

"Just thinking we can end this with a bigger payout."

"What are you selling?" Shaw asked, half enamored with a silver serving dish.

The Cramers and Alverez all drew closer, surrounding Sam, but he forced himself to look bold.

"I've got Simons wrapped around my finger. He won't notice any of this missing, and we can get more. We can get everything. What he's most protective of are his stateside accounts. The offshore ones barely touch the surface. He's already asked me to stay on full-time. He hasn't given me his account numbers or passwords yet, but if I play this right, I can get him to turn over everything.

"I'm talking a real long con. Another month, six weeks tops, but I'll have him so head over heels, he'll be gifting me half of what we want to steal."

"You're seducing the fucker?" Shaw snorted.

"Hope he's worth it," Alverez said.

"You don't know what he looks like, do you?" Sam gauged their responses carefully—they didn't. "He's worth it. A nice bonus for me. But the best part of going back in for more is that everything new we take, you won't have to split with your source."

"He's got a point," Celia said, crossing her arms with a contemplative glint in her eyes.

"Cece," Brock reproached.

"Come on, baby. What do we owe Midnight anyway?"

Midnight?

"So what if he brought us the job? What has he done since, and he expects half? Let him have it." She gestured at the loot on the coffee table. "And we take a hundred percent of the bigger pie."

"Ninety," Sam corrected. "I get ten. And ten from this take too."

"You're sure confident tonight." Alverez glowered.

"Because I earned it."

"Hang on," Fitz called, spinning around in the computer chair. "If you're willing to take such a risk, why bring us in on it? You could have kept everything for yourself."

"I'm no idiot. If you'd seen me in town or caught wind of me still being in that house, you would have thought I was betraying you to Simons or the police. I don't make enemies where I can make friends. I want things right between us," Sam said, looking to each of them. "But if this all goes sideways, you already got the original payday, and the only one they can pin anything on is me."

"My, my," Celia said. "Maybe you're not just the pretty face we took you for. I say it's a deal."

"For now," Brock interjected, "but we're going to expect updates. Progress reports. Regularly. There could be a lot of heat coming down if Simons catches on, and even if that's only on you, we don't want our source finding out either."

"Who is this Midnight anyway?" Sam tried to ask casually.

"Oh no." Alverez pushed forward, following up with a rough push at Sam's shoulder. "So you can go over our heads right to him? No fucking way."

"Enough," Brock said in warning, and Alverez backed off. "You want to know about Midnight, Goldman? We never met in person, but he made it clear it would be in our best interest to take the Simons job when he offered it. Remember Lawrence Santini?"

"Drug and gun runner, right? He ran off about the time you came to town. Made sense to me, since you would have fought over turf."

"He didn't run." Celia chuckled. "Who knows what really happened? But we got his finger in the mail as a nice incentive to do as Midnight asked, sporting the Santini family ring."

Sam didn't try to hide how that disturbed him.

"We have work to do transferring the money and getting all this lovely merchandise appraised for sale," Brock said. "By morning, your initial cut will be in your account, and you and your friends can move out of that shithole."

Sam hadn't thought about Mim or Gerry much yet, but even with just the stack of cash Ed had let him keep, he could take care of his friends for a long time, which would hopefully soften the blow of no longer leaving town.

That still wasn't going to be an easy conversation.

A knock at the door gave Sam more of a fright than he'd admit, suddenly wondering if it was Ed, and if he was going to kill them all right away anyway. These were bad people, the worst, but the thought of watching Ed tear into them and seeing more blood churned his stomach. Maybe he couldn't go through with this….

"Must be that late runner," Alverez growled, storming past Sam for the door.

Sam held his breath, but when Alverez lurched the door open, it *was* a runner, some gangly teenager, ragged-looking and far too thin.

He passed a backpack to Alverez, who checked it and pulled out a wad of cash.

"That's it? Get in here!" Alverez grabbed him by the hair, tossed the backpack into the room, and slammed the kid face-first into the wall. He twisted his arm behind his back, and while he kept one hand on the kid's head, the other started to bend back his first two fingers.

"S-stop!"

"You make us wait, don't offer the full payload, and think I'll go easy?"

Sam glanced warily at the others, but while Brock was watching with mild interest, the rest weren't even paying attention, back to sifting through their haul. Sam didn't know what the money was from—drugs, guns—but Alverez kept bending the kid's fingers, ignoring his screams, until the bones snapped.

"Ah!"

"Shut up. Next time, it'll be the right hand."

He shoved the kid out the door again and slammed it in his face, laughing as he picked up the bag on his way back to the coffee table.

"Aren't you glad you're playing nice with us now?" Alverez sneered at Sam.

Fuck them, Sam thought with a surge of anger. They deserved everything Ed did to them.

"I'll give you my first status report next week," Sam told Brock.

None of them moved to stop him as he reclaimed his empty backpack and turned to leave.

The kid was about a block down when Sam exited, whimpering and still nursing his hand. At least he wouldn't have to worry about the Cramers for much longer.

Sam didn't expect Ed to show himself while he was still near the warehouse, but now that his next destination was home, he started to grow wary again. Ed would know who Mim and Gerry were. Wherever he was, watching, he'd know their faces. With that thought came dread again, but Sam had to trust that Ed would keep his word.

"So?" Mim ran up to him as soon as he entered the loft, Gerry on her heels.

"The money will be in our account by morning, ten percent, and I got a bonus." Sam grinned, pulling the wad of cash from his pocket and tossing it onto the table. He set the backpack down too, much lighter now holding only his possessions.

"Sweet!" Gerry snatched up the cash. Everything was already packed behind them, ready to be loaded into Gerry's car. They weren't taking any furniture, since they planned to buy everything new once they decided where to stay.

Had planned. Had.

"The bonus is from Ed," Sam said.

"What?" Mim turned to him with a frown. "What do you mean, from *Ed*? He gave you a stack of cash before you robbed him?"

"No. He gave it to me after. When he caught me."

Mim and Gerry both froze.

"It's okay. Everything is going to be fine. We just have a change of plans."

He sat them down at the table and explained what had happened. Well, he explained that Ed had caught him and their new deal, leaving out the vampire part and the man Ed had eaten. The important thing was for them to understand that while Ed was dangerous, he was still on their side.

"Are you saying your blushing, swooning, stuttering—"

"Don't start that again," Sam interrupted. "But yes. He's a lot more dangerous than the Cramers, but he's going to let me work this off. We'll still get paid, and when it's over, we won't have to worry about the Cramers or their goons ever again."

"What about Simons?" Mim demanded.

"We won't have to worry about him either."

"You don't sound sure about that."

"He promised me."

"He's apparently pretty good at lying to you."

Sam had to admit that was true, but what other choice did he have?

"You're scared of him," Mim said with a start.

"I thought you had, like, all this chemistry," Gerry added.

"We did. We *do*. He's just not… what I thought. But it's going to be okay."

"You're not telling us something," Mim insisted.

"I'm telling you everything you need to know. It'll be fine. I'll handle it."

"You keep saying that," Gerry argued, "but are you really okay with letting Simons kill the Cramers? I mean, that's what you're implying he's going to do, right? I thought we didn't like working for murderers."

"We do when one of them's on our side."

"Sam—"

"I'm tired." Sam pushed from the table. "I'm going to wash up. Then we're going to pack everything in Gerry's shitty Volvo and get a nice fancy suite at a hotel. So start picking one."

Before either of them could say more, Sam escaped into the bathroom, the only place he could be alone without leaving the loft.

He collapsed against the door, letting his eyes close and taking several shaky breaths.

"You did well."

Sam gasped as he opened his eyes—to see Ed sitting in the window. It hadn't been open when he entered, had it? But he hadn't heard a thing.

It was a large window that faced the alley and usually had the curtains drawn. Ed sat casually on the ledge with one leg propped.

"I saw the account numbers they're transferring everything to," he said.

"From Fitz's computer? How?"

Ed didn't answer but held out a piece of paper with several numbers on it. "Which one is yours?"

Sam inched forward, struggling to get his pulse back under control. "That one."

"Which means one of these others belongs to whoever sent them after me."

"Could it be another vampire?"

"No. We don't play games with each other like that."

"Do you have enemies?" Sam asked.

"None breathing," Ed said absently. When he looked up, he seemed to come back to himself, but his expression was hard to read. "We'll discuss next steps later, but the Cramers will pay, and so will whoever hired them.

"Go find yourself that hotel room. Tomorrow, come at your normal time. If you don't show," he said sternly, "I'll come looking. Please don't make me do that."

"You can be out in the sun?" Sam couldn't help asking.

"It's uncomfortable, and I don't like the glare, but that wouldn't stop me—"

"I'll be there! I was only curious."

Ed looked away with a sigh, stuffing the piece of paper back in his pocket. Sam wasn't sure what to say or do or anything else to expect, but after a few beats, Ed said, "I suppose you fancied yourself Hades until tonight."

The soft tone startled Sam as much as Ed's arrival and occasional chilling coldness. He sounded sad now, and that made Sam consider the question carefully.

"I still do," he said, and when Ed's eyes flashed to his, he willed himself to not start trembling. "Weren't you listening to the last line so far? Persephone is the one to watch out for."

A small smile twitched at Ed's lips, and for a moment, Sam wondered if he was going to ask him to finish the tale, but he simply nodded—and leaped from the window.

Sam stared, startled yet again but also curious. He moved forward to peer outside.

Nothing. No sign of Ed.

But no bats either. He'd at least had to check.

Because Ed was a vampire. And now, Sam only worked for *him*.

CHAPTER 3

SAM THOUGHT yesterday had been rough, arriving for his workday knowing the entire time that he was about to betray a man he genuinely liked. Crazy to think that had only been twenty-four hours ago.

Now he was heading into work for his vampire master so they could plan out several murders.

At least the Cramers hadn't lied; that morning, there had been so many fresh zeroes in the joint bank account Sam shared with his friends that they'd be able to survive for a long time. Once his debt to Ed was paid.

"I'm here!" Sam called as he entered the house—fifteen minutes early. The foyer smelled of lavender, with no remaining traces of ammonia at all.

From the *blood.*

He shuddered. He told himself he had nothing to fear as long as he followed Ed's orders. He'd been so concerned with pleasing him this first day, but maybe being early explained Ed's absence.

The silence in reply to his arrival drew his attention to the living room. The patio doors were shut with the curtains drawn like always. Sam approached them slowly, visions of last night assaulting his senses like flickers of apparitions—Ed's eyes and fangs as the man's throat lay torn open, drops of blood trailing on the carpet, the way Ed had held the man afterward and lapped at the remaining dribbles....

But the carpet was clean now, Sam had made sure of that himself, and when he peeked behind the curtains, Ed had obviously disposed of the body and hosed off the remaining blood into the drains, because the patio looked empty and spotless.

"Dammit!" A distant voice made him jump.

"Ed?" Sam returned to the foyer.

"Up here!" Ed called. "Just one more minute!"

Now Sam was curious and ascended the stairs, following Ed's voice to the bedroom. He found him grumbling to himself in front of his dresser mirror, fumbling unsuccessfully with his bow tie.

"Urg! This is impossible today!" Ed huffed, roughly tugging the ends loose.

Sam chuckled, and Ed's eyes snapped to him so furiously that dread coursed through him like before. Only for it to crumble, because Ed crumbled, turning fidgety in familiar embarrassment.

"I-I-I was just—"

"Going to all that trouble for me?"

"I like looking presentable for myself too!"

Sam chuckled again, reminded of why he'd been so charmed by Ed in the beginning. "Come here." He strode into the room and reached up to finish doing the bow tie himself.

His fingers were good for more than lifting wallets and the occasional sleight of hand, and he finished the job almost as quickly as he'd undone Ed's tie the other day.

"There. Or you could go without," Sam teased, but the intense way Ed stared at him made him shrink back uncertainly. "N-not that you… have to listen to me."

"I like listening to you." Ed followed him, as if he hadn't meant to make him worry. "You're so much better at some things. And you're right," he said with finality, undoing the bow tie once more. "Maybe you can help me look for some updates to my wardrobe."

"Sure," Sam said, taking a breath to steady his pulse. He felt so foolish, caught between two ways to act around Ed and completely unsure which was right.

"Did you sleep well?" Ed asked, pulling the tie out from around his collar and setting it on the dresser.

"At the Marriot?" Sam chose his words carefully. "Well enough."

That cold stillness settled over Ed as he turned to face Sam.

Shit.

"I know you're lying. I waited and followed you to the Hilton."

Shit.

"I-I was going to admit the truth even if you didn't call me on it, I just—"

"I understand. You need to know what you can get away with, and you want to protect your friends. They seemed nice, like they really care about you."

"Please…." A tremor shivered up from the base of Sam's spine.

"I'm not threatening them."

"Yes, you *are*."

Ed paused and glanced away with a pinch of sorrow. "Yes, I am. I don't want to, but I need to know I can trust you."

"I get it. No more lies."

"Thank you. I do believe you're trustworthy, Sam. After all, you're here. That's why I'd like you to do what you can to trace the other account numbers." Ed took out the piece of paper from last night and handed it to Sam.

"I can do that," Sam said. Or rather, *Gerry* could.

"But first, shall we get back to those investment ideas?"

"Oh. Uhh...."

"Since we didn't get to finish everything yesterday. We ended early so we could get ready for our... I mean...." Ed shut his eyes, as if pained to remember their "date" that never happened. "If you don't mind still helping me with things like that?"

"I don't mind," Sam said quickly.

"We have all day to discuss other things."

Like murder, Sam filled in.

"Shall we go into the office?"

Sam could do this. *This* was easy. And even though relaxing around Ed proved difficult, once they were in their customary seats—Sam in his roller chair, Ed in his straight-back—mulling over investment portfolios almost felt normal.

Until Sam knocked a pen from the desk.

"I'll get it," Ed said just as Sam leaned down too, and suddenly, he was lunging for Sam's throat!

Sam kicked at the carpet to send the roller chair flying back a foot.

Ed startled, looking confused, because he hadn't been lunging at anything. He frowned and finished claiming the pen to set it back on the desk.

"S-sorry," Sam stammered.

"It's all different now, isn't it?" Ed said sadly.

"Just hard to forget I saw you eat someone last night." Sam cringed, wishing he hadn't said it like *that*.

"I never would have hurt you," Ed affirmed. "I won't hurt you. Or your friends—"

"Unless I give you a reason," Sam said.

Ed sighed, and with it cracked the remaining coldness until there was only sorrow left. "Then forget all that."

"What?"

"I can't do this. I can't bear to have you look at me like…." He winced and clenched his eyes closed as if to stay tears. "Just go. You don't owe me anything, and you never have to see me again." He stood abruptly and tried to turn for the door, but Sam stopped him with a hand on his wrist.

"Wait. There's something bigger going on here. I want to understand it too."

"No, you don't. You're just afraid of me."

"You'd let me walk out the door?"

"I shouldn't." Ed's eyes drifted back slowly, but he didn't try to pull from Sam's grip. "I know I shouldn't, but I can't bear to see you hurting, and I have your picture when I want to remember you."

All those weeks Sam thought he'd been reading Ed so easily, and he'd been proven wrong, but he swore there was no con in Ed's eyes now, the way they'd conned each other for so long.

He let his hand fall from Ed's wrist. "I'll stay."

"Really? Why?"

"Because I work for you." Sam mustered a smile. "And I'm too wrapped up in this to walk away without seeing it to the end. I owe you that. But no more threats. I won't betray you, but my friends—"

"I swear." Ed nodded, reclaiming his chair.

"And no more games. You don't need to play a role for me."

"What do you mean?" Ed looked at him innocently, endearingly, something he easily could have let fall away now, but that was just it.

"This is the real you too, isn't it?" Sam said softly.

"Who else would I be?"

Sam took a breath, watching carefully for Ed's reactions as he slid the roller chair closer. "And so… Hades took Persephone across the river Styx."

Ed's eyes widened—honest and interested, just as Sam had hoped.

"She had lied a little. She was afraid. Of the future. Of the unknown. But not of him. Her darkness could be greater than all the Underworld she saw around her, because what was more violent and terrifying than a summer storm that brought the floods and great lightning down from Zeus himself?

"The spring brought life and beauty, the summer warmth, but it all ended in death, one way or another. Hades was merely the guardian of it all, not the cause.

"Persephone wondered just how many dead she'd laid at Hades' feet."

The deep longing in Ed's expression tempered the fear that kept finding its way into Sam's stomach.

"Hades knew all that," Sam continued. "As they'd talked on their way down from Mount Olympus, he'd realized who she was—daughter of Demeter, goddess of natural life and the rebirth and return to death of spring fading into summer and giving way to autumn.

"Hades was afraid too, but not of her. He feared he'd love her and lose her as fleetingly as when a storm passed."

They'd started to gravitate closer while Sam talked, whatever doubts he might have had pushed aside as he reached for Ed's cheek.

"Don't." Ed drew back. "Don't play a role for me either. If you think you need to, to protect yourself, you don't—"

"Eddie," Sam said, daring to grasp his face anyway, because he did need to know what he could get away with—and what he wanted. If Ed could be willing to let him go, maybe whatever this was between them was worth going after, even if Ed was far more dangerous than any god. "Humor me."

And then he kissed him.

SAM *KISSED* him.

And oh, his lips and mouth were so much better than the man from last night.

Ed had longed to feel the pliant press of Sam's mouth, the slow tilt of his head, the subtle slip of tongue between his teeth, and the gentle prodding to push the kiss deeper.

He shouldn't let it go deeper. He shouldn't let them kiss at all. It would only make him want more, when he knew how risky this was, even just to steal a simple taste.

"Wait," Ed gasped, unsure where to put his hands as Sam held him captive with that palm on his cheek, "we can't."

"Why not?" Sam panted back, twisting his fingers in Ed's shirt. "You want this. I know that part wasn't a lie. I see you now, Eddie. All of you. I get it. And I still want you too. I'm sorry I lied and used you like that."

"I'm sorry too." Ed melted at the sweet words. "I wish you hadn't seen—"

Sam captured his words with another kiss, then another, each reconnection growing more frantic. Ed had to stop it, but all he could think about with each new plunge of Sam's tongue was tearing his shirt open, climbing into his lap like he had with that unworthy man last night, and rutting until he felt something real.

Their knees knocked together, and Ed spread his apart, letting Sam get closer. Sam's hand dragged down Ed's stomach, reached the waistband of his slacks, and paused only a moment before continuing down between Ed's legs and squeezing.

"Sam," Ed moaned, dizzy from having the smell of Sam all around him, stronger with their arousal. "A-aren't you... still afraid?"

Sam pulled back to gaze into Ed's eyes as if looking for a reason to be afraid, but didn't seem to find any. "I don't care," he said and kissed Ed again.

Ed tried to tamp down the urge to seek out the rush of blood he could hear in Sam's veins, tried to pull away, but Sam kept following him, kept rubbing between his legs with the same deft fingers that could tie a bow tie so effortlessly and just as easily make it disappear.

Clawing forward to grip Sam's thighs, Ed couldn't stop kissing him back, but between licks and nips and harried breaths, he tried talking sense. "S-sometimes, if I get too excited, I...."

"It's okay," Sam said, continuing with firm, rhythmic strokes, "let it happen."

"N-no, I mean, I... I-I...."

Ed's eyes sharpened, fangs lengthening, as he pulled back with a hungry growl and lunged for Sam's throat.

"Fuck!" Sam cried, kicking away with the roller chair, only this time, it caught on the carpet, sending him toppling backward, the wheels spinning as they nearly struck Ed in the face.

Which finally snapped him to his senses.

"Sam!" he cried, leaping to his aid, but when he tried to reach down, Sam frantically scrambled away from him on his elbows. "I'm sorry!" Ed held up his hands, forcing his face to shift human. "I'm sorry."

They were both breathing hard, the terror on Sam's face unmistakable and the passion of the moment ruined. It took a minute, but eventually Sam raised a shaky hand and let Ed help him to his feet.

"*That* happens, huh?"

"I'm so sorry. I won't hurt you. I won't hurt your friends. I promise—"

"I believe you, or I never would have kissed you. Maybe you just need practice." Sam offered a weak smile, reaching for Ed's face again.

"Sam…." Ed placed his hand over his, touched that he was still willing to try.

"We'll go slower."

"I don't know if—"

A knock at the door made them both jump, and Sam snatched his hand back again.

"S-sorry," he stammered, clearly more afraid than he wanted to admit.

"No, I'm the one who—"

Another knock cut Ed off with an anguished scowl.

"I'll get it," Sam said, casting Ed a yearning glance, "but I am not running away."

WHY WASN'T Sam running away? He definitely hadn't imagined the lunge that time, but he couldn't deny how he felt.

He was drawn to Ed, had been from day one, but especially now, realizing that Ed was equal parts monster and blushing, swooning, stuttering mess. Kissing him felt right, if a little cold like his hands, but more invigorating than off-putting, and certainly heated enough once they started pawing at each other.

Because Sam wasn't being forced to stay; he'd chosen to.

Mim and Gerry would think he'd lost his mind.

"Daniel." Sam exhaled as he opened the door, heart still pounding in his ears. "Hey. You know, now isn't the best—"

"Sorry, Sam," Daniel broke in, no neighborly smile this morning. He was dressed for work, the usual three-piece suit with his badge and gun very apparent, and he carried a thick file folder. "But even if Mr. Simons isn't in right now, I'm going to have to wait for him. I'm surprised to see you here on a Saturday."

"He… convinced me to stay on longer," Sam said, since the best lies were the truth. "We needed to work out some new arrangements. What's going on?"

"I'd prefer to explain that to him. I need to ask him a few questions. Are you okay?" Daniel frowned as he looked Sam over.

Sam was breathing hard. At least the scare had minimized any other telling signs of what had been going on. "Yeah, I just ran down from upstairs to answer the door. What do you need to ask Ed about?"

"Well…." Daniel obviously didn't want to tell him, which meant it was police business.

Oh no.

"It's all right, Sam," Ed called from inside. "Let him in."

Not once in the three weeks Sam had known Ed had he seen anyone cross that threshold other than them—and the man Ed killed last night.

"Mr. Simons," Daniel said with an attempt at a smile, still far too serious. "It's nice to finally meet you."

Sam quickly closed the door as Ed came forward to shake Daniel's hand, like two disparate worlds colliding.

"My apologies it took so long," Ed said, smiling cordially. "I've been far too busy since I moved in, and keeping Sam busy too."

"I understand. Ooof, must be cold in here," Daniel said with a shiver.

That was just Ed.

"Smells lovely, though."

"Thank you. Would you like something to drink, and we can sit in the kitchen? Or would you prefer the living room?"

The living room—where there had been blood all over the carpet.

"Living room is fine, thanks. You know, Sam was right. You're not at all what I expected."

That's because he was a vampire.

Sam had to get a hold of himself. Just because this looked bad didn't mean Daniel was going to accuse Ed of anything. It didn't mean Ed would be forced to retaliate. Sam hoped it didn't. But even though he believed he had nothing to fear for himself or his friends, that didn't protect others if Ed perceived them as a threat—not even a nice family man with a wife and two kids.

"I hope that means I'm a pleasant surprise." Ed was all charm, like he'd been when Sam first met him. He'd proven easily ruffled, but he kept it together around others, around prey.

"Only if you promise to come to our barbecue next weekend," Daniel said, already growing more relaxed as they gathered around the coffee table, with Daniel taking an armchair and Ed and Sam the sofa.

"I suppose I at least owe you a pie." Ed chuckled. "So, what seems to be the problem, Detective? Oh, and I'd like Sam to stay, since he's been handling all my affairs."

Like cleaning the house and pool, unknowingly helping get rid of evidence for three weeks.

Sam had to *stop*.

"I'm glad you'll be sticking around, Sam. But I thought you had another gig?" Daniel turned to him.

"Ed… made a better offer," Sam said, still trying to catch his breath.

He couldn't help it; when Daniel glanced down at the file folder, he shot Ed a panicked look.

Ed stared him down, stone-faced and cold again.

Not Daniel, Sam pleaded silently. *Please not Daniel.*

"As you may have heard," Daniel began, prompting Ed to look forward again, "there have been an increase in missing persons lately, and several bodies found with similar MOs in the past few weeks. Very messy, bloody business. We've identified the victims, and two of them have your cell number as recent outgoing calls."

What?

"That's why I have to ask, Mr. Simons: How do you know these people?"

Daniel passed two photographs to Ed, one of a middle-aged woman, the other of a young man. They were normal, happy photographs, but deeper in the file folder, Sam caught a glimpse of the carnage they'd become.

"That's Kathryn Deckard," Ed said in genuine surprise. "My realtor. And Mr. Lepke was the carpenter I hired for renovations before I moved in. I haven't spoken to either of them in weeks."

"I'm going to need your alibi for the nights we believe to be time of death."

That should be easy, because these weren't Ed's victims. He'd told Sam as much, and he was too smart to go after anyone connected to him. Plus, he honestly seemed sad to hear that they'd been the ones killed.

"He was with me," Sam said after Daniel gave the dates, which was true, but that might not matter if anything else connected Ed to the deaths.

"Working late?"

"We always do."

"Detective, may I know the names of the other victims?" Ed asked.

Daniel gave them and pulled out their photos too.

"This other man put in my pool," Ed admitted. "And the woman was my travel agent when I came to town."

"They *all* knew you," Daniel stated the obvious. "Could be a coincidence."

"But you don't believe that." Ed handed the photos back to him.

Sam tensed, because he saw Ed's muscles grow taut too.

"You know what they say, Mr. Simons: Two's a coincidence. Three's a pattern. Four is deeply concerning."

As soon as Daniel glanced away to gather everything back into the file folder, Sam grabbed Ed's hand and shook his head in pleading. Not Daniel, not with those twins next door. They could figure something else out. These weren't even Ed's kills!

Ed almost looked cold again, almost maintained the visage of the monster, but for Sam, he hesitated.

"You might be next."

Their eyes snapped back to Daniel in tandem, hands releasing before Daniel looked up.

"You think someone is after *Ed*?" Sam asked.

"It's a possibility. Is there anyone who might want an inside look at this place, Mr. Simons? Someone who could be picking those people off to get more information on you or details about this house?"

"I don't know," Ed said. "No one springs to mind. I tend to keep to myself."

"I'd say I'm even more glad that you're staying, Sam, but as someone who's worked with Mr. Simons since he arrived, you could be a target too."

Sam's fears had been so focused on the Cramers and even on *Ed* that he hadn't considered another threat.

"As of now, I don't need either of you to come down to the station, but I'd appreciate your cooperation if anything comes up. And it would be best if you both made sure you were around more often."

"Absolutely, Detective," Ed said. "I want you to catch this person. Those were good people who died. Let us know of anything you need."

After a solemn nod, Daniel pulled on a smile. "I'll leave you two be, then, but we'll see you next weekend?"

Ed laughed, falling easily back into the part of unassuming neighbor. "A barbecue may be a bit too much sun exposure for me, but you might twist my arm. I couldn't get that pie out of my mind the entire evening."

If Sam hadn't been so preoccupied, he might have smirked at that, since he had a feeling Ed meant it.

"I'll tell Marie," Daniel said as they stood to head for the door. "I mean, *I* baked it, but she likes to brag about me sometimes. Thanks again, both of you."

"See you soon, Daniel," Sam called and promptly shut the door behind him.

Fuck.

"FUCK," SAM said aloud.

Ed couldn't have agreed more.

"Do you really think someone wants to kill you?"

"Or frame me," Ed said, gesturing Sam back into the living room. "This is too coincidental. The timing, all of it revolving around me."

"And the Cramers." Sam scowled. "This has to be the same person who hired them."

"I wondered that too."

Ed had never had deaths surround him like this when he hadn't fed from any of the victims. He was being targeted, but there was no one living who he could imagine hating him this much.

"We're back to the same goal," Sam said. "We have to find out who it is. You overheard them call him 'Midnight,' right? Does that name mean anything to you?"

"I don't think so. Can we glean anything more from your employers?"

"The Cramers don't like me asking questions. We can still trace the account numbers, but it might help if you started tailing them, since you can stay hidden and move so fast. I'd follow Fitz first, the one from the computer. He's the wild card."

"I'll do that tonight," Ed agreed.

Their eyes met, and the serious air of careful planning gave way to all the other emotions lingering, like the many phases Sam had gone through since his arrival. Ed never would have guessed that all that fear and distrust could lead to them kissing.

Before he ruined it.

"Thanks, by the way," Sam said, startling Ed again.

"For what?"

"You know."

"For not attacking my neighbor?"

Sam huffed a laugh. "Would you have?"

"Only if I had no other choice."

"And what does that mean?" Sam asked carefully.

"If he had been here to arrest me, I wouldn't have let him take me in."

That seemed to sober Sam, but he didn't lean away from Ed or tense like before.

"We need to make sure things don't steer in that direction," Ed continued. "It's going to be bad enough if the police are watching me more closely."

"At least it's Daniel. He likes me. The whole family does. And they can learn to like you too. At that barbecue," Sam said pointedly.

Ed grimaced.

"I know it sucks, but we need the Neu-Ryans to be so charmed by their dashing neighbor, they'd never suspect you could be a killer. You can wear those sunglasses I gave you." Sam smirked.

"Fine, but *you're* baking the pie."

The laugh that escaped Sam was so honest and carefree that it washed away most of Ed's worries.

"Meanwhile, I'll get my team digging into those account numbers."

"Your team?" Ed frowned again.

"My friends. It's okay. They just think you're John Wick."

"Who?"

Amusement on Sam's face was far better than terror. "We'll rent the movies sometime. I still owe you a date."

But that wasn't good either. Ed wanted them on good terms, he wanted all they'd had these past few weeks, but they couldn't go too far down this path where Sam's sweet mouth and skillful fingers had tried to lead them.

"I also have a rejuvenated myth to finish telling you."

"Sam...."

"You didn't mean it," Sam beat him to the punchline.

"That's the problem. I can't always control myself."

"You seemed in control with that guy last night until you *wanted* to bite him."

"That was different. I wanted a meal, not...." Ed considered what he meant to say. "I didn't want to kiss him or touch him or have his hands on me. It's easy when it's an act. But when I really want someone, I... lose myself."

"That's why you kept me at a distance for so long?"

"You did too. You didn't ask me on that date until you were going to leave me."

"Technically, you're the one who called it a date," Sam said, grin widening when Ed pouted at him. "And I agreed. But how else was I supposed to handle things, knowing it was all going to end?"

"So... if you weren't a thief?"

"If you weren't a vampire?" Sam volleyed back.

There were too many ends to that sentence for Ed to voice them all.

"Wait...." A new realization dawned on Sam with a furrowed brow. "If you can't get intimate with someone you like, when was the last time you...." His eyes sprang wide, and Ed felt his cheeks burn hot. "You're not a hundred-year-old virgin, are you?"

"N-no!" Ed sputtered. "I slept with people before I was turned. I've slept with people since. My own kind."

"Like long-term immortal boyfriends? Girlfriends? *Both*?"

"Brief, passing tension releases." Ed stopped him, because if his face turned any redder, old cartoon steam would start coming out of his ears. "There's a certain unwritten understanding that if you go into another vampire's territory and they don't want you there, you leave. If they don't mind your presence, you're friendly and don't step on each other's toes. Alternatively, if you're both of the same mind, you might...."

"Fuck like bunnies?"

"Sam!"

Sam laughed again, obviously enjoying the discussion, though Ed wasn't. He wasn't a prude; there were just some things you didn't talk about!

"When was the last time you had that experience?" Sam asked.

There was also *that*. "A long time ago."

"Then I maintain what I said before." Sam reached over as if to take Ed's hand but spread his fingers over his thigh instead. "You need practice."

Ed huffed his own laugh, amazed and a little enchanted that, even after everything, Sam could still be so adorably insufferable. "You are being very unprofessional, Mr. Coleman."

"Um, it's Goldman, actually."

"Oh. Are you even really Sam?"

"Of course. I mean, that's not what's on my birth certificate."

"Samuel?"

"Solomon."

Ed smiled. He liked that. "Is there anything else you haven't told me?"

"Well, I never want to college, so most of my references are fake, but the knowledge is real. I have a GED, and everything else we ever talked about, things I like, that book you gave me, music, art, all of it was true." His hand was still on Ed's thigh, and he squeezed gently. "What about you, Mr. Simons?"

"Eadric," Ed said, a name he hadn't spoken aloud in longer than he'd last… fucked like bunnies, with a touch of his old-world accent slipping in too. "Or it was, originally. I went through many variations."

"Which eventually led to Ed?"

"I like Ed."

"I like Eddie more."

"A-a-and as for being *one hundred*, that is a very conservative number."

"How conservative?" Sam pressed.

"I don't think that's something to reveal on a first date."

"This isn't a date, but does that mean I get one?" Sam squeezed his thigh again, lightly rubbing down to his knee, and then up to rest near his hip.

Ed sucked in a breath. He didn't need to breathe, but the habit never went away, even down to pants and gasping shudders.

This time Sam leaned in slow, just a press of his lips to Ed's at first, a gradual opening of their mouths and light flick of tongues. A gentler and more languid kiss didn't mean Ed's arousal was slow to remember where they'd left off. He felt it stir low in his belly, and with it, his hunger stirred too. He'd fed only last night, but the two animal sides of his id were intimately entwined.

His vision intensified, and he fought to keep his eyes green.

"That's it…." Sam whispered. "You can do it. I trust you."

He kept kissing Ed, letting his tongue sink deeper, connecting with Ed's in an unhurried caress. Sam's hand started to drift between his legs again, but Ed stopped him, keeping Sam's hand on his thigh, and reached to seek out Sam's hardness instead. It was firm and ready for him, straining against his slacks. Giving Sam pleasure with tentative strokes made it easier to stay in control.

Until Sam groaned, and the sound shot a signal straight to Ed's primal side that made his eyes flicker again and his fangs start to grow. He pulled away to catch his breath, leaning their foreheads together to fight back the beast that kept roaring to the surface.

He didn't want to hurt Sam. He never wanted to hurt him or scare him again, but even with his face changed, Sam didn't look as afraid. He took Ed's hand from between his thighs and simply held it, hesitated with a brief shudder running through him, and then kissed Ed very softly, fangs and all.

"We'll work on it."

"I'd like that." Ed took a few beats to rest so he could make his face look human.

But he wasn't human, and he never would be again.

"Sam… I'm still going to have to kill those people. I always have to kill someone."

"I know." Sam stared at their hands, thumb circling Ed's knuckles.

"You can't tell me you're okay with that."

"I'm okay with the Cramers. And their flunkies. I won't mourn anyone like them." He glanced up, finding whatever it was he kept looking for in Ed's eyes and smiling. "If I'm around to keep your life organized, maybe I can make sure those are the only types of people you ever need to kill again."

There would be more to it than that. This couldn't go as well as Sam hoped. It never did. Because eventually it had to end. But things between them finally felt like back during those first few weeks together. This was *better*, and Ed did so love the way Sam kissed.

"S-so...." He peeled his fingers away and took a steadying breath. "Back to investments?"

"Sure." Sam stood and reached down to help Ed up too. "But be honest. Those Apple shares you have. Were you there, in on the ground floor, or did you buy them recently simply because you could afford it?"

SAM COULD have afforded whatever fancy meal he wanted that night, between the cash Ed had given him and the cut of the take in his bank account, but for some reason, they still ended up at Lucifer's Rest.

"We have a nice suite at the Hilton. Why are we eating here?"

"Because Gerry has a new lease on life now that we're not leaving," Mim said.

They were in their usual booth, which was easy to acquire, since the place was seldom packed. Mim sat beside Sam, leaving Gerry by himself with a nice clear view to Lara, who he kept gazing at like a lovestruck puppy.

"If that means you're actually going to ask her out, great," Sam said, tossing aside his menu. He had it memorized anyway. "If not, I'd rather stop choking down greasy food every night. We should be enjoying some of that hard-earned cash."

Gerry didn't seem to hear him, perched on the edge of his seat, waiting for Lara to reach their table.

"You're in a better mood," Mim said.

"Things went really well with Ed today." Sam shrugged.

Ed was out somewhere in the city tailing Fitz right that moment, like an impossibly fast shadow moving as an unseen predator through the streets. He was a predator, a vampire, a storybook monster, and yet, Sam had enjoyed every kiss and touch they'd shared and trusted him despite everything. Ed had no reason to lie to him or fake anything anymore, not when he could have gotten everything he wanted through fear alone.

"You're smitten again." Mim all but rolled her eyes.

"We just know where the lines are now, which parts weren't lies."

"You like Simons again?" Gerry returned to the conversation.

"I always liked him."

"You were pretty freaked last night," Mim reminded him.

"Sometimes I still am, but I know we can trust him. And he trusts me." Sam covertly slipped the list of account numbers from his pocket to pass over the table.

"What are these?" Gerry snatched the list closer.

"The accounts where the Cramers moved his offshore money."

Mim and Gerry stared at each other, and then at Sam.

"One of those belongs to their source. Ed wants to see if we can trace it."

"Sammy…." Mim shifted in the booth to face him. "You realize that with these numbers, Gerry could just hack into all of them, steal the whole take, and we could—"

"We're not running. The real payoff will be worth it."

And Sam wasn't going to try betraying Ed again.

Before Mim could protest, Lara made it to their booth, and Gerry shoved the account numbers away. They'd already put in their drink orders, each of them having a beer. Sam's was light enough that when Lara set it down with a napkin already stuck to it, he could see what looked like writing through the bottom of the glass.

If she was passing him her number, she was barking up the very gay tree, and Gerry would be devastated. Sam hoped he was wrong, waiting to peek at the napkin until she'd taken their orders and left. Once he saw what was written there, however, he sincerely wished it had been a phone number.

We need to talk, Mr. Coleman.

CHAPTER 4

SAM DIDN'T want to alert Mim and Gerry that anything was amiss, but if Lara knew his alias with Ed, they were in trouble.

He waited until she disappeared into the back and then excused himself. He didn't see anyone at first, wondered if she was just in the bathroom and someone else had slipped him that napkin, but when he turned around to head back to his friends, the Employees Only door behind him opened and a pair of hands wrenched him into the dark.

Sam spun around to take a swing at his attacker, but a knife pressed to the side of his neck as he was slammed against the closed door.

"For someone who gets jumped on the regular in this place and knows he's being watched, you're not very good at this," an unimpressed voice spat.

It was Lara, but she didn't sound like the sweet waitress they'd known for the past—shit, *three weeks*, just like Sam's time with Ed.

"*You're* behind this?" he said, holding still to avoid the sharp edge of her blade.

"Behind what exactly?" A wicked smirk curled her lips, her dark eyes glittering with previously veiled mischief.

Sam needed to get better at reading people, but he couldn't exactly come right out and ask: Are you the one trying to frame the local vampire?

"You hired the Cramers," he said, sticking to what she must know if she knew the name Coleman. "You're Midnight?"

"Not me," she admitted, "but my boss is, which means he basically hired you through them. And you are really throwing a wrench into our plans." Keeping him at knifepoint, she got up very close and personal for someone so much shorter than him. "You finished the heist but still went back to see Simons today. Why?"

"I… thought of a new deal with the Cramers that pushes your boss out." No point in making up another lie to keep track of. "Figured I could take Simons for even more than his offshore accounts."

"Really?" Lara studied him carefully, finally adding, "Or did you learn that his bark isn't as bad as his *bite*?"

Sam tried to keep from reacting. He really did.

"You *know*." She chuckled. "And you still went back. Are you hiding teeth marks somewhere, Mr. *Coleman*"—she glanced down his body—"or has he just got you that scared?"

For one terrifying second, Sam wondered if Lara was a vampire, but then she wouldn't be threatening him with a knife. "I don't know what you're talking about."

She huffed. "Maybe you should wise up, then, because you've seen the news, the bodies that keep showing up, haven't you?"

"Ed had nothing—"

"You were supposed to be next."

Sam froze, suddenly much more concerned with that knife.

"That's right," she purred, clearly enjoying his fear. "The final nail in the coffin, as it were, to make sure the police suspect him."

"You *are* trying to frame Ed. Why? They'll never be able to bring him in."

Lara just kept grinning and tapped the blade a few times, making Sam hiss as it finally cut into him. "We need updates, intel, so we can rethink our game plan. You've made Midnight wonder if there's a better angle."

"For what?" Sam couldn't believe how much he wished Ed was stalking *him* again tonight instead of Fitz.

"Updates," she ignored the question. "The inside scoop on Ed Simons, what he knows, what he's planning."

"I'm already doing that for the Cramers," Sam said miserably.

"Caught between a rock, a hard place, and a woodchipper." She laughed, pressing the knife down hard enough that Sam whimpered at how deeply it cut into him. "Guess which one *we* are?"

"Okay!"

"You keep coming here like clockwork and giving me updates, no questions asked."

"I got it. Fine. Yes."

"Good boy." Seeming satisfied, she stepped back, taking the knife with her.

Sam reached up instinctively to check the cut and pulled his hand away with a smear of red. "What am I supposed to tell my friends?"

"Whatever you want. You're the one who put them on the chopping block. Should have told them to run while they had the chance. Now...."

Lara shoved the knife at him, flat against his chest for him to scramble to keep it from falling and taking out one of his toes. "I'm going to go bat my eyes at Gerry a little more, and you're going to keep quiet and play ball, or you or one of your friends will be the next body found by the police." Grinning wickedly, she twirled her fingers in a dainty wave and pushed past Sam out the door.

He threw the knife into the corner, wondering how the hell he was supposed to play triple agent when he'd finally calmed down enough to play double. After exiting quickly into the bathroom, he took a moment to wash out his wound, got a bandage from Logan behind the bar, and told the others he'd scraped it on one of the stall doors.

"Might need a tetanus shot." Mim snickered.

Sam tried to laugh it off and act normal, but it wasn't easy with Lara smiling sweetly and oh so convincingly every time she neared their booth, prompting Gerry to finally ask her out.

She said *yes*.

At least Gerry was so busy celebrating, and Mim so busy patting him on the back, that neither noticed anything was wrong.

SOMETHING WAS wrong.

"I'm here!" Sam called, but as Ed met him in the foyer, he could already tell Sam's gait was off.

"What happened?"

Sam bolstered himself as if ready to lie, but then he paused, sighed, and looked at Ed squarely. "I know who's framing you."

He knew *one* of the parties involved, it turned out, but hearing about him getting accosted by that guilty party and that they'd planned to make Sam the next mutilated victim made Ed's fists clench and his temple twitch.

"They can't know I told you," Sam said, sitting with Ed at the kitchen island, nursing a cup of coffee. "I have to keep acting like I'm playing all sides."

"Of course. I won't let anything happen to you or your friends. I promised you that."

Sam relaxed, sagging onto his elbows, and Ed's hand raised of its own accord to alight gentle fingers on the bandage on his neck.

"I won't tail your employers anymore. I'll—"

"No, you have to." Sam reached up to cover Ed's hand. "If you watch me, they might catch on. We don't know who Midnight is. He could be a vampire like you."

Ed hadn't wanted to believe that, but anything seemed possible now.

"Nothing has changed," Sam insisted. "I'll give them intel like they want, make them think you know nothing, and meanwhile, we keep trying to figure out who's behind this. Then we take them all out."

"Then *I* do," Ed said.

Sam nodded and slowly dropped his hand so Ed could pull his away too.

Normally, Ed was good at planning in a new city, but he'd never encountered a situation like this. "What do we do next?"

"Did you find anything out about Fitz?"

"Yes." Ed sneered. "He goes to a club on Forty-seventh. The girls he fancied barely looked eighteen. He spent most of the night there, in a back room with young women, drugs, and drink."

"Classic creep," Sam agreed.

"I almost made a premature move against him when he got rougher with a girl than is allowed, but a bouncer intervened."

"You see why I won't mourn these people."

"A few more nights will teach me his other haunts. I followed him home afterward. He keeps to himself when not with his partners. He'll be easy to get alone."

"Um… and how are we going to do that when the time comes?"

"I will do it. You don't need to be there."

"But you can't just kill him. It'll raise an alarm with the others. We need to think of the staging, the aftermath, make sure they don't realize it has anything to do with us."

"Who's to say they won't think it's this Midnight?"

That brought a smile to Sam's face. "That's it! Everyone knows about the murders. If we get the Cramers thinking they're being targeted, picked off by their former employer to clean house, we can get both sides to work against each other. They'll get sloppy."

"And give us the perfect openings." Ed smiled too. He'd never had someone to plan things with before.

"I need intel I can feed them, true things so they think I'm getting closer to you. Actually getting closer is a bonus." After a playful pause, Sam leaned forward to kiss Ed very lightly.

"You know so much already," Ed said with a wider smile, "but there is one thing I haven't shown you yet."

Sam looked wary but went along willingly when Ed led him to the library, behind the bookshelf that hid his secret staircase, and down into the basement. Sam must have expected something vile or concerning, because he gave a great exhale when he saw what the basement held.

Some things were practical, like the extra washer and drier and a small incinerator. But there was also an extra bookcase, and photograph after photograph from decades past with Ed in them, always the same age in appearance, even one of him in front of Big Ben that matched the larger one upstairs. Ed had a darkroom down there as well, and several old paintings and sketches on the walls in intricate frames.

Sam took it all in with awe, but eventually turned to Ed, studying him as if summoning confidence to speak his next words. "Can I... ask you things about what you are?"

"You can."

"Do you sleep?"

"I don't need to anymore."

"And the sun won't burn you up?"

"No. Prolonged exposure can be painful, but I can go outside without bursting into flames. Most of the other lore you've heard are superstitions people told themselves to feel safer."

"Like needing to be invited into a person's home?"

"Crosses, garlic, traveling over water."

"Sleeping in a coffin?"

"Can you imagine?" Ed scoffed, pleased that it made Sam laugh.

"Are you invulnerable?" he asked.

"Are you asking for my weaknesses?"

"N-no, I just...."

"I'm only teasing. I heal quickly. I lost a finger once and it grew back. But I imagine if I lost enough blood, was beheaded, set on fire, things that would kill most people would still kill me."

"Do any other supernatural creatures exist?"

"Perhaps, anything is possible, but I've never met any werewolves or unicorns."

That cracked a fresh smile on Sam's face. "What about other vampires? Where are they all?"

"Who knows? I keep in contact with a few, but we never stay in one place for very long. There aren't many of us. A few hundred years ago, those of us who were left agreed we wouldn't create any more without real purpose or reason behind it. It's too dangerous, brings too much attention on all of us, and honestly, most of us had no desire to.

"I don't think more than a handful have been created since then, if they're all even still alive. Many of my old acquaintances have gone dark in recent decades. I think some decided they were done living."

"And you?" Sam asked, looking disconcerted.

"I love life," Ed assured him. "I never tire of anything. There's always something new to enjoy, and so many old things I adore centuries after they've gone out of fashion. Like bow ties, apparently." He laughed, making Sam laugh again too. "But it is lonely sometimes."

"I bet. *Centuries*," Sam repeated. "But there was never a vampire lover you wanted to keep with you forever?"

"No," Ed said softly.

Sam's smile was unmistakable, maybe because jealousy had prompted the question, but that was also when he cast another perusing gaze around the basement and landed on the most unique and prominent of Ed's pictures.

It might not have stood out so much if there were others like it, but while there were many rough sketches Ed had drawn before he had the luxury of a camera, other than the few photographs of himself, this was the only picture of a person.

The sketch was simple black and white, drawn meticulously a very long time ago, of a young woman with fair hair and light eyes.

"Shall we go up?" Ed said, noticing how Sam's attention lingered on the picture. He wasn't ready to talk about her yet.

"Sure." Sam glanced back slowly. "We have a lot to do. But thank you for showing me."

SAM WAS amazed by everything Ed had shown him, the trust he had in him.

He did wonder who that woman was, though.

Their plan from now on was straightforward, mostly revolving around Sam reporting separately to both Lara and the Cramers, while still attending to the job Ed had originally hired him to do—housework, groundskeeping, finances. It was comforting to dust and vacuum and clean the pool, monotonous and habitual enough to help Sam clear his head and not think about how different all this might feel once Ed was ready to claim his first victim.

It was getting dark out. Sam had wanted to get most of his basic chores out of the way so that the rest of the week could be focused on how to pit their two antagonist groups against each other. He was exhausted, probably because he hadn't slept well in the past two days, but when he was ready to call it a night and looked around for Ed, he was surprised to find him outside, already in the pool. Sam was usually gone before Ed took his swims.

The tricked-out radio by the patio doors was blasting loud enough to carry outside, playing Blue Oyster Cult and making Sam smile. He didn't *fear the reaper* so much himself anymore either.

Ed wasn't doing any complicated strokes, just floating serenely on his back, arms gently moving to keep him up while he gazed at the stars beginning to glitter above him. He'd left the doors open as if to invite Sam to watch, so it was easy to do so without calling much attention to himself.

Ed didn't look like a predator while swimming, his trunks clinging to him, chest bare. Sometimes it was hard for Sam to accept that dissonance—this version of Ed compared to the swift, brutal one—but then, wasn't a lion capable of seeming like a housecat even if it was always dangerous?

"Would you like to join me?" Ed called without turning to look at him. "I have an extra suit upstairs."

Sam wondered if that made him the lion *tamer*.

Mim and Gerry weren't expecting him at any particular time, and checking in with Lara and the Cramers could wait until tomorrow.

Enjoying the way Ed's eyes fixed to his mostly bare body when he descended from upstairs in the spare trunks, Sam took his time walking to the edge of the pool, set his clothes on one of the lounge chairs, and stepped off for a simple, smooth drop into the water. He shook the excess from his hair and face when he resurfaced, seeking out Ed at the other end.

"Tell me," Sam said, lifting up to float lazily on his back, "even without your telescope, how many of those can you name?"

"The stars? Or constellations?" Ed lifted as well, both watching the sky as they orbited each other.

"Does it matter?"

"No. I can name most of them."

"Then where am I?"

Ed navigated to drift up beside Sam, tracing over invisible lines in the sky. "Gemini. Sort of like two stick figures holdings hands."

Sam chuckled. "And you?"

"Pisces is there." Ed dragged his finger the other direction. "See the way the ends connect and then it makes a sort of tilted *V*?"

"Doesn't really look like a fish."

"We had to be more creative back then."

Blinking as what Ed was implying sunk in, Sam righted himself, not sure if he could ask, "You mean…?"

"I'm not *that* old." Ed grinned. He didn't clarify how old he was, however.

"You know, one of these days, I'm going to get you up on that roof to use your telescope properly."

Ed scrunched his nose. "I wasn't lying about not caring for heights."

"I figured. Any particular reason?"

"I don't know. Maybe because there weren't as many tall buildings in my time."

"Which was…?" Sam tried again, but Ed glanced away.

"Is this our first date?"

"If it was, would you tell me?"

"I said my age wasn't a first date reveal, so…."

Sam read Ed's hesitancy and didn't want to push. "I don't think this counts." He smirked when Ed looked at him with a start. "We need to leave the house for a real date."

"We'll have to start thinking about our rain check, then." Ed smiled back at him.

Drifting closer, Sam slid his hands around Ed's waist to finally connect and pull him in. Even in the heated pool, Ed's skin felt bracing. "I guess we will," he said and started to lean forward.

"Sam." Ed wrapped his arms around Sam's neck, but his hands fidgeted, and he held back from letting Sam reach his lips. "You're not only pretending because you think this is the only way to be safe from me, are you?"

"What?"

The idea that Ed still expected treachery surprised him, but then, Sam almost had betrayed him again, scared as he'd been. Ed was the most powerful and deadly creature he'd ever met, but he was still vulnerable, still so human.

"According to you," Sam said, "I'm putting myself in more danger by being with you. You gave me an out, Eddie, and I chose to stay. I want to stay. Which is a fitting segue, actually."

"Segue?"

Sam smirked, not trying to steal another kiss just yet, but floating with Ed and running his hands up Ed's back to keep him close. "Persephone was entranced by the Underworld," he began, and Ed's face lit up. "The areas for the condemned and the lost, the Elysian Fields for those who'd lived well, darkness and light crossing over each other just like on Mount Olympus and just like on the earth too.

"She didn't understand why so many condemned Hades and yet praised her, her mother, and all the other gods who actively caused the deaths of mortals. How could Hades look at her and still have offered to let her take up space in his home?

"'How long can I stay?' she asked, after Hades had shown her every expanse and nuance of the Underworld. 'As long as you want,' he said. 'If you want.' 'But my mother will look for me. I'll need to go back eventually and tread the earth when it's time for winter to end.' 'Then stay until then, and when the frost returns, if you wish it, you can return too.'

"Persephone considered the offer, relaxing with Hades in his personal rooms. He maintained a respectable distance, unlike most younger gods, brutish and leering whenever she passed. They each lay across their own sofa, facing one another, with food on a table between them.

"Persephone reached for a beautifully red, ripened fruit, but Hades cautioned her, 'Eat of the Underworld and you are bound to my bargain— you'll have to stay, leave in the spring and return every autumn. This place isn't meant for living mortals or other gods, so I am cursed to be alone or make deals for my company. Take your time and decide.'

"He might not have warned her, she thought. He might have let her eat and kept her all the same, but that was what made Hades different from Demeter or anyone else Persephone had met. He let her choose her own fate.

"She picked up the fruit, split it in two, and took a ravenous bite of the dripping seeds."

Finally, drawing Ed closer, Sam punctuated the ending by capturing a kiss.

Ed shuddered against him, kissing back heatedly, their bodies flush. Sam lowered his hands over Ed's ass to prompt him to wrap his legs around his waist, but Ed gasped and moved away with his eyes flickering yellow.

"I-I thought… *you* were Hades."

"Can't we both fit each role?" Sam said fondly.

He moved his hands up again to give Ed a reprieve but ducked in close to plant a sweet kiss below his ear. Then another. Then *another*, letting his tongue dart out, all while rubbing his hands up and down Ed's back, seeking a sign that he could push further.

Ed whimpered, and then growled like releasing a pleased purr. He dug his fingers into Sam's hair to hold him at his neck, encouraging him to keep kissing.

Smiling to himself at the reversal, Sam licked and bit down gently—until he felt Ed's breath on his neck in turn and the light scratch of fangs. He froze, but the fangs didn't press down. They dragged along his skin and pulled away, replaced with a tender kiss.

Sam kept licking at the salty remains of chlorine on Ed's skin, sliding his hands down like before, but this time, he continued beneath the elastic and found the smooth skin of Ed's ass.

"I-I can't." Ed snapped away so fast, Sam saw water treads between them. Ed's eyes were clearly yellow, glowing in the dark of the backyard at night, the patio lights glinting off his fangs. "I'm sorry. I am. I want all that, but it has to be slower. *Much* slower." He closed his eyes, and when he opened them, the inhuman aspects were gone.

Sam closed the space between them, heart pounding, but he wasn't deterred. His heart was mostly pounding from how good that had felt. "I'm sorry too. You're just really hard to resist." He smiled and slowly placed his hands back on Ed's hips.

"So are you." Ed leaned into the touch. "Although that is part of what concerns me…."

"You won't hurt me," Sam said, cupping Ed's cheek to reassure him, though yesterday the one who would have needed reassurance was him.

"I want to be certain. Think about our future date more, and... I'll see you tomorrow?" Ed said, even as he nuzzled into Sam's palm.

"Are you still going to tail Fitz tonight?"

"I should."

"Then, if we're both getting out of the pool, we could rinse off together."

Ed laughed. "*Very* hard to resist, but we better not."

"Okay, but I will be back tomorrow."

"And the next day?"

"And the next," Sam said, though it would all stop eventually; it had to.

He wondered if there was a way for it to not stop, but if he could be with Ed longer, what would that mean? What would he be willing to offer or ask for to stay?

Not yet ready to dwell on that, Sam rinsed off in the pool house shower, and only after he'd changed back into his clothes did Ed appear to take his place.

Sam stole another quick kiss before Ed could get past him.

"May I join you?" Ed startled him not long after, just as Sam was about to mount his bike.

"You mean, as a bat flying beside me?" Sam joked.

"That's a lie too," Ed assured him with a chuckle. "I mean, *with* you. When we get close to town, I can simply jump off."

"Jump off?" Sam repeated. Ed had said he'd grown a finger back once, but that didn't make it any easier to imagine. "I guess I don't need to lecture you about not wearing a helmet."

"I'll be fine," Ed said, climbing on behind Sam with his usual bashful smile.

Sam put his helmet on and kicked off onto the road. That chill always clung to Ed, and Sam loved the way it felt pressed against his back, even through Ed's clothes. He hung on to Sam's waist, an echo of what they would have shared if they'd had their real first date Friday night. This was different, but in some ways better, with no lies between them.

The city lights were upon them far too soon.

"Whichever one of us is Hades," Ed said, soft breath on Sam's neck at the edge of his helmet, "I'm glad we're weathering this *winter* together."

It was spring, but Sam got the meaning. "Now is the winter of our discontent," he called over the rushing wind.

"Made glorious summer," Ed said and kissed Sam's nape.

Then he leaped from the bike with a rush of extra cold striking Sam's body.

Sam glanced back in surprise—he had to at least look—and when he did, he swore he saw Ed simply standing there like he'd stopped time, before he vanished in a blur.

ED WISHED the night would vanish in a blur, but watching Fitz was more grating than the night before. He knew it was necessary, but it would have been so much easier if he could have torn the man's throat out.

Thankfully, maybe because it was Sunday, Fitz didn't stay out late. He stumbled home alone, confirming Ed's hopes that he would be easy to take out once the time came. They just needed to leave the right trail so their enemies conspired against each other instead of them.

Ed should go home. He could read, take out his telescope, swim again.

Or relieve some of the sexual tension building in his gut.

Sam was just so careful with his kisses. So precise. Ed hadn't been with a human since he *was* human, and as much as he feared losing control, it was a wonderful thrill.

Zipping through the streets unseen, he just wanted to see Sam again before he left the city. He made his way to the Hilton and up to the top floor balconies where Sam and his friends were staying. He could just barely peer inside with the curtains drawn, but that's all he needed, able to hear everything even with the balcony door shut.

The group had just returned from a late dinner.

"No more Lucifer's Rest, I'm serious," Sam was saying. "Or at least not so often. You're going to see Lara tomorrow on your date. You don't need to stalk her."

Ed felt a wave of guilt that he was basically stalking *Sam*, but he only wanted to ensure his safety.

"Or maybe don't go out with her at all."

"Why so against Lara all of a sudden?" Gerry asked, sporting a prominent pout.

"I'm not against her. I just think you should get to know her better."

"That's why people go on dates!"

"Will you two drop it," Mim said, reclining on the sofa with a stack of papers in her hands. "I want to turn in these job applications tomorrow. If I have to sit on my ass one more day listening to Gerry wax poetic about his dream chick, I'm going to strangle him with his laptop cord."

Gerry scowled, but Sam just smirked. That kind of harmless ribbing was what proved they were friends. Family. Ed had been that way once too.

With *her*.

"It's not like I was mooning over Lara the whole time," Gerry defended. "I finished tracing those account numbers."

"You did?" Sam moved across the room to crowd Gerry at the desk, looking over his shoulder at the laptop screen.

"They were all easy to find and hack into. If Simons's plan is to screw over the Cramers and take all his money back, he'll have no trouble.

"Well, except for one number. See that last one? I found it, it's the only one that's its own offshore account, but I can't get inside. Someone who knows what they're doing picked one hell of a secure bank. I might be able to get through all the firewalls eventually, but it's going to take some time."

"Do it. That's the account we need," Sam said. "I'll tell Eddie tomorrow. Maybe he'll recognize the bank."

Ed didn't; he could see the name and location from where he was spying.

"Anything to please 'Eddie,'" Gerry droned sarcastically. "How come you get to complain about my dating choices, but everything's fine and dandy with you dating him?"

"We're not—" Sam stopped himself short. "You don't even know him."

"Exactly. At least you've met my girlfriend."

"She's not your girlfriend."

"*Yet*. So, when do we get to meet your murder boyfriend?"

"Never if you call him that."

"You know, Gerry's got a point," Mim chimed in, sitting up straight and dropping the applications on the coffee table. "When do we get to meet Mr. Simons? Unless you're just using him and planning to hit and run when we're finished?"

"That's not what this is," Sam said, which made Ed smile—not that he'd doubted anymore.

"Long-distance relationship bros?" Gerry reached up to offer Sam a fist bump.

"No." He swatted it away. "I don't know. I'm not ready to think about that yet."

"Then you don't get a say about Lara."

"Gerr—"

"And I'll keep working on *Eddie's* project."

"Fine." Sam turned with a huff, arms crossed as he leaned back against the desk beside Gerry's chair—aimed right at Ed.

Sam couldn't see him, but Ed still took that as his cue to stop eavesdropping.

He wasn't ready to think about what came next either, but it warmed his usually cold heart to know that Sam really did care for him.

Leaping from the hotel, Ed crossed the street in a blink. He landed quietly in the alleyway on the other side, pausing to glance up at Sam's room one last time before he headed home.

He heard a shuffle, sensing that someone was in the alley with him, but when he darted after the noise, the street proved to have too many pedestrians to pinpoint who it might have been.

Damn. He should have listened to Sam.

CHAPTER 5

THE FIRST morning in too many days that Sam entered the house without feeling distracted or agitated, and Ed was the one wringing his hands.

"What happened?"

Ed dove into a rapid-fire explanation of how he'd checked on Sam last night. "Just to see you and make sure you were okay. I only lingered because your friend mentioned the account numbers, though I don't know the significance of the one that stood out.

"Then I left, pausing in the alley across the street. Someone was there. They saw me but ran off before I could see who it was."

"Another vampire?" Sam asked, feeling a cold chill trickle down his spine.

"It couldn't have been. We can sense each other when we're close."

"One of the Cramers, then? Or maybe Alverez or Shaw watching me?"

"No, I know all their scents. This was someone new."

"You know their *scents*?" Sam startled at that. "Mine too?"

"Of course."

"So, even if you weren't following me, you could find me pretty much anywhere at any moment?"

Ed's eyes widened, hands fidgeting in front of him. "I'm sorry. That must sound terrible. I promise I'll never spy again!"

"Eddie." Sam smiled, stopping him with a gentle hand on his arm. "It's okay. You were worried, and you didn't hear anything I didn't want you to."

That, finally, made Ed smile too. "I couldn't find you anywhere at any moment. I'd still need to catch your scent first. It can take time moving through the streets, even at my speed."

"It's kind of nice, actually, knowing you could always find me." Sam moved his grip down Ed's forearm to take his hand and led him into the living room to sit. "Maybe it was just some random person you freaked out."

"I hope so, but I don't know. People don't tend to lurk in alleyways near the Hilton, and this person was definitely trying to stay out of sight."

"Like you?" Sam teased.

"I'm so sorry," Ed said again. "I put everything at risk by not listening to you."

"It doesn't matter. If it was Lara or her boss, all they know is that you were looking in on me."

"I'm usually better at this." Ed continued to pout. "It's basic rules. Don't show your face where it might be suspicious. Don't retrace your steps or return to the scene of the crime. And never leave behind evidence that someone might use against you."

Sam paled as he realized he'd broken that rule too.

"What?"

"You were an idiot because you worry about me. I was just an idiot." He proceeded to remind Ed of his encounter with Lara and the *knife* he'd thrown away. "With my blood and fingerprints on it."

"You were distraught. It's understandable."

"But we can't afford to be sloppy." Taking his phone from his pocket, Sam showed Ed the text he'd woken up to that morning from the Cramers.

First check-in tonight or we're pulling our investment.

"Someone seeing you doesn't change anything, Eddie. We just have to make sure that when the bodies start dropping, they suspect each other instead of us. I have an idea...."

SAM HAD a marvelous idea, and it meant using one of Ed's cameras.

They worked hard all week—and stole several more intimate moments. Kisses. Furtive touches. Sam pressing Ed up against walls throughout the house. Even another swim, but each time, Ed put a stop to things before they could get too heated, afraid his passion would stir to hunger.

Now it was Friday again, and he was only getting hungrier.

The photos he'd taken wouldn't be useful for blackmail, but following someone with the occasional click and flash of a camera, only for no one to be behind them when they turned, was a great way to build paranoia. It had also given Ed an excuse to take more shots of the city. And steal the occasional shot of Sam.

"I wish Gerry didn't think Lara was so perfect, but I can't tell him the truth," Sam said, watching Ed hang up his most recent photos in his darkroom. "They've gone on two dates now and are going on a third tonight. He's completely smitten. If he and Mim didn't have those new jobs to keep busy, he'd probably be at Lucifer's Rest all day."

"Gerry's heart may be broken eventually, but we'll keep him safe," Ed said.

Sam hummed noncommittally but soon said with a teasing chuckle, "You know, maybe one of these days you can take a picture of me when I'm paying attention."

Ed had gotten quite a few impressive shots of the city and their quarries, but his favorite was one of Sam leaving the Cramers' warehouse with no discernible landmarks in the background, just brick and glass and Sam's profile bearing a smirk.

"Are you offering to pose for me?" Ed said, then blanched when he rethought those words. "N-not that I mean—"

"Eddie, if you asked, I'd happily pose for you."

Ed swallowed hard, transfixed by Sam's gaze. He made Ed feel very hungry, which meant he couldn't possibly entertain any more stolen moments until after he fed. He thought maybe Sam had been avoiding the topic, but they couldn't ignore the inevitable forever.

The doorbell rang before Ed could say anything, and they shared a smile at the familiar interruption.

Heading swiftly up out of the basement, Ed followed Sam but let him answer the door since it wasn't yet dark outside.

"Marie. And hey, kiddos. What can I do for you?"

"Hey, Sam. Is Mr. Simons home? I wanted to ask him something about the barbecue."

"Sure, come in."

They'd agreed that any more house calls from the Neu-Ryans were to be met with friendly acceptance.

Ed stepped into the foyer as Marie entered with her twins at her coattails. "Mrs. Neu-Ryan, what a pleasure. And these must be your lovely children." He shook her hand and smiled down at the curious five-year-olds eyeing the inside of his home.

"Wow," Marie said, but then shook herself to attention. "Sorry, it's just that my husband described you well. I'm glad we can finally meet. It's a little embarrassing, though, since I'm here to ask a favor. Do you have an extra table we could borrow for Saturday? No matter how I look at it, I think we're going to be one short."

Ed had been trying to forget about the barbecue, but he kept his smile cordial. "You know, I think I do, in the garage." It was just a basic table, which was why he hadn't bothered finding a place for it yet.

"I can show her, see if it'll work," Sam offered. "You can handle the kids for two minutes, right?" His grin was teasing, like he expected Ed to panic.

Ed did no such thing. "I can. How about I give you two a tour." He bent to their level, and the twins nodded eagerly.

Sam led Marie through the dining room toward the side door that connected to the garage. Ed had a car for appearance's sake, though he rarely used it. Meanwhile, Ed brought the children the other way into the living room.

"Don't worry about not touching anything," he said. "I'm not strict. Why have possessions if you don't plan to enjoy them. But a few pieces are fragile, okay?"

They barely responded, too preoccupied looking over the radios, photos, and odd vase, clock, or figurine. They stopped at an old wooden chest against the wall, expensive, with intricate carvings, but it was heavy, which was probably why it hadn't been on Sam's to-steal list.

"Do you want to know what's inside?" Ed asked, crouching beside them.

They nodded like before, still shy.

"Go on, but be careful. The lid is very heavy."

Working together, the twins lifted the latch and brought the lid up, revealing a collection of additional photographs, mostly from the past few decades, of landscapes and cities like the others. Ed might still put them up somewhere.

The children seemed disappointed, not interested in photos, but Ed reached inside to grab on to the false bottom.

"This chest holds a secret. It's actually much deeper than it looks." He set the shelf aside, allowing the children to peer in at his most prized comic books, in plastic sleeves and stacked in neat piles at the bottom. "I have more in storage, but these are my favorites."

"You like Spider-Man?" Dawn asked in awe, gazing at the cover of Amazing Spider-Man #42, with Mary Jane's iconic first appearance and the quote: "Face it, Tiger, you just hit the jackpot."

"I do," Ed said. "Superheroes are like modern myths, epic stories of good against evil with lessons to be learned, and all with very pretty pictures. Spider-Man's my favorite," he added in a whisper, making the twins giggle as they agreed.

They continued gazing at the stacks as if the comics were treasures to be delved into.

Ed grabbed the book on top, revealing an identical copy below it. "I actually have two of this one, so I wouldn't mind if you wanted to borrow it, as long as your mother says it's okay." He held the book out to whichever twin would be brave enough to grab it first.

Joey started to, but Dawn was faster than her brother.

"Hey!" he protested.

"And as long as you share," Ed said.

Dawn let Joey take a corner, both looking reverently at the comic.

"If your mother says yes, you can take it home and look at it out of the plastic. I'd like for you to take good care of it, but if something happens, I won't be mad."

That seemed to put them at further ease, and eventually, Dawn let Joey hang on to it alone while they turned from the chest to explore the rest of the room. It didn't take long for them to part the patio curtains and find the pool outside.

"Can we see it?" Joey asked, both children rushing back to take Ed's hands and drag him toward the doors.

A strong waft of their scent struck Ed, and he felt his mouth water. Children smelled different from adults, fresh and new without the pheromones of adolescence, like they'd taste different too—sweeter.

Ed shook his head. He was definitely too hungry.

"I-I don't know if I want you getting close to the water without your mother," he said, resisting their pull before they could yank him right outside. "And I'm allergic to the sun, so I only swim at night."

"How can you be 'lergic to the sun?" Joey scrunched his nose.

"Can we swim during the day?" Dawn asked before Ed could answer.

"Well...."

"Kids," Marie chided, having returned with Sam.

"I wouldn't mind." Ed turned to her. "It's spring, warming up every day. As long as you give me fair warning, you can bring the children over and use the pool sometimes."

"Are you sure?"

"Please, Mama? Can we?" Joey pleaded, and Dawn parroted him.

"Please, Mama?"

"We can't today, and tomorrow's the barbecue, but… maybe another day, if Mr. Simons really doesn't mind."

"Not at all. And call me Ed."

Sam gave him a warm, satisfied smile. The kids were ecstatic, and Marie looked like Ed had given her a wonderful stress relief for the busy summer ahead.

"Thank you, Ed. For the table too."

"And the comic!" Joey held it up with a grin.

"Comic?"

"If it's all right," Ed said.

Sam had already helped Marie load the table into her father's truck that she'd borrowed, and after they left, Ed felt Sam's eyes on him.

"What?"

"You're pretty good with kids yourself."

Ed just wished they didn't smell like appetizers.

That thought made him very aware of the time, of the sun close to setting, and of his growing hunger that made Sam smell appetizing too.

"You had some of your comics in that chest the whole time? I need to be a better thief." Sam's light chuckle cut off abruptly as he looked at Ed's stiff expression. "What?"

"It's time, Sam. I know where Fitz will be tonight, judging by his patterns—back at the club on Forty-seventh."

"Tonight?" Sam's mirthful expression vanished.

"I'm hungry. Best not to tempt that." Ed looked to the front doors, as if to indicate the family that had left.

"R-right. Okay."

"I'll carry it out exactly as we planned."

"I'm coming with you."

"What?" Ed snapped back to him. "You don't have to. You don't need to see me like that."

"I know," Sam said determinedly, "but I'm coming with you anyway."

SAM HAD to go with Ed. Even if what was about to happen made his pulse ratchet like it was a week ago all over again.

Ed was meticulous in how he prepared for the evening, choosing a simple outfit and warning Sam as well, "Wear as little extra clothing as possible. No jacket. Less chance of leaving evidence behind. You'll park your bike at the Hilton so it's assumed you were there all night, and I'll pick you up."

"In your car?"

"No."

"But the Hilton is across town from where Fitz will be."

"I'm aware," Ed said with a smile.

All Sam could think about then was Ed whisking him through the city at hyperspeed, which at least helped distract him from what they were going to do.

Fitz deserved it. He was a terrible man who'd done terrible things. Sam had investigated their backgrounds, and every single one of them had assault charges, worse in some cases, just not full convictions for murder. That didn't mean they hadn't committed any, and even if they hadn't....

They deserved this. They all did.

The ride into town felt strangely short, and in no time Sam was already at the Hilton, parking in the underground garage, where cameras easily caught him. He went into the stairwell, finding a blind spot from security as he waited for Ed.

The only warning he got was two whispered words: "Hang on."

The lurch in Sam's stomach was like the drop from a roller coaster, a mad rush of speed, with nothing but the haze of city lights and motion all around him. He was conscious only of Ed's chill, and clawed for purchase as if he might drop any moment, finding Ed's neck and clinging tightly.

When they came to a stop, they were on a rooftop, looking down at Fitz's favored strip club from across the street.

Sam teetered as Ed released him, afraid he might throw up once his stomach caught up to him, but Ed's hand settled at his waist, the other at the back of his neck, and the cool touch chased away any nausea.

"Are you okay?"

"We're going to have to do that more often," Sam said.

The smile Ed graced him with was lovely, but as they started to drift closer, he took a breath, like catching Sam's scent, and his eyes flickered yellow.

"B-better not," Ed said. "I can smell Fitz, but I'll check to make sure he's inside. When he heads home, we'll follow him and end this, right in his apartment."

It was even more important that they do things carefully, because they wouldn't be destroying all the evidence, only everything that pointed at them.

Ed vanished and returned in moments to report that Fitz was indeed enjoying one of the back rooms of the strip club. They settled in to wait, and Sam thought this would be the hardest part, like the proverbial watched pot waiting to boil. But, like the ride into town, it was over quickly, and Fitz was soon exiting to stumble unsteadily down the street.

For once, Sam got to experience tailing someone from Ed's perspective. Suddenly, they'd be down one alleyway or another, on different rooftops, behind different buildings, always out of sight but within view of Fitz. When they finally reached his building, the coast clear down his hallway, as soon as he unlocked and opened his door....

"Ready?" Ed whispered.

"Ready."

Ed zipped them inside, hiding in the shadows but leaving Sam standing in Fitz's living room.

"The fuck are you doing here?" Fitz slurred, slamming his door shut behind him.

"If you know anything about Midnight," Sam said calmly, "now is the time to tell me."

"Are you fucking kidding me?" Fitz laughed, taking out his switchblade.

"Anything at all could go a long way to making this easier on you."

"You got some nerve, coming in here, not even armed. I don't know shit about Midnight, but if I did, I'd still carve up that pretty face before I told you anything." He lunged forward with a snarl, taking an angry, intoxicated swing, but Sam didn't bother dodging.

Fitz's hand froze in midair, his wrist snatched up by Ed.

Eyes glowing and fangs already extended, Ed squeezed Fitz's wrist so hard, Sam heard bones crack. Before Fitz could cry out or his fingers could slacken on the switchblade, Ed swung his arm down, still holding Fitz's wrist, and stabbed into his side.

Fitz tried to scream, but Ed spun him so fast and slammed him up against the wall with such force that the sound was knocked out of him. His eyes blinked in disbelief, staring at Ed's monstrous face.

"My apologies. I don't usually cause my victims unnecessary pain, but we need to make this look believable."

Ed swooped in to bite Fitz's neck and twisted the knife in the same motion, Fitz's scream once again getting lost, though he managed to sputter.

"The fuck…. Wh-what the *fuck?*" He tried to push Ed off, but Ed was an immovable wall.

Sam watched from the same spot Ed had left him, in the middle of the room but still only a few feet from where Ed was feeding, much tidier than last week, not spilling a single drop.

Until he yanked the knife free to let Fitz bleed out onto the floor.

"We don't want them questioning how much blood you'll be missing," Ed said, swinging the knife up, still in Fitz's hand with Ed's wrapped securely around it, and sliced through his bite marks to hide the puncture wounds. He returned then to drink from the pulsing gash, finally letting the knife drop.

Fitz's glazed eyes found Sam and stayed on him, pleading silently through his pain for Sam to help him. Sam wouldn't, even if he thought this was wrong or cruel, but he kept waiting for the freak-out to hit him.

His stomach was in knots, pulse racing, breath coming in pants, but it wasn't like last week. Back then, he'd feared for his life too. Now, he knew he didn't have to.

Ed drank slowly, but Fitz's eyes eventually went blank, and Ed dropped him in his own puddle of blood. Once again, Sam saw satisfaction and sated desire on Ed's face as he licked his lips clean, the only blood on him being a little on his sleeve.

"Did you touch anything?" Ed turned to Sam with his eyes still glowing.

"N-no," Sam said.

"Then stay still."

Ed moved around the apartment like the same blur Sam had seen before, and when he'd finished, he stood beside Fitz's body.

"All is well. The only fingerprints here are his. Sam? Are you okay?"

Reality snapped back into place. Sam was unsure of the passage of time, but Ed was Ed again as he came over, with green eyes and a concerned scrunch to his brow.

"Yeah," Sam said, surprised maybe, but honest. "I'm good."

ED WAS so, so good.

All the drink and drugs hadn't soured Fitz's blood. It still tasted amazing, and Ed felt that wonderful ecstasy he always did after feeding. He kept waiting for something else to spoil the evening, for Sam to admit he couldn't handle what Ed was or seeing him take someone's life again.

Ed brought them back to his home to clean up. Sam's bike was still at the hotel with footage of him going inside and never leaving. They were ghosts, with no proof that they had been anywhere else at all.

But Sam was quiet.

"Would you like to shower?" Ed asked.

"Do I need to?"

"No. There's nothing on you, but we should still wash your clothes to be sure."

"Yeah. Good idea."

They went to the basement and stripped down to their underwear to load the clothes into the washer. Ed thought it would be impolite to stare at Sam's bared form, because while they'd seen each other in swim trunks, the tight fit of boxer briefs left far less to the imagination.

Then again, Sam had already seen Ed naked, and the memory of that made him blush. He reddened further when he realized Sam was staring at him.

"Are *you* going to shower?" Sam asked.

"Just to rinse off. Sam—"

"I keep waiting to feel afraid," Sam cut him off, calm despite his words. "To be disgusted or horrified. Is there something wrong with me that I'm not? That all I want to do right now is kiss you?"

Ed straightened in surprise, but whatever hammer he'd feared might fall, that Sam had apparently feared too, didn't seem to be coming. "No. We ended an evil man, giving me something I need and keeping you safer. It isn't wrong not to mourn him."

Sam nodded like he knew that but was still conflicted by his lack of… feeling conflicted. He stepped closer to Ed with clarity solidifying in his gaze, as the washer filled the basement with white noise. "I think I like how terrifyingly powerful you are, and that you can still be so gentle with me."

"W-well… you're worth being gentle for," Ed said, grasping Sam's hand to lead them back upstairs before his nerves could get the better of him.

He still wanted to rinse off in case he'd missed any errant spots, but he didn't want to lose sight of Sam. He even left the bathroom door open a crack. When he returned from the shower a few minutes later with a towel wrapped around his waist, Sam sat on the bed with his phone beside him, looking bemused.

"My calendar just reminded me."

"Of?"

"We need to make a pie for tomorrow."

Ed laughed. "Tonight?"

"I'd have to come over pretty early in the morning. Or…."

"Or?" Ed approached him slowly.

"Or I could stay."

"Or you could stay," Ed repeated.

"So, I'll tell my friends not to expect me?" He waved his phone at Ed.

"You can message them in a minute."

Ed got closer, and when Sam parted his legs, he walked right between them. He took the phone and set it aside, and then grasped Sam's face to kiss him. He wasn't hungry now. If there was ever a time when Ed believed he could control himself, it was this moment.

Sam clutched his waist, and as they kissed, he tugged the towel loose to let it fall to the floor. Ed felt his face heat up, knowing he was now naked between Sam's legs, but he didn't pull away. He tipped Sam back and started to climb onto the bed.

Sam scooted up the mattress, trying to keep in contact with Ed's mouth, but they had to part eventually to situate themselves. He stared at Ed hovering over him and looked down the full length of his body. Ed wanted to look at Sam the same.

Reaching for Sam's underwear, he waited for a sign that it was okay, and Sam's frantic nod was clearly permission. Ed slid them down

Sam's legs and tossed them to the floor. He was so beautiful, every human scar and mark and tantalizing tan line.

Sam grabbed Ed by the back of his neck to drag him in for another kiss, and Ed finally lowered his body to settle on top of him. The slide of their bare bodies made Ed tremble. They writhed against each other, rolling to be side by side, and Sam's hand drifted down to take hold of Ed between them. Ed thrust into his grip, feeling a growl build in his throat.

"You can do this. I'll show you," Sam said, rolling them further until Ed was on his back, and then he slithered down to get between Ed's legs.

Ed's eyes sharpened, flashing yellow, his fangs growing no matter how hard he tried to keep them back, but he thought, this time, maybe he could keep it to just that. Sam looked at him and had to see it all, his bestial side, but it didn't make him flinch or pause as he descended to take Ed into his mouth.

Ed roared and clutched at the sheets.

He was uncut, and Sam quite the opposite, but that didn't give Sam pause either. He used his tongue with delicate reverence around the skin, down beneath Ed's balls and up to his tip, where he took him in deeper and sucked hard.

It was wonderful, how fervently Sam attended to him, but Ed didn't want to come like this. He wanted to pleasure Sam too.

Coaxing Sam upward, Ed grasped his shoulders and flipped them, careful as he kissed Sam since his fangs were out. He didn't trust himself to tend to Sam in kind, but the wetness Sam had left between them made it easy to grind together with a smoother slide.

Ed reached down to grip Sam, his long fingers stroking firm and slow, and then speeding up as he took hold of himself too, and thrust against Sam's hip.

"*Shit*... I'm not... gonna last long," Sam huffed, neck arching as he pressed his head back into Ed's pillows. He shook amid their desperate, messy rutting, and so did Ed.

Ed started to slow them, lifting Sam's hips while keeping their cocks aligned. "We won't get as far as I'd like tonight, but I want a preview of how you'll moan once we do."

He brought his fingers to his mouth, but Sam stopped him and brought those fingers to *his* mouth instead. He sucked them between his lips, and Ed thrust harder against him at the reminder of where those lips had been—and of that sinful pie all those weeks ago. Once the fingers were sopping, Sam released them, and Ed brought them down to tease Sam as promised.

He started a slower, rhythmic rocking with their cocks connected as he penetrated Sam. The first knuckle brought out a whimper, but a wicked twist of the full finger pulled out the moan Ed wanted to hear.

Again, Ed growled. He could admit that part of him wanted to devour every inch of Sam, but focusing on giving pleasure kept him steady.

Sam tempted him so terribly, moaning louder with Ed's gentle thrusts and grabbing the back of Ed's neck for another kiss. It was strange to kiss someone with his fangs out when the other person didn't have fangs of their own. It forced Ed to be careful, helped him keep his nature in check, even as he pulled away to sniff along Sam's neck and dragged his fangs down the skin. Ed didn't bite, and Sam didn't flinch, and it was all so marvelous.

He was getting close, his thrusts increasing, but he wanted to get a second finger in Sam and kept a steady pace until Sam was open enough for that other digit to breach him. They were both moaning then, because they were close, closer, right there—

Sam came first from the twin sensations of their rocking and Ed's fingers inside him, and Ed followed soon after. They kept rocking into the mess that stained them until their panting slowed and Ed finally pulled his fingers away.

His eyes dimmed and his fangs retreated as he rolled to lie beside Sam in the sticky afterglow.

"Told you… you could do it." Sam laughed, making Ed chuckle too.

"I'd like to finish that thought sometime." Opening Sam up and taking him fully.

"Definitely. But for now…." Sam tilted his head to gaze at Ed with a heartfelt smile. "Is all your hunger sated?"

Ed had to admit, "Very."

CHAPTER 6

SAM FOUND Ed's bed unbelievably comfortable. Though that was probably because it was never used.

He woke up at that perfect natural pace of having had a good night's sleep, with the sun coming in through the curtains. That made him blink more fully alert, because even though the sun was only just rising, Sam wasn't used to Ed having his curtains parted.

"Oh! Good morning," Ed's voice drifted from the dresser. "Is the light bothering you? I thought you might prefer it. I don't really know much about morning etiquette anymore."

Sam took in Ed's figure slowly. He was dressed in one of his less garish cardigans but had on those bunny slippers again, fussing in the drawers for a second set of clothes. He'd let the sun stream in *for Sam*, and now he was trying to pick out an extra outfit for him, since his was being washed.

Stretching out on the spacious bed, Sam enjoyed the feeling of being very naked still beneath covers. "I can't think of a better way to wake up. Unless you were in bed with me."

Smiling back at him with a faint blush, Ed went to the window first to block out the light, and then prowled toward the bed.

"You are seriously sexy, Eddie. Especially in slippers." Sam winked.

Ed blushed deeper at the tease, toeing off the slippers to kick them aside. "I can undress again, if you like?"

"Mmm…." Sam hummed as Ed crawled up to join him, trapping him against the mattress. "Tempting. I don't suppose you went ahead and made that pie?"

"That falls under *your* duties." Ed scowled at him.

Sam chuckled. "Then you're going to have to let me up."

"In a minute," Ed said softly, leaning down to kiss him.

Even with Ed clothed, it felt so good to have him on top like that while Sam was nude beneath the sheets, teasing his skin with the gentle slide of cotton. Ed's hands weren't as tentative as they used to be, sliding down Sam's body.

"I could get used to this," Sam said.

"Me too." Ed settled comfortably atop him and gently stroked the side of his neck. "Though we need to be more careful. I left marks. Faint but still noticeable."

Sam reached up to feel them too, but they were just two light scratches where Ed had dragged his fangs. They blended right in with where his knife cut had been. "The perils of gardening," he said, since it was as good an excuse as any.

Ed snickered before kissing him once more, but as they started to deepen the embrace, Sam bucked his hips up into Ed, and the familiar flash of yellow overtook his eyes.

"W-we better focus on baking." Ed carefully rolled away from Sam. "Your clothes are done, but I thought you might want something new to wear." He indicated the jeans and blue button-down he'd chosen. They were close enough in size.

"Thanks. I want to jump in the shower quick," Sam said, snatching his phone from the nightstand, "while you start getting out everything I need to make that pie." He had a recipe on his phone, but as he brought the device to life, he noticed a few missed messages.

"The Cramers?" Ed asked. "Did they find Fitz's body?"

"No. They might not even notice he's missing for a couple days. These are from Mim." Sam pulled up the messages as Ed peered over his shoulder.

Hope you had a fun night, Romeo, was first.

Followed by, *Gerry sure did.*

"Urg," Sam groaned. "Third date rule, apparently."

"Third date?" Ed questioned, then seemed to seriously consider that. "What does it mean that we technically haven't had our first?"

"That we both really wanted it," Sam said, setting his phone aside to pull Ed close again and kiss him soft and slow. "And like you said, we still have to… finish the thought."

Ed shuddered against him. "I-I'd like that. But we should wait again. To be safe."

"Are you really that worried?" Sam asked, running his fingers through Ed's slightly mussed strawberry hair. He didn't look like a vicious killer, lying in bed beside him.

"When it comes to your safety, I will always put caution first." Then Ed smiled. "But we can see how things go, as long as we're careful. Now—" He reached across Sam to grab the phone. "—do we even have everything you need for this pie?"

THEY DID have everything Sam needed—save the rhubarb, planted in the yard, which Ed refused to retrieve since he was already going to be outdoors for longer than he liked today.

"Do you tan that badly?" Sam teased, fresh-smelling and looking very smart in Ed's clothes when he came back in with the red ripened stalks. "Burn?"

"Implode," Ed muttered, but when Sam's eyes widened, he thought better of the joke. "Not really! The redness might become noticeable after too long, but it'll go away once I'm indoors again. It just hurts."

After setting the rhubarb in the sink, Sam turned to him with a frown. "I'll keep an eye on you, make sure you don't get too baked. We'll save that for the pie. I wish we didn't have to go at all, but it'll help your image."

"I know. Now, how can I be of service?" Ed looked over the ingredients and supplies they'd set out on the kitchen island.

"Wash and chop the rhubarb?"

That was an easy task given Ed's speed, and he set to work, already finished with a pile of rhubarb pieces before Sam had even started measuring sugar.

"And yet I do all the chores." Sam shook his head.

"I *pay* you. And just because I'm quick or good at something doesn't mean I enjoy it." Ed meant for more than just menial tasks, but then, that wasn't always true, because when it came to killing, especially someone like Fitz, he did enjoy what he was and what he did.

"Sometimes I enjoy it," he spit out before Sam could go back to baking. "I *did* enjoy it. Last night. I need to know you understand that."

A stillness settled over Sam like a wave of reality crashing on his shoulders. He dumped the sugar into the bowl and set the measuring cup aside. "I didn't only take this job—the original job to steal from you—because I don't have other prospects or needed the money. I *did* need the money, but I like being a thief. We said this could be our last job if we made enough to move, start over, but a part of me always planned to return to old habits, at least for the thrill.

"Carrying out a plan, getting one over on someone, especially a bad someone, can be... fun. You're the first person I felt guilty over."

"Sam," Ed said, catching his wrist before he could reach for the next ingredient, "stealing and killing people don't exactly compare."

"I know. But I enjoyed last night too. It felt... justified. If things had gone differently, and you'd killed Daniel—"

"I would have felt awful," Ed said, thinking of those children, his wife.

"That's good enough for me." Sam smiled and pulled his hand away to go right back to baking. "Preheat the oven?"

This couldn't last, Ed told himself, trying to make the inevitable blow softer, but every passing moment with Sam made him wonder if it could.

While they waited for the pie to bake, they remained in the kitchen, discussing tactics for the barbecue: keep Ed in the shade or inside whenever possible and mostly just be a charming neighborly presence.

"We can enjoy ourselves," Sam said. "It doesn't have to be an act. Let's have fun."

"And if someone questions our relationship?" Ed asked.

"I don't mind being honest if you don't."

That was an unfair answer, because it passed back to Ed to define what they were. "Our professional relationship got away from us, and... we're exploring options?"

"Hoping we'll eventually move on from hand-stuff to an actual date?"

"S-Sam!" Ed sputtered.

Sam's smile and gentle chuckle always made the hardest of this seem easy. "I'll try to avoid saying that part out loud," he said, scooting closer to Ed to draw him in for a kiss.

That part was getting easier too.

Once the pie was finished and cooled, Ed made sure he had his sunglasses and that he was dressed coolly but in long sleeves, and they used his car to cross the short distance to the neighbors'. It was not an overcast day, and being so close to noon now, the sun was high and painfully hot and glaring. Ed gritted his teeth regardless and painted on a smile.

The Neu-Ryans were the closest house to his, but there were several other homes that could be considered neighbors, and all of them appeared to be in attendance. Along with dozens of children and many police officers.

"Mr. Sam! Mr. Ed!"

Oh, Ed hoped "Mr. Ed" didn't stick.

Dawn and Joey ran over to greet them, Joey wearing a T. rex shirt and Dawn a sundress with what appeared to be nondescript monsters all over it.

Sam's hands were occupied with the pie, so each child grabbed one of Ed's hands to drag him toward the food tables.

"We took good care of your comic, Mr. Ed!" Dawn said.

"No jelly stains or nothin'!" Joey chimed in.

Ed had to laugh. He wasn't used to having children hanging on him, in the middle of the day, putting so much attention on him. Then he realized that a lot of attention was on him. The neighbors must all realize who he was—or it was just the cops recognizing him as a recent suspect in a murder case.

"Don't tear his arms off!" Daniel called, hurrying over to save him. "I'm so glad you both came."

It was the first time Ed had seen Daniel out of a suit. He looked very young and rugged in jeans and a T-shirt, and every bit the family man as he scooped up both kids and hung them over his shoulders, to which they giggled wildly.

Ed understood why Sam was so taken with this family. He didn't want to see any harm come to them either, especially not because of him.

"Help yourselves to food," Daniel said, setting the kids down to go running off to join the other children. "Marie has drinks inside. I'm sure she'd love to give you a tour. Which we haven't had of your place yet!" He patted Ed's shoulder in jest.

"You haven't, have you? That makes me feel like a terrible neighbor," Ed said. "We'll have to remedy that sometime. Maybe when you bring the kids over for a swim."

"Marie mentioned that. Are you sure? Let those kids over once, and they're going to want to move in." He was clearly enjoying being host, bright and boisterous. "You might recognize some of the other neighbors, but that's Marie's dad and her brother over there." He gestured to a handsome older man and a younger man about college age. "I'm sure some of my family is around too. The rest are coworkers, so sorry that it's mostly cops."

He got called the other direction, but before heading off, he motioned for Marie's brother to come over.

"Mikey! Show Ed and Sam down the food line, will you? And add this to the dessert table." He passed off Sam's pie.

Mike was a nice young man, easygoing and friendly, as was his father, Joe, where little Joey had gotten his name. Ed and Sam were soon caught up in the din of it all, the bustle of meeting people whose names and faces Ed would probably forget. A simple smile from him, however, seemed to go a long way toward banishing the suspicious and curious glances from neighbors and cops alike.

"Stupid question I should have asked before," Sam whispered as they went shuffling down the buffet line, "but you *can* eat, right? You just don't need to?"

"Yes. It tastes fine. I just don't crave it and it isn't sustaining." Ed took small amounts to fill his plate since he'd only be picking at it for appearances.

The excuse of his "condition" made it easy to head inside rather than get herded to the tables. Sam reached to take his hand, a mostly unconscious act, Ed thought, but the brush of his thumb along Ed's wrist that had been sitting in the sun for too long made him hiss.

Sam frowned and tugged Ed more gently the rest of the way inside, stopping in the entryway to run the cooler backside of his hand along Ed's reddened skin.

"It's okay. Watch," Ed said, pulling his arm away and holding it in the shadows. The redness vanished after only a few seconds.

Sun exposure aside, Ed didn't feel strange being surrounded by so many people trying to get to know him, not with Sam beside him. As long as he didn't stay too much in the sun, everything would be fine.

EVERYTHING SEEMED to be going fine—until they met up with Marie in the kitchen and she introduced them to one of her coworkers.

"The mysterious Ed Simons in the big house down the street," Linda said, a charming woman, but with a bit more *reporter* shining in her eyes. "Marie talks about you all the time, but I feel like I know so little. Tell us about life before Riverside. What brought you here?"

Sam felt like an idiot for not preparing Ed for those kinds of questions, but that's when the smooth liar reappeared from centuries of experience.

"I've lived abroad most of my life," Ed said with a small shrug. "I've been in Europe for the past several years, but I missed the States and settled on Riverside mostly because of the house. I was a grand staircase away from choosing Long Beach, but the house here had more of what I wanted."

He *was* good at this. It was just Sam who tripped him up.

"And how did you two meet?" Linda asked.

"I work for Ed," Sam said. "I'm his assistant."

"I'm sorry, I thought you were a couple."

"Oh, uhh...."

"Well...."

"I knew it!" Marie exclaimed, and then immediately reeled herself back in. "Sorry, I'm being a totally shameless busybody of a neighbor, but I kept thinking there had to be something between you two."

Even if they hadn't just confirmed it with their rambling, Ed's blush said plenty.

"Robbing the cradle, huh?" Linda nudged Ed playfully.

"Linda! They aren't that far apart in age," Marie said, rushing on to add, "not that it matters."

"You must think me a terrible predator," Ed said with a bashful duck of his head, which would have made Sam laugh if he didn't know Ed was being genuine, "seducing my employee."

"Not at all!" the women practically spoke over each other.

"And well they shouldn't," Sam said. "The seducing was all me. Mostly for a raise."

Ed scoffed, but Sam laughed, which prompted the ladies to join him.

"Relax," Sam assuaged Ed with a chaste kiss to his cheek, "I wouldn't tease if you weren't such an easy mark."

"Aw, you two are the cutest," Marie said, sharing an adoring look with Linda. "Now I get why you were sequestering yourself in that house. You had a love story to play out. I'm just glad we finally got you into the sunshine, Ed. Only it doesn't bother you too much, does it?"

Ed had the sunglasses hooked into his shirt. "I just need to balance my time indoors."

"I don't think I caught what you do for work," Linda returned to grilling him.

"I'm mostly a collector. I've been a curator for museums in the past and acquired items for other collectors. I thought I'd take a break, though, inventory my own possessions, which Sam has been helping with, and figure out what to do next."

"Any hobbies?" Marie asked.

"He's a pretty great photographer," Sam said.

"Really? We're always looking for freelancers at Channel Five."

"Oh, I'm hardly a professional."

"Looks professional enough to me," Sam argued. "Could be a real…. Spider-Man opportunity for you."

Ed chuckled helplessly, cheeks going red again.

"That reminds me," Marie said, "I need to give you back that comic book. The kids really loved it."

"Let them keep it," Ed said with ease.

"You don't have to—"

"Really, I insist. I have another copy. They can have it."

Sam was honestly proud, not only because Ed was schmoozing the neighbors with such skill, but because it was honest. He wondered how seldom Ed allowed himself to get close to people, to know them and make friends. Almost never, he figured, because in Ed's own words—it got harder to say goodbye, since being a vampire, he always had to move on when the people he met grew older and… died.

Like Sam would someday.

The conversation drifted away from him as he spent far too much time dwelling on that. When he came back to himself, the others were talking about Ed's photography again.

"The least you can do is show me your work. Let me be the judge."

"I don't know if I'd want to see my name on the nightly news."

"Shouldn't be a problem if it's for a good reason," came a new voice, drawing their attention to the kitchen doorway. "And not a bad one," finished the stranger with a wide smile that didn't seem to reach his eyes—blue and piercing.

He had short blond hair and made a tall, striking figure. Daniel was with him, and their equally Aryan appearances made Sam wonder if this was one of his relatives.

"Ed, Sam, this is Detective Cheroneau," Daniel said—*not* a relative, then, unless he was a distant cousin. "He's a transfer, working with me on the, um… murders."

"Daniel!" Marie scolded.

"But no shop talk at the barbecue!"

"I wouldn't mind," Linda muttered.

"Hon, didn't you want to introduce Linda to Mikey?" Daniel deflected, like he was used to deflecting hungry reporters.

"Right!" Marie said. "You haven't met my baby brother yet. We'll be right back," she said to Sam and Ed before dragging Linda out of the kitchen.

Almost immediately, Daniel was called away again, the perils of being host, which meant Sam and Ed were suddenly alone with Cheroneau, who didn't seem at all like he was going to scamper off and leave them be.

"New in town, Detective?" Sam tried to read him.

But all he said was, "Call me Hal."

His smile was dangerously calculating.

Like a cop with a lead.

If Ed noticed, he didn't let it show, reminding Sam again that he did know how to navigate these things. "I'm new in town myself," Ed said, "moved in next door a little over a month ago."

"I know. You did all those renovations."

"That's right. Well, I didn't do them myself."

"Of course. You hired a contractor. Who was he again? Oh, wait. He was murdered."

There came that gripping chill Sam thought he'd banished. He knew this had been going too smoothly.

"Not to worry," Cheroneau said with his false smile, "even if there was a conflict of interest with you and Daniel being friendly, I've also looked over the case, and you have an alibi. Don't you, Mr. Simons?" He stared evenly into Ed's impressively neutral expression. "Mr. Coleman vouches for you. I mean, it would be different if you two were sleeping together."

Shit. Maybe they shouldn't have been so cavalier about their relationship.

"Sorry, I had to detective my way through that one. But full disclosure? That's not enough either. There isn't evidence to put you at any of the murders, just suspicion and coincidence, and Daniel thinks very highly of both of you. As of now, you have nothing to worry about."

He patted Ed's shoulder like Daniel had earlier, but with an entirely different connotation, as if to say he was not as easily swindled as the Neu-Ryans.

"Enjoy the barbecue."

Just when Sam had thought they had nothing to worry about.

"I REALLY thought we had nothing to worry about," Sam said once they'd returned to Ed's house. "We *don't*. We know who the other detective on the case is now. He has to act like that, because they don't have any leads. He's desperate, trying to get us to reveal something—"

"Sam." Ed stopped him, since Sam had started a hurried pace across the foyer.

"Sorry," he said, one of the rare times he'd shown his age and inexperience compared to Ed. "I'm rambling."

"You are." Ed smiled. "It's cute on you. But I really do think we're fine. We're doing everything we can. We've done everything right. Like you said, he's desperate, trying to scare us." Ed had to believe that until they had real reason to suspect otherwise. "Were you heading back to the hotel now?"

Sam calmed with a drop in his shoulders, finally releasing some of his tension. "I know Cheroneau spooked us—well, *me*—but I had something else planned for tonight, if you're up for it?"

Ed was always up for whatever Sam wanted.

Until he grabbed Ed's hand and dragged him to the widow's walk. Ed almost refused and said he'd had enough adrenaline for one day, but Sam looked so eager as he gripped his hand.

The stars were just starting to twinkle when they made their way up onto the roof, and a pair of lawn chairs and Ed's telescope were waiting for them.

"How…? *When…?*"

"I'm still a meddler in misdirection," Sam said. "After spending all day with other people, I thought we deserved some alone time."

They got comfortable in the chairs, chaise-like and easy to lie back in, and Sam pulled the telescope closer to peek through. Then he gestured for Ed to do the same.

Ed had to admit, the view was much better from the roof than poolside.

They watched the stars awhile, Ed pointing out constellations and Sam looking at him adoringly through all of it, until finally, he moved the telescope aside to climb across the space between them and crowded onto Ed's chair.

Under the stars, Sam kissed him sweetly, moving his tongue like a slow memorizing of the moment. Ed tried to memorize it too, to hang on for as long as he could. When Sam's hands drifted from Ed's face down his body, he realized how much he never wanted any of this to end.

"T-tell me more…." He pulled away before Sam's hand could stray beneath his beltline. "About Hades and Persephone."

"What more is there?" Sam chuckled.

"What happens after they decide to stay together?"

The weight of the question hung between them, and Sam pulled away to look Ed in the eyes. "I don't know. It's easier for them. They're both gods. Immortal."

"You think that makes it easier?"

"I don't know…," Sam said again.

Ed could map Sam's face and memorize it like he had their kiss, and a hundred years from now, he'd be able to recall exactly how Sam looked tonight. He wasn't sure if that was enough, but the alternative….

Ed liked what he was, but that didn't mean he didn't have regrets.

"It doesn't make everything easier," he said.

Sam's hands returned to Ed's face, their bodies close, scrunched in the lawn chair. He stroked his thumbs beneath Ed's eyes as if to say, even if they were yellow, fierce and glowing, he wouldn't mind. He accepted all that Ed was, but that was very different from giving up humanity.

"We don't have to think about that right now," Sam said.

"Okay." Ed kissed him before anything else could be spoken, because he wanted to enjoy what time he could steal before the days collected again and his hunger returned.

As their kissing grew more heated, Ed pawed past Sam's clothes and rucked up his shirt to feel the contours of his stomach. Frantic, feverish in his want, Ed undid the clasp of Sam's jeans and then his own, wanting to get his hands on them both again and feel that connection of skin.

Sam panted, breaking from their kiss to move his lips down Ed's neck while rocking into his touch.

Ed's bestial side stirred, making him want to drag his fangs along Sam's scratches again. He didn't. He didn't want to make the marks worse, but his eyes flickered and his fangs grew long as he licked the marks instead. Sam smelled wholly unique to him, and the desire to *bite* was always there, but focusing on the rut of their hips kept Ed centered on better things.

Sam bared his neck with ease, and when they tumbled over the edge together, breaths short and uneven, he rolled up to kiss Ed square on the mouth.

"Want to rinse off together *now*?" Sam teased with a wicked grin.

Ed laughed. "That would be wonderful."

EVERYTHING WITH Ed was wonderful, even the parts that shouldn't be. Sam didn't even mind his regularly scheduled trips to see his blackmailers, which included facing the Cramers after they finally discovered Fitz's body.

"I swear, Goldman, if you know something," Alverez snarled in his face, but that didn't make Sam afraid anymore.

He knew Ed was watching.

"I don't," Sam said.

"Maybe it was Midnight," said Shaw. Scared was a strange look on her, usually so tough and unruffled.

"Then who *is* he?" Alverez barked, still holding Sam by the collar. "Do *you* know? Huh?"

"I don't," Sam said again. "Simons doesn't either. I swear. Not that he's let on."

"We need to get ahead of this," Brock said, almost betraying that he was scared too. "Extend an olive branch, let Midnight know we'll give him a cut of our new deal if it'll keep him off our backs. That must be what he's after. No enemies where we can make friends, right, Goldman?"

They weren't exactly broken up about Fitz's loss, more just worried what it might mean for them, but without reason to suspect Sam, they let him go.

Checking in with Lara went less smoothly.

"I hear the knife cuts on Fitz were too clean and simple to have been done by the original murderer," she said, having dragged Sam into the back again to slam him up against the wall. "He died much too quick."

"It wasn't me," Sam said, taking her words for the threat they were. "And knife cuts aren't Ed's style."

"Still could have been you, working alone."

"You really think I'm capable of that?"

The look she gave him said she didn't.

"Not that we're opposed to the Cramers *biting* it—" She eyed him warily. "—but we don't like you and Simons shaking things up without us knowing."

"It wasn't us. Ed figures the Cramers took out Fitz to have more money between them. I thought it was you who killed him, but I think Ed's right, with the way they've been fighting. I wouldn't be surprised if they tried reconnecting with your boss to get more of the original money."

"They wouldn't dare."

But right that moment—Sam couldn't have planned it better—Lara's phone buzzed, and the expression she gave the message was worthy of framing.

"Those idiots. They really are suicidal. The Cramers just messaged Midnight to meet."

"Do you need me to tell you where they are?"

"We know. But you can tell me which of them they could stand to lose most."

"Alverez," Sam said, trying not to sound too pleased, as the tides of this meeting changed for the better too.

Especially since Lara had been on her way out for another date with Gerry but had to cancel now to address the new play in motion. With any luck, Alverez would be dead next, and Ed could feed from one of the others come Friday.

That night, Sam slept at the hotel, ignoring the ribbing from his friends, who mentioned his lacking presence lately but said nothing about Fitz, if they knew.

The less they were involved, the better.

By Wednesday, the late nights were catching up to Sam. It was easy to ignore the time when he was with Ed. So he returned to the hotel again to catch up on sleep, beating Mim and Gerry back from their day jobs.

He figured he'd make himself a drink, take a hot shower, and collapse into bed. He got five whole feet into his room too—*his*, with his own door, separating him from the rest of the suite—before he noticed the body.

Shaw's body in the middle of his floor, with her eyes wide, blood everywhere from her gruesome wounds, and a knife sticking out of her neck.

The one with Sam's fingerprints and blood on it.

Chapter 7

SAM HAD seen several dead bodies now. He'd thought he could handle it after Fitz, but he was wrong.

It didn't get easier when it was a surprise.

"Are you okay?" Ed asked for what must have been the dozenth time.

Sam had called him as soon as he got his breathing under control. Ed arrived only minutes later, and while sitting on the bed with him was soothing, having Ed gently stroke up and down his spine, Sam couldn't stop staring at Shaw's body.

"No," he said.

He'd told Lara that she and Midnight should take out Alverez, and instead Shaw had been laid at his feet.

"Midnight has to be a vampire."

"But the other night," Ed countered, "whoever was watching you and noticed me in the alley—"

"Then that was Lara, but this… how else could anyone get away with this without someone seeing?"

Ceasing the strokes of his hand on Sam's back, Ed moved closer to wrap his arm around him. "Vampires aren't the only ones who can be clever and resourceful. Just look at you."

The laugh that left Sam sounded pitiful. "I don't feel like much of either of those things. I should have known they wouldn't buy all that bullshit we've been feeding them."

"It doesn't matter. If Midnight wants to scare us, he can't scare me. He's the one who should be afraid. I'll take care of this, Sam. It's going to be okay."

"Mim and Gerry will be back soon."

"I'll be done before then. Just sit. I'm going to steal supplies from housekeeping. This isn't the first time I've had to get rid of a body from an unfortunate place."

Sam nodded, grateful but still numb and queasy about it all. He hardly noticed Ed leave and return, unsure of the time passing until Ed told him to look away.

He needed to cut up the body in order to dispose of it.

As soon as Sam registered that sentence and what Ed was going to do, bile rose up in the back of his throat, and he raced for the bathroom to throw up.

Ed called to him to take his time, that he should stay out of the room until it was over. After emptying his stomach, Sam gladly obeyed, staggering from the bathroom back into the main room to pour himself that drink so he could wash the bitter taste from his mouth.

He couldn't have said if an hour passed or only minutes, but Ed announced he was done before there was any sign that Mim and Gerry might be returning.

"I need to finish this, but I will be back for you, and you can stay with me again tonight. Text your friends or leave a note. I'll be back soon."

Again, Sam nodded, only briefly glancing at Ed, whose hands were bloody even though he'd managed to not get anything on his clothes.

Sam knew he shouldn't go back into the room, but he had to. He had to see if it was all really gone.

Remarkably, it was—every stain, every shred of evidence, the knife. If Sam didn't know exactly where Shaw's body had been, he could have believed it was never there.

"Sam." Ed's voice was suddenly at his ear, his hand, cold as always and clean now of any blood, wrapping around Sam's and taking the empty glass from his grasp. Sam hadn't realized he'd finished it. "Did you message your friends?"

"No... I...."

"I'll do it." Ed took the cell phone from Sam's pocket and rapidly fired off a few texts. "It's going to be okay. I promised you, and that promise remains. I won't let anything happen to you."

"But Mim and Gerry.... Aren't they in danger? Maybe I shouldn't leave them tonight."

"If Midnight had wanted to send *that* message, it would have been one of their bodies instead."

Sam shuddered at the thought.

"They'll be all right."

"Yeah...."

"*Sam*," Ed said more urgently.

Sam turned to him, really looking at him for the first time since he'd arrived. He was pristine, just like the room. He'd cleaned up, kept himself from getting too dirty to begin with, and had protected Sam just like he promised.

And he looked so scared for him, so genuinely worried and sorrowful.

The crease in Ed's brow and sympathy in his eyes almost made the bile surge up in Sam's throat again, but instead, he fell forward into Ed's arms.

"I promise, when we discover who Midnight is, I will tear him and Lara apart. I will kill all of them for you, anyone who ever threatens you until no one would ever dare again."

It was a dark promise, but it comforted Sam, and he nodded against Ed's shoulder, seeing his shirt stained after all, just with tears.

"Hang on to me," Ed said, wrapping his arms more firmly around Sam. "I'll bring you home."

ED DIDN'T want to keep Sam like a pet or a prisoner, but part of him never wanted to let him leave his home again.

He'd buried Shaw and all the evidence deep in the woods where no one would find her. Now he'd incinerate his and Sam's clothes to be absolutely sure there was nothing left, since this death had not been part of their plan.

Not so soon, without any of the blood going to better use.

It all unfolded so similarly to Fitz, the two of them in the basement, quietly undressing. But that night last week, Sam had turned it all around and shown that he was okay, that he could handle this and what Ed was. Shaw's death had clearly hit him harder, reminding him of his own mortality.

They might have been safe enough to simply wash their clothes, but when Ed piled it all into the incinerator, he heard a sigh of relief from Sam, who clearly wanted it all gone. Ed was soon ready to lead them back upstairs when he noticed Sam's gaze drift to the sketch of the fair-haired woman.

"What if this is personal?" Sam said.

"What?"

"All this." Sam stared at the picture like he'd stared at Shaw's body. "What if it's someone who knows you? Another vampire, maybe even the one who made you." He whirled to face Ed with a wild expression in his eyes. "What if it's *her*?"

Ed laughed. He didn't mean to, a terribly insensitive thing to do when Sam was so distraught, but the idea was so much more absurd than he realized. "Sam, she can't be Midnight."

"Just because they've been saying 'he' doesn't mean—"

"It can't be her because she's not the one who made me."

"She isn't?" Sam said, looking back at the picture like he'd been so sure he'd figured it all out.

"She died, human, a long time ago. That's Hypatia. My wife."

Sam whirled around even faster, and Ed couldn't blame him, since he hadn't told him any of this yet.

A few charged moments passed before Sam finally said, "But you're gay."

Ed laughed again, offering a small, somber smile that didn't quite carry as much of the sadness as it once would have. "So was she." He moved past Sam to stand in front of the picture he'd drawn so long ago. "She was my best friend. Times were different then, so marrying kept us safer."

"Then?" Sam pressed with a tentative edge.

"Mid-eleventh century," Ed said, even though this was hardly a date, but he knew it was silly to wait any longer. "Last March, I celebrated my nine hundred and ninety-eighth birthday."

He let that sink in before glancing back at Sam to take in his reaction. If Ed was being honest, Sam looked relieved to finally know the last of what had remained unsaid.

"We never consummated the relationship," Ed continued. "Everyone assumed she was barren and felt pity for us, which made it easier for them to leave us alone. We both had lovers over the years and kept each other safe."

"Lovers?"

"Not *love*, but partners. Pati was my love, just platonically. When she died, I wasn't as careful about hiding what I was. Luckily or unluckily for me, my last lover as a human ended up being the vampire who made me."

"Who was he?"

"Ødger," Ed said, with a hint of his ancient accent. "I suppose he looked like Pati. Maybe that's why I was drawn to him at the time—

blond hair, blue eyes. Not my *type*," he added quickly with a fond look at Sam's darker coloring and curls, "and not someone to love or that good of a partner, but we speak from time to time still.

"He would have no reason to wish me ill like this. We had our time together. We've had our time apart. It's amicable. I've said before that I have my regrets, but I was always grateful for what he made of me, and he knows that. I didn't have to be afraid anymore of someone discovering what I was. If they did, I was something else too, something much more dangerous than what anyone might accuse me of."

"I don't know why I thought it would have been easier back then," Sam said softly.

"It could be in some places, but in others it was considered unnatural and the laws of the land upheld that. Vampires never really cared, though. After I became one, I… experimented with women of my kind, but I maintain my preferences."

Sam laughed lightly but eventually frowned again. "Are you sure… Ødger… doesn't feel differently?"

"I am, but I can contact him if you'd like."

"Maybe. I just can't imagine anyone having you and not going crazy living without you."

"W-well…." Ed tried miserably to keep from stuttering, meeting Sam's adoring gaze. "He was never like you."

A thousand years and too many of them spent alone, but of all the men Ed had been with when he was human, all the vampires he'd been with since, all the people he'd met over his lifetime, no one had ever affected him like Sam did.

Sam was still the one who'd been wronged and threatened tonight, whose expression held an edge of sorrow like he was close to breaking, so stuttering fool or not, Ed crossed to him when there was nothing left to say.

He remembered how scantily clad they both were as he gathered Sam against him but ignored the way it made his skin flush to feel Sam all down the length of his body. Instead, he kissed him, holding Sam too tightly maybe, as a rush of possessiveness overcame him.

"I-I get it!" Sam gasped in Ed's hold. "You can't imagine life without me either."

Ed really couldn't.

He kissed Sam once more, gently. "Come. I'll make you some tea and put you to bed."

IT AMAZED Sam that tea and being tucked into Ed's bed was all it took to put him right to sleep.

He'd already been so exhausted, but he'd feared Shaw's lifeless eyes and bloody wounds would haunt him into his dreams, along with the looming unknown shadow of Midnight. Sam didn't dream, though, maybe because Ed lay down beside him and stayed there until he fell asleep.

The messages waiting on Sam's phone in the morning were just Mim and Gerry teasing him again about spending so much time with "Mr. Simons." There was nothing from the Cramers. They likely didn't know about Shaw yet.

Part of Sam wanted to stay with Ed, to hide with him and just wait for it all to blow over, but he still worried about Mim and Gerry and asked for the day off to see if Midnight's message would be followed by any obvious demands. He'd expected a text or call from Lara, but so far there had been nothing. They were letting him sweat, and if that was the case, he'd rather sweat where he could keep an eye on his friends.

"I can come with you—"

"No, it's fine. You'd have to stay in hiding all day. Or meet my friends. Both of which sound like torture for you right now."

Ed laughed but clearly didn't want to let Sam out of his sight.

"I'll be fine," Sam assured him. "They wanted to scare me. They probably expected I'd stay with you last night. But eventually, Lara or Midnight will have to contact me. I'll let you know as soon as they do."

Sam's bike was still back at the hotel, so he called a Lyft. It was still early when he entered the suite.

"Lover boy returns," Mim said, lounging like usual on the sofa and not looking in any hurry to do anything but dawdle on her phone.

Gerry was at the desk on his computer. Neither seemed like they knew the place had been a murder scene last night. "Hey, Sam! I feel like we've barely seen you for weeks."

"Does this mean you're skipping 'work' today?" Mim tipped her feet back to the floor. "Coz neither of us have any hours either."

"Not until I see Lara," Gerry said.

"You consider that a job too?" Sam griped, since it brought up a fresh gurgle of bile.

Mim laughed.

Gerry scowled. "No. The benefits are way better than a paycheck."

Urg. "Listen, Gerr...." Sam trailed off before he could think of what to say.

He couldn't tell them what was going on. If Gerry ended things with Lara, Midnight would know they were in on this, and then they'd be in danger for sure.

"Do you even know her last name?" Sam asked instead.

"Uhh... well...."

"Seriously?" Mim spun toward Gerry with another laugh.

"It hasn't been important!"

"*Wow.*"

"What do you like about her, anyway?" Sam pressed, continuing into the room to drop down on the sofa beside Mim.

"We have a lot of the same interests."

Lies.

"She loves listening to my ideas and rants. Even about tech stuff."

Pandering.

"And she's uhh... not too bad in other ways."

That... might be true, but considering how seldom Gerry got any, maybe she was only mediocre.

Regardless, Sam didn't want to think about it. He didn't want to think about any of this. He'd asked for a day off and that's what he wanted. "Do you guys want to get out of here? Get some breakfast? Something *good* for once."

"Hell yes," Mim agreed only too easily.

"But I was going to work on that firewall again. I am *this* close." Gerry held his thumb and index finger a millimeter apart.

They needed that account, maybe now more than ever since Midnight obviously knew everything about Sam, but he couldn't face the threats against them if he wasn't calm and centered. He needed a break—and coffee. "You can do that later. Come on."

They were at the Hilton, so finding a nice place to get quality breakfast within walking distance wasn't hard. All their years together scamming people, stealing food when needed, meant they weren't the frivolous type.

Today, though, Sam didn't care, even if the inevitable check they had coming would have normally made him turn up his nose.

He was pretty sure Gerry's fruit parfait alone was twenty bucks, and that was just for starters. All Sam wanted was coffee, but he upped it to a latte and ordered an omelet too.

"To what do we owe the pleasure of your presence, anyway?" Mim asked once the food was served and they were digging in with gusto.

"Like you said, I've been working nonstop. I missed you assholes."

She snorted. "You gonna give us a timetable, then?"

"A few weeks yet, but if Gerry can narrow down that last account, maybe sooner."

"And then we'll hit the road like we planned?"

Sam froze with his fork dug into a bite of omelet. He'd been trying not to think about that either.

"You want to stay, don't you?" she said. "With him."

Gerry paused in his eating too, the whole table going suddenly still.

"I get it," Gerry said, never one to enjoy a comfortable silence, let alone a tense one. "I don't want to leave anymore either with Lara here."

Sam set down his fork and stared at his half-full latte.

"Sammy," Mim said, more hushed across the table, "I obviously don't want to know anything about how that creep Fitz ended up dead, or however the rest of them are going to be following, but I don't trust Simons. You're wrapped up in some much heavier shit than we ever planned on."

"I trust him," Sam said, having expected this conversation, just not at breakfast. "Even if you don't, I do. With my life." He looked up unwaveringly to meet Mim's stare. "I want this over with and all our threats gone, but Ed isn't one of them."

"So, it's all about him now?"

"If you still want to leave town, I won't let that mean things are over between us. You're my best friends. And if you choose to stay, I'll still want to do everything we planned, just here. With Ed part of the equation too."

"You love him, huh?" Gerry said with a soft smile.

"I didn't say—"

"Sam." Mim stared him down.

He sighed. "Yeah. I think I do."

"*Fuck*." She dove back into her pancakes. "So much for a final haul from the mall. Maybe I'll keep the job even after we're rolling in dough. It's kinda fun kicking brats out for shoplifting. And letting a few get away with it if they do it with enough style." She grinned as she took a large bite.

Sam smiled back at her, because she knew love wasn't something any of them admitted to easily. They'd spent too much of their lives with a very limited amount.

"Then we're staying?" Gerry bounced in his seat.

"Yeah, Gerr, we're staying," Mim droned.

"I can't wait to tell Lara!"

"Gerry...." Sam's stomach dropped again.

"I want you guys to spend more time with her. And same with Ed! We have to meet him finally."

There was an idea—Sam, his friends, Ed, and one of their blackmailers, all enjoying a friendly chat.

"You'll meet him, I promise."

Eventually. After all, Ed was charming with the Neu-Ryans; he could be charming with Mim and Gerry, and they never needed to find out what he was.

"So, grooming the next generation of shoplifters." Sam finally dug back into his breakfast. "What about you, Gerr? How's the Nerd Herd going?"

It was good to catch up. Mim and Gerry might still be wary of Ed, but even before meeting him, they accepted him and Sam's feelings for him.

Because Sam loved him. He was *in love* with him.

Now he just needed to tell Ed that.

They took their time getting back to the hotel. If they were going to stay in Riverside, they'd need to find someplace more long-term, though Sam wondered how much time he'd even spend there once they did, more likely to just stay with Ed—if he was allowed.

"Start working on that account, Gerry. I'm going to take a shower. Whether you make headway or not, how about we catch a movie later?"

"I'm game," Gerry said.

"And while Gerry does the heavy lifting," Mim said, dropping back onto the sofa with her phone, "I'll check showtimes."

Sam smiled, feeling relaxed and confident again despite the dread that accompanied going into his room for the first time since last night. There was hope and promise and acceptance on the horizon. He could do this, and it started with going into that room for a fresh set of clothes.

The carpet was still clean when he entered, with no sign of anything amiss.

Which was why he jumped so high when a voice spoke from behind him.

"Mr. *Coleman.*"

Sam spun on his heels so fast, he nearly tripped. He could scream, his door was still open, but then he realized who was there, hidden by the closet in his room's armchair.

With blond hair and blue eyes.

BLOND HAIR. Blue eyes. Just like Hypatia.

But this was Ed's *sire.* He couldn't possibly be Midnight.

"Hello?" A stranger answered when he attempted to call Ødger.

"Uhh… yes, I was looking for…." Vampires didn't often use their true names, and Ed wasn't sure what his sire was going by these days. He'd always known him as simply Ødger.

"Mr. North? Are you a friend of Oscar North?"

"Yes, exactly." Bit on the nose, but then, Ed hadn't gone too far from *Eadric.* "This is Ed Simons, an old friend. This was my most recent number for… Oscar. Is he available, or is this no longer correct?"

"I'm so sorry, Mr. Simons. I've been hoping for your call," the man on the other end said with a genuine drop in his tone. "Almost all of the information for Mr. North's contacts and associates was either taken or destroyed. I wasn't sure if I'd get any calls on this phone, but I was hoping to hear from you."

"Forgive me, I'm not sure I'm following. What's going on? Who are you to Oscar?"

"I'm Mr. North's lawyer. And the executor of his will."

Ed felt the blood drain from his face. "His *what?*"

WHAT?

It was Cheroneau.

"I'm sure Gerry out there will get everything he needs about my account soon enough, but in case you're antsy… my real name is Black. You understand why Midnight works so well."

Sam stood frozen in the middle of his room.

"Best close that and give us some privacy, don't you think?" Cheroneau—Black, *Midnight*—gestured at the door, smiling even more unnervingly than he had at the barbecue.

Remembering Shaw and all the other mutilated victims, Sam hurriedly swung his door shut. Black couldn't be a vampire, Ed would have sensed it when they met, but that didn't make him any less dangerous.

He'd managed all this because he was a cop.

Slowly, Black stood and approached Sam with that unsettling smile. He wore a neat suit with a long trench coat, very fitting of a detective, especially a partner of Daniel's, but Sam doubted Daniel had any idea who this man really was.

"Someone's going to kill you eventually, Mr. Coleman. Or *Goldman*. But now I know it won't be Simons. He likes you. I think he'd do anything for you. A smart man, even a vampire," he said with a pointed widening of his eyes, "who didn't care beyond that pretty face would have let you take the fall for Shaw. Instead, he saved you."

Whoever Black was, Sam felt the same chilling sense of dread around him as he did around Lara. "Tell me what you want."

"Leverage. That's all I've ever wanted. Now, I have it."

"For what?"

His smile widened. "Keep picking your way through the Cramers and their crew. I'm patient. You're making my job easier. Go ahead and tell Simons who I am too. I know you've told him everything else. Make sure he understands that it won't be easy to take out the detective working a case that mostly points at him. Especially since there are so many ways this could all *really* point at him—or you—if I'm not feeling generous.

"And if he thinks he can go after Lara, assure him that you will be a lot less recognizable than Miss Shaw if it comes to that. Or I could start with Daniel. Or his wife. Or—"

"I get it." Sam knew what Black was implying and just how little he cared about collateral damage. "I'll tell Ed whatever you want."

"Good. It's very simple: do as I say, and I swear, once the Cramers are dead, what I want from you and *Ed*… you can both survive."

"Are you picking out matching accessories in there?" Mim called from the living room. "Get in the shower! The best movie times are in less than an hour!"

"I'll be right out!" Sam yelled back through the door. "I got a call!"

"From lover boy? Tell him you're ours today!"

Sam grimaced, especially since Black looked so smug. "You're not a vampire, so what are you? Some sort of slayer?"

Black chuckled. "This isn't cable TV. I won't be leaping from the window. I'm just a normal human like you. Which means I'll be making myself comfortable and leave after you and your friends head to that movie. Best behave and go enjoy your shower. And don't do anything stupid."

He turned and sat right back down in the armchair.

Sam gathered his clothes, made sure he had his phone, and hurried across the suite to the bathroom, mostly ignoring Mim and Gerry, who teased him to hurry up.

He immediately slumped onto the edge of the tub and called Ed.

"Sam...? I was about to call you. I... I have concerning news."

"You too?"

"What do you mean? Are you all right?"

"Sort of. No. I don't know." Sam clenched his eyes shut and took a steadying breath. "You go first."

"I think Midnight killed my sire."

"What?" Sam's eyes snapped open again. "The vampire who made you? He's dead?"

"I contacted him, but... his lawyer answered. I'd informed Ødger that I was moving to Riverside. He knew, one of the only people who did. But he was found dead a month ago with all my information gone, other than what was in his will. What if it's my fault?" Ed's voice hitched. "If I was the end goal...."

Sam felt that same nausea from last night, because Black was still there, with Gerry and Mim the only thing between them, and he'd killed a vampire, enough of a blow that Ed sounded more distraught than Sam had ever heard. "It wasn't your fault. I don't think you're the end goal because you're you, Eddie, just the next target because you're a vampire. Taking out your maker simply led them to the intel they needed for who to go after next."

Ed was quiet for a moment, a shudder coming through the phone before he spoke again like he was stifling tears. "I've been trying to contact others. A few are fine, but several aren't answering. If you're right, Midnight may be picking through every one of us he can find."

"I just wish we knew why." Sam tried to understand what could possibly be gained from this. "What does he want? Lara said it isn't only about money, and he said he isn't a slayer or hunter or whatever."

"Such people aren't as prevalent as modern media would have you believe. But wait... *he* said?" Ed's voice took on a note of alarm.

"I know who Midnight is," Sam admitted. "He's here."

CHAPTER 8

SAM TOLD Ed not to rush over to the Hilton, not with Mim and Gerry there and so many unknowns concerning Cheroneau—Midnight.

Black.

If he'd managed to kill so many vampires, including Ed's creator, then it was dangerous to underestimate him. They needed to find out everything they could, even if Black seemed prepared for that too.

So, Sam went to the movies with his friends and tried to forget how fucked they were.

He tried to relax, to have fun, but he was even more terrified of that room than before when he walked back into it after they returned. Black was gone, but that didn't make Sam feel any better.

The rest of the evening, Gerry finished hacking into Black's account and came up with everything Sam had hoped to discover—even Black's name—but all of it seemed moot now. Sam pretended it was great news, thanked Gerry and said he'd tell Ed right away, but inside, he felt trapped and unsure about what they could do without making everything worse.

They couldn't kill a cop, and if they tried, Black was sure to have contingency plans.

When Sam was finally ready to turn in for the night, he called Ed again.

"Would you like me to come get you?"

"No. Come—yes, please. I want you here. But I can't leave Mim and Gerry again. Will you just be here and stay with me tonight?"

"Of course."

OF COURSE Ed could be there for Sam; it was easy enough to traverse into the city now that the sun was set, and he had many ways of sneaking into the hotel without anyone noticing. He wondered how Black had managed the same but figured a police detective didn't need to use subterfuge.

Once Ed was in the room, Sam sank gratefully into his arms. Ed sank against Sam too, probably holding him too tightly, unable to shake the aching loss in his chest.

"Shit, I'm being so selfish," Sam said, looking up at him as they embraced beneath the covers. "Yeah, I'm scared, but you... you just found out someone important to you died." He raised a hand to Ed's cheek and smoothed a thumb across the skin. "And your eyes are red. I've never seen them red before."

That's because Ed almost never cried, and when he did, his natural healing tended to take care of any puffiness or other telling signs. This time, the tears had been too recent. "It's silly." He choked on his words. "We rarely talked, and I haven't seen him in... I don't remember when."

"It's not silly," Sam said, petting his cheek again and then letting his hand drop to rest atop Ed's heart. He must have been able to feel how it didn't beat, if he hadn't noticed before, but he didn't look troubled, only traced his fingers lightly over the spot.

Neither was undressed, but the gentle touch over Ed's shirt felt nice too.

"I never met my parents," Sam continued, "but if I found out who they were today and that they'd already passed on, even though part of me hates them for giving me up or whatever happened to put me in the system all my life, I think I'd cry too. I wouldn't be here without them, and even without knowing who they are, sometimes it still feels like this great gap...."

"Yes," Ed whispered, thinking he understood, because he hadn't lied when he said that Ødger had never been his love or the best partner, but he was his sire, and Ed wouldn't be here without him. "I've kept myself from knowing people to try to avoid feeling this way ever again."

"Like when you lost your wife?"

"Yes."

"Would you give up having known her, or your... sire, to never have felt that loss?"

Ed smiled, because it always came down to that, and he knew the answer. "Never. I suppose that makes me a hypocrite for going so many years without making new friends."

"Maybe, but at least you were smart enough to make an exception with me." Sam grinned up at him, almost like his usual self, holding only an edge of the sorrow and fear that clung to him.

Dipping his head, Ed pressed his lips to Sam's in a chaste but lingering kiss. He worried that allowing more than friendship with Sam was a far worse mistake than staying solitary, but that concern did nothing to loosen the hold he had on him.

Ed told Sam to sleep, to not worry about anything else tonight. They could discuss it all in the morning. Sam agreed and snuggled into his arms like he had the night before.

While Ed didn't sleep, he didn't mind dozing, lying there with the warmth of Sam beside him. He got up from time to time to stretch, and at one point discovered the book he'd given to Sam, the one on myths, and brought it back to bed to read while Sam burrowed unconsciously against him.

The sun was starting to peek through the curtains when Sam groggily asked, "Which one are you on?"

"Psyche and Eros." Ed peered down with a warm smile. "My favorite."

"They get their happy ending too," Sam said, smiling in return. "After Psyche joins Eros as a god."

"Sam...." Ed set the book aside.

"I know you're not a god. Black still managed to kill someone like you."

"Maybe more than one."

"I really am sorry about your sire."

"Thank you," Ed said quietly.

It was the first time he'd mourned anyone in ages. He'd lost other vampire friends over the years, but all because they'd chosen to stop living. This was different. This was having someone taken from him that he hadn't been prepared to lose.

"He left everything to me, but most of his assets were stolen the night he was murdered. There's insurance, but I don't care about money. I never would have thought that the last time I saw him... would be the last time."

Sam squeezed him tightly.

"His lawyer needs me to go to him, meet in person to sign off on everything and get what Ødger left me, but I told him that now isn't exactly a good time. We'll finish this first, bring Black to justice. I still want to know why he's doing this."

"I don't care why," Sam said with a boldness lighting his eyes. "I'm so sick of being scared. Of him. Of the Cramers. He and Lara are the ones who should be scared, and we're going to make them feel that way." He looked at Ed, his expression softening. "It's Friday again. You need to feed, and it has to be Alverez."

"Are you thinking we should frame Black like he tried to frame me?"

"That'll be tough until we have more intel, but I have some ideas. Most of it can't go down until tonight."

"What shall we do in the meantime?"

Sam shifted, legs tangling with Ed's and hands grasping him closer to kiss him sweetly on the mouth.

"Rise and shine, Sammy!"

"RISE AND shine, Sammy!" Mim called—seconds before opening Sam's door and walking right in.

Sam bolted upright. It wasn't as if they didn't know Ed existed, but finding them in bed together was very different. He fumbled to think of an explanation, while simultaneously realizing that he could no longer feel Ed at his side.

Because Ed wasn't there.

That vampire speed was a godsend.

"Hey, lazy ass," Mim said, leaning in the doorway. She was dressed in her security uniform, which shouldn't be flattering on anyone, but she was an exception. "We're heading into work. You gonna be a lump all day or go play house with Simons?"

"I'm up. I'm getting up right now. And yes, I'll be with Ed most of the day, but… how about you guys meet me for dinner at Lucifer's Rest?"

"Really?" Gerry peeked his head in too.

"Yes, Gerr, really." Sam chuckled. "We need to make more of an effort with Lara, right?" Much as it nauseated him.

"But she works all night." Gerry pouted.

Sam knew that—Gerry never shut up about her schedule—but that was the point. "Why do you think we're going to her? Now, will you two get the hell out of here and go be useful to society?"

Gerry looked gleefully appeased, while Mim snorted.

"Don't work too hard," she said and blew Sam a kiss.

As soon as they were gone, thankfully shutting the door behind them, Ed reappeared as if materializing out of the wall.

"You want to see Lara?" He crawled up from the foot of the bed.

"I never *want* to see her. I have to. We have a long day ahead of us." Sam opened his arms, letting Ed nuzzle against his neck. It was like lying on the cold side of the pillow; Sam was cozy warm beneath the covers, but the chill of Ed was invigorating. "Morning can be for planning, but I need food first. Did you bring your sunglasses?"

"Yes." Ed frowned. "But I was hoping we wouldn't get out of bed yet. Besides, I don't have a spare set of clothes."

Sam pushed the covers aside to get Ed under them with him, making it clear that he was perfectly fine with stealing a few more quiet moments. He kissed Ed, grinding his hips against him to feel that morning hunger rise.

The hunger was stronger for Ed after a week, and his eyes flashed yellow.

Sam kissed him anyway but slowed the writhing of their bodies until Ed's growls became a rumbling purr.

"The clothes I borrowed from you are still dirty, so I guess you'll have to borrow mine for once." Sam liked the idea of Ed in one of his Henleys. "Maybe we can finally get some shopping in today. Breakfast for me, hit a few stores for you, then home before lunch? Minimal time in the sun, I promise."

"What are we going to do once we're home?" Ed asked.

They'd both started calling Ed's place *home*, and Sam was of no mind to correct that.

He wished his plans for the day involved pinning Ed to the nearest hard surface—the mattress beneath them would have been adequate—but that would have to wait until after Alverez was dead.

"We're going to invite the Neu-Ryans over for a swim."

ED DID not invite people over—ever—least of all to swim in his pool. But he'd promised those children, and Sam had several ideas brewing for how to turn things in their favor.

First, Sam ate. With Ed's sunglasses firmly in place, they found a back corner of a coffee shop, and Ed got a simple black coffee for appearances.

The shopping afterward was surprisingly pleasant. Ed usually avoided it, kept his clothes in good shape to hang on to them well after their normal wear, or shopped online, but with Sam, it was… fun.

Sam chose things for him, gave critiques and hums of approval. Ed found himself enjoying dressing for someone other than himself, catering to Sam's opinions, which he had to admit were flattering. Ed liked everything they purchased, even if he wouldn't have thought to try some of it on if he'd been alone.

Like a green-and-black bomber jacket that Sam said brought out the hazel in his eyes. Very chic.

They used Sam's bike to get around, and to eventually head back to the house. Even with the sun glaring and hot, Ed didn't mind the drive, closing his eyes beneath his shades and clinging to Sam's waist. The smell of him so close still roused the part of Ed that was growing hungry, but the more time he and Sam spent together, the more certain he was that he could control himself even at the worst of times.

"Why are we pretending we're having a garage sale?" he asked later, while aiding Sam in carrying boxes into the living room.

"We're not pretending. These are things I didn't originally think I could get away with stealing, but that you either don't need or don't seem to care you have."

"I…." Ed was poised to protest, but then took notice of what was in the boxes and couldn't disagree. "So, we're going to sell all of it?"

"We're going to sort it and decide what might sell and what could be donated or given away. Getting ready for a garage sale is the perfect excuse for why Marie and the kids can come over. It's tedious work we won't mind them interrupting, and it'll give us the perfect chance to learn more about Black."

Not that Marie needed any convincing to accept the invite. She showed up not much later in a swimsuit, cover-up, and hat that Ed wasn't sure would fit through his door, with the twins in tow and a couple bags filled with snacks and pool toys.

"I promise we'll clean up whatever mess we make," she said, already out of a breath, likely just from packing up the kids for the short drive there.

"Nonsense. That's what I pay Sam for," Ed said.

Sam shot him a dirty look, and Ed chuckled, which made Marie chuckle too.

"Anything I can do to help today?" she asked as she ushered in the kids, who had floaties on their arms as if ready to dive right in—which, considering they beelined past Ed and Sam for the patio doors, was probably what they planned to do. "No running!" she called after them but didn't bother giving chase. "And say thank you!"

"Thanks, Mr. Ed!" the twins parroted without slowing their momentum.

He really needed to get them to stop that.

"We invited you here to relax," Sam said, taking the bag of snacks from her, "not get roped into our manual labor."

"Besides," Ed put in, "it'll just be us scrutinizing my possessions, trusting in Sam's keen eye for what might sell. By all means, if you see anything that catches your eye, don't hesitate to ask about it. If I'm going to get rid of it anyway, I'd rather it go to a good home."

Marie cast an interested gaze over the boxes in the living room. The kids had successfully hefted the doors open, darted outside, tossed their towels onto chairs, and were already in the water. "I might do a little window shopping, but I actually have a lot of work to do. There is something amazing about being able to work on a news story while basking in the sunshine, though." She indicated the laptop tucked into her tote. "Seriously, let me know of any way I can help repay you for letting us come over."

"This is our repayment for the barbecue," Ed insisted, "and just to be good neighbors. Finally meeting more people from the area was a delight, like your work friend, Linda, and Daniel's partner, Mr.… umm… oh, I'm terrible with names. Did he say Hal?"

"Cheroneau." Marie nodded with a scrunch to her nose. "Harold Cheroneau. He's uhh… hard to read, isn't he?"

"You think so?" Sam played into her obvious dislike. "Seemed friendly to me."

"That's what Daniel says, but he sort of rubs me the wrong way. I don't know. Daniel says it's my old reporter instinct on overdrive, but I think I have a right to worry about the man who's watching my husband's back day in and day out.

"He's fine, I guess. Real sweet with the kids. Has his own, I think, but I never heard of a wife."

"Cheroneau has children?" Ed asked.

"I don't know for sure. I just got that impression. I suppose if he's nice to those little rascals—" She smiled toward the doors. "—he can't be all bad. I really wish they'd get some leads on those murders, though...." She snapped her attention back to them after letting that slip. "Not that you heard anything from me, but since you got all wrapped up in it, it only seems fair.

"The whole thing sort of stalled," she said, more hushed. "There was another murder last week, but not as brutal, so they can't say if it was the same killer. Honestly, I'd be glad if it all just blew over, maybe gang related, and it really was all coincidence that, well...."

"That I knew everyone who was killed," Ed said with a wry smile. "Aside from last week. I hadn't heard about someone new," he lied.

"Oh, I don't think you'd know him, just some thug. Maybe he was one of the ones doing the killing and they're cleaning house. Daniel swears he's never noticed any weird behavior around the neighborhood, but I was really worried about you for a while there.

"That you were being targeted!" she rushed on. "Never that you were involved. Certainly not after meeting you." She passed her gaze from Ed to Sam with an equally warm smile. "If you're sure you don't need any help in here, I better get to work. Thank you both so much again. And feel free to yell at those two if they get too rowdy."

They both laughed as Marie took the bag of snacks back from Sam and went outside to claim a chair.

"What do you think?" Ed asked. "Will Black up the death toll now that we took care of Shaw?"

"I don't think so," Sam said. "He's biding his time. He wants us to take out the Cramers, because then he doesn't have to. He doesn't need any more murders to frame you. He knows we'll be committing plenty of our own."

"Then maybe we shouldn't go after Alverez."

"We're still taking out Alverez. We need the case to stay hot."

"But we're not going to frame Black?"

"Too risky now that we know he's a cop, but we can do better." Sam grinned. "We'll talk more when there are less ears around. Now, come on. We actually need to go through this stuff."

Most of the items had already been cataloged by Sam in previous weeks and simply needed to be put in a keep, sell, or donate pile. During a break from working, Marie claimed a Tiffany lamp that she said reminded her of one her grandmother used to have, and Ed gladly let her have it, but she wouldn't accept anything else since he refused payment.

She reapplied sunscreen, made the kids do the same, and let them head back into the water. When she was finished with work, Ed showed her how to use his digital jukebox, and she played some classic rock while sunning herself.

As it was nearing dinnertime, another knock at the door turned out to be Daniel. Having yet another person in his home usually would have made Ed edgy, especially so close to his feeding time, but this family had won him over as easily as they had Sam, and seeing Daniel at the door made him smile.

Until Daniel entered to reveal *Cheroneau* behind him.

"I hope this is a friendly call?" Sam said, managing much better than Ed at maintaining a cordial expression.

"Sorry," Daniel said right away, "I didn't mean for the both of us showing up to make you sweat. Hal's just coming over for dinner tonight, and I figured I'd help Marie wrangle the kids. Telling them pool time is over can be a challenge. You two wouldn't want to join us, would you?"

"I promised my friends I'd meet them later," Sam jumped in, which was just as well, since Ed blanked on a response, "and Eddie already turned down my offer to tag along."

"Right! I... have too much on my mind to leave the house tonight," Ed fumbled to add, "but rain check for sure."

A chorus of complaints rose up from the patio.

"It begins," Daniel said in apology and headed to his wife.

Leaving Ed and Sam alone with Black.

Ed growled, letting his vampire aspects flash in warning. It didn't matter if Black saw him; he *should* see him and fear the power that simmered beneath the surface.

"Down, boy," Black said snidely. "If you're as old as I suspect, you have to have better control than that. Or maybe you haven't been eating well." He cast a glance at Sam that made Ed growl louder. "Careful, how would you explain my sudden demise to that sweet family in there? Of course, you could always kill them too."

This was why Ed didn't make friends or get close to...

He glanced at Sam.

... anyone.

"But you won't, will you?" Black said, almost pityingly. "You're a nice guy who cares. Fascinating...."

Ed forced his face back to normal, but with a firm mask of hatred in place. "Whatever you want from me, ask it now."

"Not yet. We haven't finished cleaning up our messes yet."

The anger that spiked through Ed made it difficult to stop his true nature from coming out again, and he clenched his fists to stay the change. "You murdered a friend of mine."

"Did I?" Black leaned closer to Ed without an ounce of fear. "You might have to be more specific."

Ed almost lunged, seeing red everywhere in his vision—when squealing from the twins reminded him that they weren't alone.

"You can fantasize about sinking those pearly whites into my neck all you want," Black taunted, "but if anything happens to me or Lara, there's a timed delivery planned for more than enough evidence to blame the two of *you* for everything. Shaw was a parlor trick by comparison, so don't get cocky."

He smiled widely, putting on a façade of pleasantness, and strolled right past Ed into the living room.

"Where are my favorite kiddos?" he called.

Ed hated how powerless he felt, how powerless he *was* against a lone human, and tried to convey how sorry he was to Sam.

But Sam was not so easily broken, despite all he'd been through, because he put on his own façade, giving a comforting nod to Ed before heading into the living room too.

The children were being rounded up and dried off as they began their goodbyes. It was a bustle of real and false smiles, Marie and Daniel thanking them again and the kids chiming in with their own gratitude that ended with last-minute hugs around Ed's legs, making it impossible to be completely soured by Black's presence.

"Can we swim at night with you sometime, Mr. Ed?" Dawn asked.

"Only if you call me *Ed*. And if your parents say it's all right." He was just glad that the chlorine helped to dull any tempting smells from having them so close.

He shouldn't be making friends at all or getting so attached, but he'd already broken that rule for Sam, and it seemed he was doomed with this family too.

Though it surprised him after they all left to see Sam still smiling.

"Why are you happy?" Ed asked. "That man was in my home!"

"I know. I didn't think we'd get so lucky. Because now I know what he wants."

"You do?"

"He was casing everything," Sam said, pulling Ed back into the living room to indicate the boxes, "especially what we're planning to get rid of. Your sire was robbed before he was killed, right? Black wants what he took from you, he wants more, but I'm betting what he really wants is his next lead."

"He wants information on other vampires…." The weight in Ed's stomach flipped jarringly, and he honestly wasn't sure if he felt better or worse.

"You do have considerable wealth. I imagine others like you, those old enough, which is most of the ones still alive, you said, would be just as well off."

"Then it *is* all about money, just more than mine. To think he'd kill for that!" At least Ed only killed to survive.

"We also know where he'll be tonight. Right next door." Sam's cell phone buzzed before he could say more, and he paused to look at it. "The Cramers won't meet. They're too nervous about Shaw being missing after what happened to Fitz. That probably means the warehouse will be empty. We could lure Alverez there. You can still catch his scent, right?"

"I can find him," Ed said. His nose was often sharper when he was hungry. "The Cramers can hide all they want. When the time comes, I'll find them too."

"Then I better head to Lucifer's Rest, while you get a line on Alverez. We message each other when we're ready?"

"Does that mean you're finally going to tell me the rest of this plan?"

Despite the dangers, despite Black having been within their grasp and having scared Sam so deeply before, now he took on a look of mischief that Ed loved, proving he enjoyed the hunt just as much. "I needed to be sure, but now I am. Here's how this is going to play out…."

SAM WAS proud of how everything was going to play out. It was a risk, there was the chance that Black would throw them to the wolves before they were ready, but Sam didn't think he would. Black would have done that by now if he believed he could still get what he wanted with them in jail or on the run. They had to go on the offensive, and Sam knew exactly how.

He was all smiles when his friends joined him for dinner, especially when Lara served their table. Small talk was easy, playing things up like he really was interested to learn more about her since she was "dating" his friend. She'd hover by their booth, dawdling longer with them than anywhere else, because, in her words, "Anything to have more time with Gerry."

Sometimes Sam could almost believe she liked him—until the others' attention was elsewhere and she cast him a nasty smirk. She probably thought Sam was squirming in his seat, faking it all for Black's sake. Let her believe that. He was going to make them pay for what they were doing to him and Ed—starting by keeping an eye on where Lara touched the water glass she gave him.

Sam made sure he didn't disturb the fingerprints left behind when he slipped the glass into his pocket.

Lara had a long shift ahead, so Mim convinced Gerry to head elsewhere for another drink, but Sam said he had to take care of something for Ed, which was true.

"Does it have to do with the accounts I hacked?" Gerry whispered. "Is he going to bleed them all dry?"

Sam tried not to give away how apt a description that was. "Eventually. But promise me you never talk about any of this stuff with your girlfriend?"

"Of course not! She's a sweet, normal waitress. I prefer her thinking I'm tech support, not… freelancing." Gerry never could stomach calling them criminals.

"I'll see you guys later," Sam said.

He slipped away but didn't try to hide it from Lara, making a point of looking dejected, like he was shuffling off with his tail between his legs, unable to stand being around her.

She gave a little wave, and he turned around in a huff—to hide his smirk.

Before hopping on his bike to head to the warehouse, he texted Ed, *On my way. Find Alverez?*

Strangely, no. I've tried his apartment, his haunts. He must be on the move. I'm going to check a few more places before I meet up with you. Be careful.

Alverez must be agitated, looking for Shaw. Sam didn't believe he'd ditch town any more than he believed the Cramers had. They were all too stubborn, even if they were cowards.

The streets around the warehouse looked empty like usual. Still, Sam was cautious as he listened at the entrance and heard... something. Like frantic rummaging? Maybe street kids or vagabonds had infiltrated the place.

Finding the door unlocked, Sam took a risk and went inside.

One street kid, it turned out—the one whose fingers Alverez had broken. His hand was clumsily wrapped, and he didn't appear to be using it much as he scavenged through the room. He already had a stack of cash and items to fence that he'd been gathering on a table.

He jumped at Sam's entrance, flicking out a switchblade. At least it wasn't a gun, and this kid looked like a light breeze would knock him over.

"Relax," Sam said, holding up his hands. "I'm not with the Cramers. Not really. I'm just like you, caught up in a bad spot."

"What are you doing here, then?" the kid demanded, circling wide to keep Sam away from him, while never straying too far from his spoils.

"Just wondering where they ran off to. Seen any of them?"

"Wouldn't be here if I had. They've been gone all day. I don't think they're coming back."

Sam felt his phone buzz in his pocket but didn't reach for it.

"Watch it!" the kid cried when Sam stepped closer to him.

Halting, Sam raised his hands higher, as the kid finally gave in and started scooping what he'd stolen into his bag while his knife remained poised. "Seriously, you don't have to worry about me, but even with them gone, you should get out of here. And don't come back."

"Why, 'cause you want everything left for yourself?" the kid snorted.

"It's not like that—"

"Whatever." He finally had everything in his bag and started moving toward the entrance. "I don't want to come back here, but like it even matters." He cringed, far too aged and broken for someone so young.

Sam should know.

"We're all the same monsters eventually," he said and bolted out into the night.

Those words made Sam pause, because he'd thought he knew what monsters were once, something he'd always tried to avoid becoming, but the lines had blurred over recent weeks.

Even so, he couldn't believe the kid was right. Maybe they were all monsters, but not all monsters were created equal.

He looked around at what was left. The kid had taken anything of real value. The Cramers must have taken the computer, though, because it wasn't there and hadn't been part of the kid's stash. What Sam needed was a lead, any lead on where Alverez might be if Ed couldn't find him.

Then he remembered his phone and reached to check his messages. *I think he's headed toward you. Don't go inside the warehouse.*

Sam froze, hearing the telltale shuffle of feet behind him, but before he could turn, an arm locked around his throat.

"I knew it was you!"

Alverez.

The phone dropped from Sam's fingers as he tried to pry Alverez's arm off, but he had the upper hand and was significantly stronger.

"Sto—"

"I knew it! I knew it was you!"

"S-sto—" Sam gasped, trying in vain to get in any amount of air.

Then Alverez let go, dropping him to his knees. He saw his phone in front of him, lighting up with another message.

Sam? Are you there?

Alverez seized Sam's shoulders from behind, wrenching him up to his feet and spinning him about to face a snarling maw, before he punched Sam hard enough to send him toppling back to the floor.

Ed was on his way. Sam just had to hold out a little longer.

Pushing past the spinning of the room, he flung himself at Alverez's legs, but though Alverez teetered, he kicked Sam away and managed to stay upright. Then he kicked Sam again, right in the ribs.

"You're part of it!" Alverez kicked him *again*. "You know what happened to her! Just like Fitz! Is it Midnight?" Again. "Or Simons? Tell me, you fucking—"

A blur of motion barreled into Alverez so fast, Sam couldn't be sure through his hazy vision if what he'd seen had really happened.

"Sam!" Ed's hands were at his shoulder and face then, gently checking him.

He hadn't imagined it.

"Are you okay?"

Alverez was sputtering and groaning, thrown across the room to strike the wall with such force, it was like he'd been hit by a freight train. Sam, worst case, had bruised ribs and nausea to look forward to. Alverez wouldn't be as lucky.

Because the second Sam nodded that he was fine and started to right himself, Ed offered a tender smile—and then went cold as he stood to turn toward his prey.

ED FELT only cold as he moved on Alverez, slowly crossing the expanse between them. He'd stunned the man enough that he wasn't going anywhere. Not fast enough.

How dare he touch Sam? How dare any of them *think it*?

Grabbing Alverez by the back of the neck, Ed flung him into the wall and darted after him to hold him there. "If it's any consolation, Mr. Alverez, Miss Shaw did not meet her end by us. But you will."

He swooped in to sink his teeth in deep, drinking ravenously as he kept Alverez pinned. The man was an impressive fighter, struggling hard against him, but when it became clear that there was no escaping Ed's grasp, a whimper left him, and he started to plead.

"S-stop! I'll do anything!"

It was always those with the roughest, loudest voices who were the most cowardly.

"Shhh," Ed whispered, lapping at the wound when he pulled his fangs free. "I'm afraid there is no end to this where you survive, but how you leave this world does not have to be painful." He turned back with a faint smear of red on his lips to see Sam on his feet, holding his wounded ribs. "You decide, Sam. Does he deserve mercy?"

The mirrored coldness that overtook Sam's expression, so like Ed's, stirred something primal in Ed's gut that he never realized he could lust after.

"No," Sam said.

Ed lunged back into Alverez's neck, tearing skin and sinew anew, and making a point to not be gentle.

SAM COULDN'T say he'd ever seen Ed be gentle when he fed, but when he told him not to show mercy—not to Alverez, who was harsh and cruel and unapologetic—the cries that tore from the man's throat at the vicious assault Ed launched on him were enough to make Sam tremble.

But he didn't dislike the feeling.

He didn't dislike it at all.

Sam was sore and angry, and it made him feel vindicated, watching Ed be brutal in his name. It made him feel... invincible.

Just like the glass he'd taken earlier apparently, because when he checked it in his pocket, certain it would be nothing more than pieces now after Alverez's vicious kicks, and that they'd have to start over with their plan for tonight, he found it whole and uncracked.

One more enemy down, with Ed fed for another week, and the rest were soon to drop.

But first they had to deal with Lara.

Ed left the body with Sam as he zipped off with his impossible speed to check the back room at Lucifer's Rest. When he returned and reported it empty, he was able to move both Sam and Alverez across town without Sam ever feeling the presence of the corpse with them.

Ed laid the body down, using a knife from the back room to slice through Alverez's many bite marks and leave him in a similar state to Fitz. Then he wiped the knife clean and kept watch while Sam put on a pair of gloves.

He pulled out the glass and grabbed cocoa powder from one of the shelves. After dusting the powder onto Lara's fingerprint, he was able to transfer it to the handle of the knife using a piece of packing tape.

"Cocoa powder?" Ed questioned.

"It's easier to see, and it won't seem strange in the restaurant where it came from. Anyone coming?"

"No, I can hear everyone in the kitchen and main bar."

"Then let's get out of here."

Sam dropped the knife, and Ed whisked them out of the restaurant as easily as he'd whisked them in, without anyone seeing, until they were back at the warehouse beside Sam's bike.

"Now what?" Ed asked, holding Sam tightly like he never wanted to let go.

Sam was fine with that. "Now we call 911."

CHAPTER 9

As MUCH as part of Sam wished they could head back to Ed's place and wait out the aftermath, he knew he couldn't hide when his friends would be some of the first to react to the news of Alverez being found dead.

Ed stayed in the shadows, watching as Sam drove his bike back to the hotel. The bike hadn't been anywhere near Lucifer's Rest since earlier, and it was going to stay that way.

By the time he arrived, Ed had texted him that the police were at the bar. They would question everyone, those who'd been on shift especially, since the body had been found in the back, and from there, Lara would be out of their way, even if she wasn't arrested.

Sam was certain her fingerprints would be in the system, but even if they weren't, all eyes would be on her and the few others who'd been there that night, making it harder for her to help Black.

And he wasn't going to be happy about that.

Mim and Gerry entered the hotel room just as Sam finished packing—his things *and* theirs.

"What the hell, Sammy—"

"Grab your stuff. Check for anything I might have missed, but we need to go."

"Why—"

"*Now.*"

The urgency in his tone ceased any further arguing from Mim and Gerry. They'd been through too much together to question him when he was that serious.

All three were the picture of calm as they checked out and headed across town to the Marriot, which was closer to Lucifer's Rest. It had to be in case anyone thought it odd that they'd changed locations the same night as Alverez's murder.

Sam just wanted to be somewhere else and to make the move before Black had the chance to pay attention. He didn't want any more surprise visits.

An hour had passed since he'd made an anonymous 911 call when Gerry got a text from Lara.

Sam knew who it was immediately, because Gerry looked at his phone, looked at Sam like he'd been slapped, and turned on the TV.

This wasn't some back-alley body found the next day; this was a business with a body found during working hours when frequent murders had been plaguing the city for weeks. Of course it was on the news.

And Marie's friend Linda was reporting on it.

"Police have yet to reveal the identity of the victim," she was saying, with the sign for Lucifer's Rest clear behind her, "but he's said to be a regular at this establishment. Everyone inside, along with employees, are currently being questioned. The body was found—"

"Lara got the chance to contact me finally after being *interrogated*," Gerry said, eerily icy for someone usually so warm. "She says she recognizes the guy who was killed, thinks it's a friend of *yours*. Says she remembers you talking to him at the bar."

"Gerr—"

"It's Alverez, isn't it? Or Brock Cramer?"

Sam didn't answer. He could feel Gerry's eyes glaring into the side of his face. Mim's too.

"Tell me!" Gerry shrieked, the sudden cry making Sam shudder. "Why is he dead in our bar, and why are they looking at Lara?"

"I'm sorry," Sam said, glancing up at him slowly. "I couldn't tell you. She's part of this."

"Bullshit."

"She's always been part of this, Gerry. She threatened me. She threatened *you*. She was just using you."

"No way! You're wrong. I... I can't believe it."

"Gerry—"

"She didn't kill whoever is dead in that bar! She couldn't have!" He spun around, storming into his room and slamming the door behind him.

Sam never thought he'd miss when they used to share a loft and couldn't hide from each other. Right now, he'd settle for a normal hotel room without separate doors.

It was better to not explain further, because he couldn't explain everything, not about Ed, and he didn't want to lie to Gerry again.

"Don't tell her where we moved to, Gerry!" he called through the door instead. "Please."

"Fine! Now leave me alone!" Gerry shouted back.

Sam looked back at Mim to see her shaking her head at him. "She threatened bodily harm to both of you if I said anything."

"Like I'd be afraid of *her*."

Admittedly, Mim and Lara might be evenly matched as petite powerhouses, but still. "She isn't working alone."

"The Cramers?"

"The man who hired them to hire us."

She pursed her lips and crossed her arms in indignation. "You still should have said something. Who's the vic?"

"Alverez."

"Lara didn't kill him, did she?"

"No, but she'd do worse. Her boss would do worse. To you. To Gerry. I can't tell you more—"

"This is what I was talking about," Mim hissed, keeping her voice low, but her eyes were aflame as she stalked up to him and got in his face by stretching up on her toes. "It's all because of Simons. Look what he has you doing. Lying to us? To *us*? Framing people for murder?"

"That part was my idea," Sam said.

She rocked back on her heels, aghast, and for a moment, Sam wanted to tell her everything. But she and Gerry were already in too much danger.

"I have things under control—"

"You know, I think I need to be away from you right now too," she cut him off, pushing roughly past him to retreat like Gerry, only with a slightly less jarring bang of her door.

They were his best friends, his family. He knew it must seem awful that he was choosing Ed over them, but it wasn't like that. He was choosing all of them. He didn't want to give Ed up if he could have him and keep his friends safe at the same time.

Honestly, Sam was grateful they'd shuttered themselves away to cool off. They'd forgive him eventually. For now he just wanted them to sleep, secure here in a new location.

He made sure the main door was deadbolted and turned on the Do Not Disturb light with the press of a button. Then he retired to his own room and softly shut the door.

This time he wasn't afraid of the figure hiding in the darkness, because he knew it was Ed.

"I'm sorry," Ed said, stepping from the shadows as if he'd been made of them until that moment. He must have heard everything.

"They'll forgive me when it's over."

Ed nodded as Sam moved closer to him.

He could feel the bruises he'd have in the morning from Alverez's attack—the soreness, the exhaustion—but that did nothing to diminish how much he wanted to feel Ed's hands on him.

"Would you... like to go to bed?" Ed asked, meaning *sleep*, but that was the last thing on Sam's mind.

"With you," he said, punctuating each following phrase with another step closer. "Yes. I would. Right now. Back at the house."

Ed's eyes widened, and he cast a nervous glance at the door.

"They'll be fine. Even if Black tracks us, that won't be until tomorrow."

"He was at the scene," Ed confirmed, "so I know he didn't follow you."

"Then let's go home." Sam used the word purposely, completing his trek into Ed's arms and cuddling his chest. "You can bring me back in the morning. I don't want to miss another chance to be with you, Eddie. *All* of you."

ALL OF him.

Sam wanted....

Yes. Ed wanted that too.

He brought them back to the house, directly up to the bedroom. It amused him that he'd spent more time in that room in the past two weeks than the entire two months he'd lived there. So much had changed since Sam's first day. Ed had blown up and hung one of the photographs he took of downtown Riverside over his safe, outfitted with a more difficult to crack lock, thanks to Sam, who grinned at the bunny slippers resting beside the dresser as Ed once again led him to the bed.

All Ed wanted was to keep Sam in his arms and kiss him, but still, he had to ask, "Are you sure we're doing enough?"

"Why do you think I had you bring me back to your place?" Sam winked.

"I mean about the situation!"

Sam knew that, of course, only teasing him, but while the smile slipped from Sam's face, he looked resolute. "We need to find proof that Lara and Black are connected. Or that Black and Cheroneau are the same person. Or both. With Lara under scrutiny by the police, it'll be easier to figure that out."

"Sounds easier said than done."

"There has to be a trail. I'm also hoping that once Gerry calms down, he'll use his hacking skills to help us. With that account, he has Black's real name. From there, I know he can do it."

"It's still a tall order, but it does seem like our only option."

"Tell me if you have a better one, Eddie. You're the expert."

"At covering my tracks, not pointing them at someone else or playing detective." Ed's idea would have been to just kill them both, but if Black was telling the truth about evidence sent to the police in the event of his or Lara's deaths, then he'd have to run again.

And there were so many things worth staying for.

Sam smirking at him was one, close enough that he could feel the contact of their bodies all down the length of him from chest to thigh, with a hint of arousal and promise in Sam's eyes.

"It's late, I'm tired, but before I sleep, I want you," Sam said plainly, "and to only think about you for as long as I can. Tomorrow, once we know how things stand with Lara, we'll move forward. I have ideas for every possible way this can go, but right now, all I need to know is... how do you feel?" He slid his hands from Ed's hips down and around to squeeze his ass.

"G-good," Ed said with a shiver.

"Satiated?"

"I don't... know about that. But I'm not hungry right now for anything but this." Ed gripped the side of Sam's face gently and pulled him in for a kiss.

Sam responded with eagerness, even though Ed's mouth and fangs had been stained in blood only an hour ago. They needed to wash their clothes or incinerate everything in case there were traces remaining, but that could come later.

As they kissed, at first Ed didn't feel any of his true nature stirring, so well fed from earlier, but Sam's hands shucking up his shirt to paw at his abdomen made him rumble a growl. He let Sam tear the shirt over his head, careful not to literally tear Sam's when he returned the favor, and they both went for each other's pants.

Divesting Sam of his clothing, seeing him bare and being bare for him in return, brought out Ed's sharpness after all, eyes glowing and fangs extending. He was too conditioned to separate the two desires, since everyone he'd been with since he was turned had been a vampire and clawing and biting at each other was part of the fun.

With Sam, Ed had to be careful, and that made Sam even more precious to him, something fragile but all his. Not a possession, Sam wasn't just another thing Ed owned to fill up a long life spent mostly alone, but a companion he could imagine wanting to keep.

Gathering Sam in his arms, Ed laid him out on the bed, taking in his lean figure and tanned skin, as well as the warmth and affection in his dark eyes.

Sam touched Ed's brow, and then down to his lips to lightly tap his fangs.

"I'm sorry," Ed said, turning to kiss Sam's fingertips. "I can't seem to hold back around you, but I still want to try this. I won't let myself hurt you."

"I know," Sam said, drawing his thumb across Ed's lips. "Open me up, Eddie. Get me ready for you. Then I have plans for how this can go too."

"Do you?" Ed raised an eyebrow at him.

"Just living up to my job description as your personal assistant."

Ed laughed, and the break in tension helped his face become human again—at least for a little while.

He made sure Sam was comfortably stretched out on the bed as he settled between his legs. While Ed's fangs were retracted, he wanted to get his mouth on Sam and bring him as close to the brink as possible.

Sam's length made his mouth water more than any pulsing neck veins, that human smell of salt and sweat and pheromones assaulting him. He twirled his tongue around Sam's head, humming at the pleasant taste, and sucked him in with his teeth held carefully back.

Sam's hands went straight for Ed's hair, carding through the strawberry locks and tugging as he whined approval. "I won't... last long... if you start like *that*," he mumbled breathlessly.

"Yes, you will." Ed grinned, darting out his tongue once more with a light flick. "Now, can you reach the drawer there?" He nodded at the nightstand.

It was a struggle without scooting away, but Sam managed to open the drawer and slip his hand inside, finding what Ed intended and pulling out a bottle of lube. Usually, Ed tended to himself, but finally, he had a partner.

Tantalizing as it was to imagine Sam wetting Ed's fingers again, he needed to stretch him properly this time. The smooth silkiness of the lube helped warm his otherwise cold skin, and he reveled in Sam's contented sigh at the first press of a finger, while at the same time, Ed sucked Sam's cock back down his throat.

Sam's moan was his reward, but Ed was vigilant to the patterns of Sam's breathing, the tightening of his fingers in the bedding beneath and in Ed's hair, and the tension in his muscles. Ed didn't want Sam to come yet; he wanted him teetering on the edge without being able to topple over it.

Whenever Sam seemed close, Ed tapered off, changing his firm sucking and rhythmic bobs to slow, teasing licks and a blow of air against Sam's skin.

"F-fuck...."

Ed added a second finger.

"Eddie!"

"What are these plans of yours, Sam?" Ed asked, pumping his digits in and out slowly, scissoring every few thrusts.

"I-I want—" Sam whined louder as he hoisted his hips off the bed, presenting himself to Ed that much more wantonly. "—to switch positions so I can ride you. Keep you pinned. I'll ride you so sweetly, Eddie, you'll never want to leave this bed."

Ed grazed a third finger along Sam's rim, gradually letting the tip slip inside until he no longer needed to thrust, because Sam was unabashedly rocking his hips down with constant mewling noises spilling from his throat.

"That sounds lovely," Ed said, meaning the noises and Sam's plan. He ceased his attentions on Sam's cock, feeling his fangs lengthen again with the rise of his arousal. "Yes... I want to grip your thighs while you impale yourself on my cock until your cries fill this room."

"Ngnn," Sam moaned incoherently, dropping his hips down and seizing Ed by the shoulders to throw him onto the mattress, dislodging Ed's fingers as he scrambled to take Ed's place on top. "You need to talk dirty more often," he said and kissed Ed roughly while straddling him, rocking his hips back to tease Ed's tip along his slick and ready hole.

Ed rocked up to meet him, feeling that torturous slide and wet slap. He wanted to fuck Sam, but he wanted Sam to decide when, to guide him in so he knew how much Sam could handle and at what speed. It would be so easy for Ed to lose himself and forget his own strength with how amazing even just this felt with Sam's thighs spread across his hips.

Slowing their kiss, wet and hungry but still careful around his fangs, Ed squeezed Sam's thighs like he'd promised. Sam panted against his mouth, reaching behind to grip Ed's shaft and hold him right where he needed him to be to properly sit back.

Ed broke from Sam's lips with the force of his moan.

Finally. He could feel Sam's tight muscles devouring him, slow but easy from how well he'd stretched him. He wanted to pump upward with abandon but clenched his eyes shut to make his inner beast behave.

When he opened them again, he saw that Sam's were closed, his brow scrunched as he worried his bottom lip with his teeth, chest heaving and looking positively lost in lust as he seated himself on Ed. Then he groaned indulgently and his eyes opened, heavy-lidded with his lips reddened and his cheeks flushed.

Ed wanted to taste the robust rush of Sam's blood more than anything.

No. He had to stay focused—

Sam surged down to kiss him, sending Ed's fractured psyche of man-made-beast into a spiral of conflicting desires, because in that same motion, Sam started to rock, sliding Ed's cock in and out—*in* and out— and then slamming down to the hilt. He found a rhythm quickly, kissing around Ed's fangs without any worry at all.

But he should be worried. He should always be worried, always think of protecting himself, because Ed was a predator first, and it was dangerous to forget that.

Sam's moans came more insistently, mouth turning to the side to pant, puffing warm breath on Ed's cheek. He let their foreheads press together as he rawed himself on Ed in a frenzy.

"I knew you'd feel good, Eddie…."

And Ed knew Sam would taste amazing.

He smelled amazing. Felt amazing, every slick, hot slide of him, muscles clenching on Ed tighter with every thrust. Ed wanted to possess him entirely, to have every part of him as his—*his*. He wanted to claim Sam and take all of him as his own, the true nature of his beast overtaking him, mind reeling with nothing but thoughts of sweat and come and blood—and tearing into Sam to get it.

The primal urges grew stronger, until Ed couldn't stand it anymore when Sam made eye contact, pupils blown, and huffed, "Fuck me, Eddie. I know you got more in you."

Ed was on top again in an instant, having grabbed Sam around the waist and flipped them with such speed that Sam couldn't possibly have processed it. Ed held Sam's hips, tilting him up into his mad thrusts so that only Sam's head touched the mattress.

He slammed into him so hard, Sam shouted, a keen of pleasure that made Ed want to go harder, deeper. Sam's hands flailed up to find some part of Ed to grasp on to, barely dragging up his chest, but as he got higher, Ed snapped down to suck one of Sam's fingers into his mouth and let his fangs scrape the skin.

"*Fuck*, Eddie, I... I...!"

Sam was there, right there without Ed having to touch his cock again, merely thrusting and sucking Sam's finger like he might eat it whole.

Ed was close too, but there was still one thing he wanted, and as much as a part of him screamed, "*No! Stop!*" it was his nature and too easy to nudge that finger from his mouth, knock Sam's arms aside too, and swoop down while still fucking Sam to get at his neck.

He shouldn't need it, he didn't need it, but he still sank his fangs deep into the curve of Sam's throat for a rush of warm blood to flood his tongue.

ED'S FANGS sank into Sam's throat, and at first, it was so unexpected, Sam didn't feel it, only the continued, unrivaled bliss of Ed slamming into his prostate with a force and skill no other lover could match.

But then Sam did feel it—the fangs, the blood draining from him, the *pain*.

"Ed—"

Ed latched on tighter, sucking harder, hips still madly pumping. Sam couldn't speak, couldn't fight at first, too stunned to do more than gasp.

Then, just when he was ready to thrash and try to throw Ed off him, the pain faded. Ed's bite was warm and sharp and dizzying at once, but it didn't hurt. It was almost... nice. And as Sam surrendered to it, still right on the brink, the combined pleasure of Ed's arms around him, his fangs, his cock, finally let him come.

He felt Ed come inside him soon after but was unable to verbalize how amazing it had been because he slipped quickly into a deep... sleep.

"Sam!"

Sam startled awake like he did only after the deadest of slumbers—or after passing out when Mim got too many tequila shots in him.

For a moment he didn't remember where he was or anything that had happened, until he took in the bedroom and slowly recalled his night with Ed.

They'd had sex.

It had been incomparably hot.

Then Ed had bitten him.

Which only made it hotter.

"Thank God," Ed's voice came again, right there at his bedside.

He wasn't in it, though. He wasn't naked anymore either. He was dressed, and the room was brighter, because there was sunshine trying to steal in through the curtains.

"Here, please. You need to eat something." Ed pushed a glass of water and a plate with a very greasy and delicious-looking grilled cheese on top of it.

Sam hadn't realized how starved he was until the smell hit him. He sat up to accept the food, but almost lay right back down when the room spun. He was so hungry. And dizzy. And still really tired. So, before he spoke or gave any word of thanks, he tore into the sandwich.

"Shit," he gasped, after swallowing a large bite and downing a gulp of water. "Guess this is what donating blood feels like." He tried to chuckle, but Ed did not look amused.

He remained crouched by the bedside, as if refusing to get closer. He looked like he was sitting vigil at Sam's funeral instead of offering a much-needed breakfast.

"Hey," Sam said, speaking around his chewing, "I hope I didn't taste that bad to give you such a sour face."

"Don't joke," Ed bit out, sharp and angry, and then immediately looked sorry. "There is nothing to joke about, Sam. I nearly killed you."

"What are you talking about?" Sam set the plate on the mattress. "I call this a win. I was ready to celebrate."

"How can you say that? It must have been so painful, so frightening when I attacked. It was only after I came that I realized...."

Sam moved across the bed and set the water glass on the nightstand so he could take Ed's face in his hands. "Eddie, look at me. Yeah, the worst happened, but you still stopped yourself. Don't you see that? I'm fine. And it didn't hurt."

Ed opened his eyes to gawk at him skeptically.

"Okay, it hurt a little, but only at first. Maybe because you didn't want to hurt me, after the initial sting, it started to feel... good. Honestly, I think it helped me finish." It was then that Sam realized he didn't feel sticky anywhere, which meant Ed had cleaned him and tucked him into bed, worrying over him all night until he woke up. "I'm just sorry I fell asleep right after so I couldn't tell you how amazing it was."

With a small, miserable smile, Ed reached up to place his hand over Sam's. "You're sweet. I can say without embellishment that it was amazing for me too, better than anything I've ever experienced in all my years—until I ruined it.

"We can't keep doing this, Sam. I know you thought it would be okay, that I just needed to ease in and adjust, but look what happened. I can't risk it happening again."

"What are you saying?" Sam knew the grip he had on Ed's cheek and the back of his neck was becoming too desperate and cloying. "We'll figure things out. I'm fine. You didn't hurt me—"

"But I did. And it's too risky to try again." Ed attempted to pull away, but Sam held fast.

"Don't do this. There's an obvious fix, you already know it, and you'd never have to be afraid again." Sam spoke before he'd fully thought about what he was suggesting. They'd danced around it, but he'd never actually asked, and Ed hadn't offered.

"It's not that simple," Ed said.

"Why not? If you want me. If I'm willing. And I *am* willing. I could be like you—"

"No." Ed shook his head, the somber expression he wore tearing at Sam's chest, but not nearly as badly as when Ed pried Sam's hands off, using his superior strength to pull away and stand. "This is why I don't make friends. Why I don't take lovers or get close to anyone. Ever.

"I never thought someone could see me at my worst, at my most brutal, and still look at me the way you do, but the reality is you've only known me for a couple of months. You're young. You can't ask for forever when you haven't even lived one lifetime."

"Says who?" Sam spat, sitting up farther and feeling the room tilt around him. "You weren't that much older than me when you were changed."

"I wasn't given a choice. My maker never meant to me what you do."

"And no one's ever meant to me what you do! Go ahead and think I'm just some dumb kid who doesn't get it, but does that mean my feelings don't matter? Do you think you're not worth someone wanting to be with you forever?"

Ed looked away, shame and anguish washing over his face and making his answer clear.

"Well, I do," Sam said, dropping his feet over the side of the bed, naked still and not caring, because he needed Ed to come back to him. "I've tried not to think about it, okay? To just enjoy what we have, but you're right. Our time together has been the blink of an eye, less for you, I'm sure. That doesn't change how I feel or how much I'd…." He laughed as the phrase came to him. "How much I'd gladly stay in the Underworld if you'd give me the same choice Hades gave Persephone."

Ed's eyes flew back to him. "Sam…."

"You're afraid you'll hurt me again, or that if you make me like you, I'll regret it. And I'm telling you right now that neither of those things is going to happen." He reached for Ed's face again, satisfied that Ed didn't try to escape, and pulled him down for a promising kiss.

"I love you, Eddie," Sam whispered.

A gasp shuddered from Ed's lips, like he'd never believed he would hear Sam say that.

So Sam said it again—"I love you"—and leaned up once more.

The chime of the doorbell stopped Sam a hair's breadth from Ed's lips, and he laughed without humor.

Every time.

Ed pulled away to cross the room and peer out the curtains down to the driveway. "It's Daniel and Black. Your bike's back at the hotel. We could ignore them—"

"We can't." Sam tossed the covers aside to get up. He didn't see his clothes from last night, so he went to the dresser to grab something, impressed that he only teetered a little.

"What are you doing?" Ed raced to his side with a burst of speed, his hands suddenly at Sam's waist and elbow to aid him. "Get back to bed."

"I'm fine. We don't know what they want. You need me to go down there with you, make sure Black isn't about to try something we can't predict. Just help me get dressed, and I'll finish the sandwich on our way downstairs."

The doorbell rang again, signaling their impatience. While Ed still scowled, he helped Sam as quickly as he could so they could answer the call. Sandwich devoured and plate set aside, they arrived in the foyer just as the bell rang a third time.

"Sorry about that." Sam answered the door so Ed could stay in the shadows. "We were still in bed. Everything okay, Detectives?" He smiled genuinely at Daniel and boldly back at Black, whose cold eyes betrayed his fury.

It was nice seeing him mad.

"Cut yourself shaving, Sam?" Daniel asked with a friendly chuckle.

Sam's hand went to his neck. He hadn't thought about the bite marks, but Ed had bandaged the wound. "Perils of going through antiques, I guess. Sometimes you catch yourself on sharp edges. What can I do for you two on a Saturday morning?"

"May we come in, Mr. Coleman?" Black pressed.

"Of course. Ed!" Sam called as he opened the door wider. "It's our detective friends again."

Ed, despite how he might actually be feeling, came in as the perfect host. "Hello again. Does this have anything to do with the news and that bar Sam frequents? We heard there was a body found after I picked him up from the hotel last night."

They should have discussed alibis, but that was as good an explanation as any for why Sam was there without his bike. Lacking footage of Ed getting Sam in his car was better than conflicting footage somewhere else.

"Don't worry, neither of you is under any suspicion," Daniel assured them, while Black's eyes glowed with fierceness around his fake smile. "Logan at the bar confirmed that Sam left well before the murder could have taken place, but we still need to question everyone who was there last night. Anything you can tell us, Sam, about suspicious characters?"

Sam let himself snicker. "It's not the most reputable of places, but the food's good and cheap, and my friend is dating one of the waitresses, so you know how it is. I can't say I noticed anything out of the ordinary. Honestly, the weirdest thing would be Lara, and only because she's only been there a few weeks." A wicked pleasure coursed through him at being able to say all that and not have any of it be a lie.

"Right, we spoke with her. Of course, we can't tell you anything about an ongoing investigation or who might be suspects, but your friend is dating her? Gerry Ziggler?"

Lara must have given them the name, which could mean she was covering her tracks but could also be concerning. "That's him. I'm afraid I don't know Lara very well, though, to offer any insight."

"Logan mentioned Gerry and another friend of yours, Mim? They both work at the mall? We'll likely check in with them later too. I had a feeling you might be here, but can you give me another address to find you all?"

So much for moving hotels.

"Sure," Sam said, and gave the name and room number. "We actually moved last night to have a better rate on long-term stay, since we're all between places right now, and so Gerry could be closer to Lara. Crazy that all this is happening."

"And you weren't with Mr. Coleman until you picked him up after dinner?" Black asked Ed.

"No," Ed said simply.

There wasn't much else to say. It was still all circumstantial and coincidental that death kept happening around Sam and Ed, but Sam wasn't a fool to think that Black calling him *Coleman* every chance he got wasn't without purpose.

"Hey, Daniel, I need to come clean about something," Sam said resolutely. "Ed knows now, and I don't want to lie to you anymore. My name isn't really Coleman."

Daniel looked sincerely shocked—Ed too that Sam was admitting this now, though he did a good job of hiding it—while Black kept a cool, neutral expression.

"I lied to Ed when I applied for this job because I have a record. My real name is Sam Goldman."

"That's fraud," Daniel said in disappointment. "A name might not seem like a big deal, but if you lied about a degree or your criminal record, the state penal code—"

"I know. I swear I only did it to secure this job, and the only person affected was Ed."

"And I have no intention of pressing charges," Ed said. "He's been nothing but stalwart, and this is a private position, after all."

"Yes, it's obvious you enjoy all sorts of private positions," Black said, earning a scowl from Daniel, though there wasn't much to defend since Sam had already admitted he'd slept there last night.

"There won't be any sexual harassment suits either," Sam replied snidely.

"Look"—Daniel tried to mediate—"this isn't exactly a situation where you'd get slapped with a fine, but I'm glad you told me. I may have done a background check on 'Sam Coleman' after we met. I'm a husband and father after all, besides a detective. And I get it, you didn't think you could get a second chance if Ed knew your background. It's a good thing you were upfront about this now, or it could have looked really bad if we found out another way."

"My thinking exactly." Sam nodded at Daniel, and then looked right at Black. "I don't want my mistakes to reflect badly on Ed."

"Don't worry," Daniel said, "I don't see how this could possibly be related to the murders. I will have to run another background check on you, though."

"I'm sure you'll shake your head at my juvi record." Sam hadn't been caught or charged with any of his recent crimes.

"Just misdemeanors, I assume, no assault?"

"Never any violent crimes, I promise." Which was technically true, even if now Sam was an accessory.

"I wouldn't have thought so, but I had to ask. No offense, but neither of you really seems the violent type. We should get going—" Daniel's phone started to ring. "Shoot. It's the precinct. If you have any other questions, Hal, go ahead. I'll just take this. Thanks again, you two."

Once Daniel was out the door, all pretense dropped.

"Lara's fingerprints are in the system," Black said, "under multiple names, but no one is going to find that out. Nice try."

The grilled cheese had helped Sam's dizziness, but seeing Black squirm helped even more. "You let her do all your dirty work, huh? She must be pretty disposable."

Black's eyes burned with how much he was trying to hide his reaction. "This changes nothing. It's time for you to decide who you want this newest murder to point to, because it won't be her.

"Finish the Cramers. *Today*. And no more frame jobs. When it's over, message me." He took out his phone and purposely clicked Send on a ready message that made the phone in Sam's pocket vibrate. "I'll tell you where to meet. Then we end this, and I'll tell you everything I want. Have a nice day, gentlemen," he finished and turned on his heels to slam the door.

They *had* him.

"He's scared." Sam turned to Ed. "But I can't risk him being too scared. Can I ask my friends to come here? It'll make things easier convincing Gerry to help us, and I'd feel better having them close."

"Of course. But Sam…." Ed's voice was soft, drawing Sam's eyes up from his phone as he took it out to send a text, ignoring the message from Black that simply said, *Tonight*. "I know all this takes precedence, but we still need to discuss—"

"No, we don't," Sam said with a frown, broaching no argument, because he knew exactly what Ed wanted to talk about. "There is no discussion. It's just a question. Do you love me or not? That's all that matters." He looked back at his phone to finish the text, mostly to still his anxiety, unsure how Ed would respond.

Ed was silent, but there was an answering text from Mim immediately.

If you're finally going to be honest with us, we're already on our way.

Sam wished she hadn't worded it like that, because there was never going to be a time when he could tell them everything.

Ed still hadn't spoken, so Sam had to look up, but when he did, Ed's head turned, and his eyes went wide.

"Ed—"

"Shh," Ed shushed Sam harshly, craning his ear toward the living room. "Their car's almost down the driveway, but I can hear—" He cut off abruptly, moving lightning fast to guard Sam behind him.

Sam realized several things at once.

They hadn't heard the patio doors because they'd been too focused on Daniel and Black.

There were two people in Ed's home, and neither of them was a detective.

The Cramers both had guns.

"At last we meet, Mr. Simons," Brock said as he crested the corner from the living room, followed by his wife, both prim and pressed yet somehow haggard-looking. "So glad you could send those detectives away so easily, because we need to have this chat in private."

CHAPTER 10

BROCK AND Celia hadn't seen Ed's inhuman flash to Sam's side, but Sam could feel the tension in Ed as he shielded him from the menacing aim of their guns.

Ed wanted to tear them apart, but he shouldn't, he *couldn't*, not when they hadn't planned for this and cops had literally just left the driveway.

"Don't," Sam whispered. "We can use this."

Stepping up beside Ed and seeing the stiffness in him ratchet higher, Sam knew he had to be the one to speak.

"We can have whatever chat you want, but you don't need those." He nodded at the guns.

They would hardly faze Ed, but he'd admitted that enough blood loss could still kill him, and Sam didn't want to learn what it felt like to get shot.

"Oh, I think we do," Celia said, keeping her gun on Ed while Brock stayed focused on Sam, "considering all our friends are dead, and this all started with *you*."

They were squared off across the foyer, Sam and Ed near the main doors and the Cramers poised at the living room entrance.

"Not going to question Shaw, huh?" Brock said before Sam could answer. "She's still only missing, but I'm guessing you can tell us what happened."

"We had nothing to do with that," Sam said.

"*That*," Celia repeated with a clip of the consonant. "Which means you do know what happened."

"And Simons looks like he knows exactly who we are." Brock eyed Ed. "So either he's psychic, or you've been playing triple agent."

Quadruple in some ways.

"Listen—" Sam tried.

"Don't pretend you're not in this together," Celia spat, thrusting her gun forward. "We just want to know who to point these at."

"*Midnight.*"

"Like you're not working with him too."

"I'm not. I just made him think I was, because like you, he was threatening me and my friends," Sam growled.

"As well as pretty rich boy there," Brock said.

"Yes, Ed knows everything I know, but Midnight is the real threat. He just left."

"Those were cops," Celia said with a roll of her eyes.

"Yeah, and he was one of them."

That got the Cramers to drop their guards, glancing warily at each other.

"He pretends to be Detective Harold Cheroneau," Sam went on, "but his real name is Black. I know exactly who Midnight is, and his accomplice. Lara from Lucifer's Rest."

"The waitress?" Brock snapped back to him.

"Where Alverez was killed," Celia added with a sneer.

"Yes. We don't have to be on opposite sides. We can take on Black together," Sam said, because honestly, it was the perfect shift in the plan. If something went wrong, he had more options to place the blame. "Trust me, he won't see that coming."

They still had their guns raised, and while Celia looked contemplative, Brock was less trusting.

He shifted his eyes to Ed. "You're awfully quiet, Mr. Simons."

"You're pointing a gun at me in my home," Ed said evenly. His expression was that cold stillness that always made Sam pause, surprised that someone so sweet could also be ominous.

"Black wants us to kill you," Sam broke in to keep the attention on him, "and to message him when it's done so we can meet. But if we work together, we can set a trap, make it easier for all of us to take him down."

Celia's arm had started to lower, eyes on her husband, who stared at Sam as he considered the offer, and then finally tilted his head.

"So, Midnight, *Black*, is waiting for you to message him that we're dead—" He indicated Sam's cell in his hand that he'd nearly forgotten. "—and then he'll say where to meet him?"

Sam noticed the grins spreading across their faces too late.

"Wait—!"

The guns went off in rapid succession, and Sam's instinct was to shut his eyes, bracing for the pain of Brock's bullets striking his chest, while Celia fired at Ed—only to feel nothing after a breathless beat and open his eyes to see that Ed had moved to cover him.

Arms enveloping Sam like a shield, Ed faced Sam, eyes glowing with a furious vengeance. He pushed Sam backward as he spun and sprang forward, tackling Celia in a blur. Her gun went flying as he tore into her throat, not using any of the care or restraint he'd shown with Sam.

Sam could see the bullet holes in the back of Ed's shirt.

Then he remembered Brock, who was so stunned, he hadn't moved, arm lowered with his gun aimed at the floor as he stared in horror at what Ed was doing to his wife.

Sam dove forward before Brock could recover, grabbing his wrist and twisting it to get him to drop the gun. That was enough for Brock's fight instincts to kick in, and he whipped around, but before he could do more than clumsily grab at Sam's arms, Sam used the momentum of his body against him to launch Brock toward one of the radios. Aiming to pierce Brock's temple with the corner of the table, he slammed him down as hard as he could.

Brock crumpled and lay still, blood quickly pooling beneath his head.

The adrenaline coursing through Sam reminded him of how weak he was, how dizzy, but he fought past the spinning of the room. Ed was watching while he fed from Celia, vigilant to a single perilous moment when Sam might need his aid.

Sam had to roll Brock over to make sure he was taken care of, and when he did, Brock's jacket fell open to reveal a second gun and a knife in his coat.

"You f-fucking… *freaks*…," Brock gasped.

Sam grabbed the knife, hands trembling, but only for a moment.

Brock tried to grab his wrist to stop him, but Sam batted him away. He wasn't letting anyone take what he'd found with Ed.

Not Black.

Not Lara.

And not the Cramers.

"Just die," he snarled and rammed the blade into Brock's chest.

Coughing and sputtering at first, Brock soon stilled—this time for good.

He was dead. Sam had killed him.

Sam had killed someone and had the blood pouring over his hands….

"Sam." Ed's voice startled him, half a growl since he still had Celia on the ground, who wasn't fully gone yet but dazed and immobile in his arms.

"I'm okay," Sam said, thinking maybe he shouldn't be—*okay*; how could he be okay?—but it all kept getting easier.

Ed continued to drink from Celia until her eyes went glassy.

Sam left the knife in Brock's chest, standing and wiping his hands on his pants. They'd have to burn these clothes too. They were going to need another shopping trip.

That morbid thought almost made him smile.

As Ed wiped his mouth, messier than that first night when he killed the man on his patio, Sam didn't know how to ask if he could feed from someone who was already dead, and whether he could store up if he fed from multiple people in short order.

"Do you want... umm... I mean, *can* you...?" He gestured meekly at Brock.

"I'll drink what I'm able. I heal quickly," he said, leaving Celia and showing off the holes in his shirt, but while there had been blood, it wasn't flowing anymore and there didn't appear to be wounds, "but I need more to replenish the energy it takes. Better to feed as much as I can."

"Waste not, want not," Sam said with a grimace. "Sorry."

"Are you okay?" Ed pressed.

"Yeah. Really. More than I thought I'd be. Because you saved me," Sam said with a smile, dead bodies at their feet be damned. "Again."

"You didn't do so bad yourself." Ed smiled in kind.

There was an energy between them, like the wrong sides of connecting magnets; they wanted to touch, to kiss, to hold each other and comfort each other, but the blood staining them kept them at a distance. Even standing apart, though, there was a warmth in that energy too.

Sam didn't want to watch Ed feed again, since he began doing so much slower with Brock, being in the safety of his own home with no additional threats, but there was no point in cleaning up when they still needed to get rid of the bodies and follow the trail of the Cramers to make sure no one had seen them arrive. Everything was a mess all over again, and Sam wasn't sure how to fix it.

"What... the hell?"

Sam's head snapped to the living room entrance—where Mim and Gerry now stood.

They must have seen the patio doors open and decided to come in from there instead of the front. Because Sam had called them, told them to come here, and too much time had passed while they dealt with the Cramers.

Who were dead. And Ed was lapping the blood from Brock's chest.

A growl rumbled up from him, eyes flashing, as Mim and Gerry, terrified-looking and choosing flight over fight, backed up into the living room and turned to run. They bolted back to where they'd come from, and Sam hurried after to stop them.

"Wait!"

Ed reached the doors first, just suddenly there to block their escape, like a movie monster come to life.

Gerry screamed and grabbed on to Mim, who clutched right back at him, both backpedaling and running into Sam.

"It's okay!"

They spun and honestly looked like they wanted to get away from him as much as Ed.

"He won't hurt you," Sam tried, hands outstretched and placating.

But when they looked over their shoulders at Ed, he hadn't dropped his vampire face.

Why hadn't he dropped that face?

"Eddie," Sam said in concern.

But Ed kept looking at *them.*

"They're not a threat!" He hurried around Mim and Gerry to get in front of them. "They're my friends. They'll listen to me."

Ed's stance remained taut like a springboard ready to snap—

"You *promised.*"

The light flickered from his eyes, fading to green again, and his fangs vanished. "I… I'm sorry. You're right. I promised to protect you all, and I will."

Sam breathed relief. It had just been a stressful, unprecedented morning. He knew Ed hadn't meant it.

"The *fuck?*" Mim cried, less quick to be understanding. "What the fuck, Sam?"

"This is why I couldn't tell you everything." He turned back to them. "I didn't want to ever tell you if I didn't have to, but we didn't know the Cramers were going to ambush us."

"He's a vampire…." Gerry remained wide-eyed, staring at Ed, still clutching Mim's arm. "He's a fucking vampire!"

Sam knew things were bad if Gerry was cursing. "He's on our side. He's was just being defensive, mostly because of me. He'd never hurt me. Or you."

Mim kept her hold on Gerry to comfort him, but when her gaze landed on the side of Sam's neck, she reached out furiously to rip the bandage from his bite marks. Gerry's eyes went wider as he saw them too.

"You stay away from us!" Mim roared, pushing Gerry into Sam's arms so fast, he hardly registered her storming around him and whipping the bandage at Ed's face. "And you stay away from Sam!"

Letting the bandage strike him and fall, Ed flinched and backed away.

"I don't care if you can do to us what you did to them, to Alverez and who knows who else! I won't have you using Sam like a fucking juice box!"

"Mim!" Sam called. "That's not what this is!"

"Like hell it isn't!"

"He's tried pushing me away. He's just as afraid of using me or hurting me, but that is not what this is." Sam left Gerry and stalked forward, not to Mim, but right to Ed, who stood in front of the patio doors that were still open with too much sun coming in. "I love you, Eddie. Tell me you don't love me."

"Sam...." Ed flinched again, refusing to look at him, so Sam reached for his face and made him turn his head, not caring that Ed's cheek was smeared with blood.

"I love you," he said again.

Ed's eyes looked so soft as he pressed into Sam's touch. "I love you too, but she's right. I'm just a danger to you."

"I don't care," Sam said stubbornly, clinging to the flutters in his chest at hearing Ed say the words finally, but if they were going to argue about this again, he didn't want to do it in front of Mim and Gerry. "You're worth it, worth all of this, and I won't let you think otherwise. Now," he said as he pulled away to stare down his friends, "we're going to clean up this mess and figure out our next move."

THEIR NEXT move....

The next move should be for Ed to run and make up for all the heartache he'd caused Sam, but he couldn't let Sam sort through this alone.

Ed didn't know what to say, finally meeting Mim and Gerry under the worst of circumstances and having acted so deplorably, so he offered to handle the bodies.

"Don't dispose of them," Sam said. "Just put them in the basement and wrap them up in a way that you can easily transport later."

Ed didn't ask why, just nodded and did as he was told. It should have been a strange phenomenon, at least where it came to getting rid of bodies, but not when the orders came from Sam.

Sam said he'd take care of most of the cleaning if Mim and Gerry went out to look for the Cramers' vehicle and figure out how they'd gotten there without the cops noticing. Sam trusted them to leave and come back.

By the time Ed had finished in the basement, having cleaned himself, changed, and put his dirtied clothes in the incinerator, Mim and Gerry had indeed returned and were arguing heatedly with Sam in the foyer.

"Sammy—"

"I don't want to hear it. All that matters is that the Cramers' vehicle isn't visible."

"Yeah," Mim huffed, while Ed stayed hidden on the second-floor landing to listen. "Totally out of sight in a little off-road spot in the woods. I only knew where to look because I saw Celia's heel prints outside the fence. No one else would ever notice."

"Good. We'll take care of that later."

"Sam—" she tried again.

"Not now."

"He's a monster," Gerry hissed. "You're covering up murder for a monster!"

Ed shrank inward, understanding their concerns, because they were warranted.

"He only feeds from bad people," Sam defended. "Is it really that different from what we've always done?"

"We never killed anyone," Mim said.

"I'm the one who killed Brock. I caused the head wound and stabbed him before Ed ever touched him. Am I a monster too?"

"That's different," she bit out quietly.

"Why?"

"It was self-defense!"

"And it's survival for Ed! What's the difference if it's bad people?"

Mim and Gerry didn't say anything at first, and Ed snuck closer to risk a glance over the banister. Sam was almost finished ridding the foyer of any traces of what had happened; tile was much easier to clean than carpeting, like on that first night when Ed made Sam clean the living room.

He'd been so angry and flustered and unsure of how to respond that night, half certain Sam would turn on him the second he had a chance.

Sam had had plenty of chances, but he hadn't betrayed Ed yet.

"You want to be like him," Mim said finally, quietly again, as if she hardly believed it. "We just found out vampires are real, and you want to become one?"

"The first night I saw Eddie change," Sam said, "when I found out what he was, I was scared. I didn't think I could handle all this. But I can. I have been. It doesn't feel like a heavy price to pay when it means I get to be with him."

"But he bit you," Gerry said with a shudder.

"That was an accident."

"That doesn't make it better," Mim snapped. "God, you sound like a textbook battered spouse case—"

"That isn't what this is." Sam raised his voice enough to echo up the high ceiling. "If I become like him, it won't matter."

"What about us?" Gerry asked.

"What about you? Nothing has to change."

"If you become some creature of the night," Mim said with a sneer, "I think a few things are going to change. *Shit*. Must be some pretty impressive sex."

Sam snorted. "It is, but that's not why I want this. I love being with him. We look at the stars and tell stories and balance each other out in ways no one else ever has for me. He thinks I'm too young and that this is too new for me to know what I'm asking. I disagree. Have you ever known me to be certain about something and change my mind?"

"Yeah," Mim threw back. "This fucking job."

That made Sam snicker again. "In the beginning, but now I'm glad, because this job led me to him."

"Um...," Gerry said suddenly, pointing warily upward—at *Ed*.

"S-sorry!" Ed shrank inward again, before realizing how pointless that was now and moving to descend the stairs. "Bad habits."

"It's okay," Sam said, smiling. "You didn't hear anything I didn't want you to."

Ed felt that warmth fill him like nothing else ever had in all his years with cold skin and an empty heart. It had been easy to give in to Sam, and it would be just as easy again, but one of them had to be practical. "I can't commit to an answer about what you want from me. I need time to think. I want us to be done with this burden I've put on you first."

"Okay." Sam nodded, however somber. "That's fair. But it's our burden, not just yours."

"And I promise you—" Ed looked at the others. "—I will stop at nothing to protect Sam *and* you. I didn't mean to scare you before. I just... don't trust easily. Sam means a great deal to me. I do love him. Very much."

Mim didn't say anything.

Gerry still looked terrified but said, "C-cool. I-I mean... if you really wanted to kill us, I guess you could have done that by now, so... I'll try to believe you. Sam doesn't trust easily either."

Stilted as that may have been, it meant so much hearing it from Sam's friend.

"Whatever," Mim said with less attempt at pleasantness. "But if I ever see any reason to think you're more bad news for Sam than good, I don't care how all-powerful or freaky you are. I will kick your ass and make you regret it."

"Understood," Ed said with a nod, thinking there was something in Mim's fair form with her raging fierceness beneath the petite package that reminded him of Hypatia. "What now?" He returned to Sam.

"Now I change and clean up, and you make sure I didn't miss any evidence. Then we tell Mim and Gerry everything."

So they did. Gerry was clearly heartbroken to hear more about Lara's exploits, but he didn't raise his voice to deny it anymore.

"If she could lie to me that easily... then yeah, I'll help. I'd already been researching Black after I got his name. Now I know better what to look for."

Gerry had his laptop in a bag he'd been carrying over his shoulder, so much like an extra limb that Ed hadn't noticed. He set it up on the coffee table to begin working, with Sam helping by recounting everything he knew.

They'd decided to wait to handle the Cramers' car until after it was dark, so all Ed could do was stand around and wait, and Mim was much the same.

Until she passed Ed a swift once-over and said, "How about a tour?"

"Uh-um…."

Sam and Gerry silently eyed them, putting Ed on the spot.

"Of course! It would be my pleasure." He hastily gestured her back toward the foyer.

It really was just a tour at first. Ed showed her the kitchen and garage, led her upstairs to the sitting room and library, explaining the basement below, which she didn't press to see, and finally ended at the master bedroom and hallway leading to the widow's walk.

"You mean the roof? I want to see."

"Certainly." Ed pulled down the ladder for her.

"You too."

"Oh, I… don't go up there."

"Why not?"

"I don't like heights, and while not everything you may have heard about vampires is true, the sun does bother me."

"Badly or just makes you uncomfortable and weak?"

"The latter."

"Then you're coming with me." She shot him a challenging stare and started to climb.

Ed honestly didn't know how to refuse her, so with a breath to steal himself, he squinted and gritted his teeth against the surge of panic at being up there without his sunglasses or the comforting presence of Sam.

The sun was still beautiful to him, but it hurt to look at, even in his periphery, and the heat felt like the worst of summer days in the dry desert.

Mim didn't say anything initially, merely looked out at the view. She'd obviously been giving Ed—and everything that had been going on—a lot of thought.

"This is crazy," she said at last, not looking at him. "You're a vampire. A real fucking vampire, who I saw gorging himself on Brock Cramer's chest cavity. And you're just as hopelessly in love with my best friend as he is with you."

She looked at him, a sideways slide of her eyes.

"I have no idea what the right answer is, but if all this comes down to Sam's safety over his happiness, I'd rather see him alive. So you better think real carefully about what happens next."

There she was, with Ed in a vulnerable spot, once again threatening him, someone she couldn't possibly defend against if he chose to attack, and she didn't so much as stutter.

Ed had to admire that.

"I promise I will put Sam's best interests first. Always. He's lucky to have you."

"I know." She gave a light flip of her hair. "You know, for a vicious killer, you're not what I expected. I think I get why Sammy likes you."

"Oh?"

"He was always a sucker for contradictions."

MIM WAS full of contradictions—and there was no way in hell she only wanted a tour.

Sam was trying to assist Gerry, but his attention kept being pulled to his surroundings, looking to see if Ed and Mim had returned yet. She was probably giving him a shovel talk. She never gave *Lara* a shovel talk.

But then, she hadn't known either of them were killers until today.

Just when Sam was going to excuse himself to go look for them, they appeared, saying they were going to gather snacks.

"For *us*," Mim reiterated, and turned to Ed with a lightness she hadn't displayed before. "No snacking on the humans, got it?" She patted his shoulder, and he blushed faintly as he scurried to follow her to the kitchen.

Sam couldn't believe how much that eased him, despite the work ahead.

Well, mostly ahead of Gerry, who was fixated on his laptop, but quietly, which wasn't like him. How else should he act, though, when he'd just seen what Sam was pretty sure were his first dead bodies, a classic movie monster in 3D, and all while learning that his girlfriend was the bad guy.

"Gerr?"

"Mm?"

"I'm sorry about Lara."

The clicking of the keyboard stopped, and Gerry took a slow breath. "Me too. You're dating a vampire, and I'm dating a lying sociopath, apparently. Good times." He chuckled, but Sam could see the strain in his shoulders. "I mean, I'm happy for you if you're happy, even though this is all really, really weird. But I'm more… sad? Because my killer love interest didn't turn out to be so nice."

"I wish I could have told you."

"I get why you didn't. I probably would have thought you were nuts." Gerry opened his mouth to say more but held back before he asked, "Did you really kill Brock?"

"Yeah."

"And Simons… Ed… he killed the others?"

"Yes, except Shaw, who Black or Lara killed. Brock was my first."

"And you're really okay with all that?"

It should have been a tougher question to answer, but when Sam thought about it, he only had one thing to say. "They tried to shoot us. All these people we've killed have tried to hurt us first. And Ed only goes after the worst of the worst. I kind of can't help being okay with it."

Gerry nodded, not like *he* was okay with it, but like he could accept that answer. "He's sort of like a vigilante, huh?" He leaned into Sam's side with a small smile and then turned back to his computer. "Oh, whoa."

"What?" Mim asked before Sam could, returning with Ed from the kitchen.

"Lara is Black's daughter."

"*What*?" Mim growled more fervently, but Sam and Ed just looked at each other.

Marie and Daniel assumed Black had kids because of how he acted around the twins. It made sense. He did have a kid. She was just an adult.

"The records got buried when she changed her last name," Gerry said, "but the trail's still there. She's Lara *Black*. Her mother died when she was eight. The year it happened is when Black first started showing up with a record, then other aliases, and finally, whispers of Midnight."

"He snapped when he lost his wife," Sam said.

"And raised his daughter to be a psycho," Mim added harshly, plopping down beside Gerry and digging into the provisions they'd brought. Then she paused. "Sorry."

Gerry shrugged.

"Maybe the mom was killed by a vampire," Sam suggested. "That would explain why they're so obsessed."

"I'll keep digging." Gerry dove back into his work.

"What about when it's time for you to see Black?" Mim asked. "Is that what the bodies are for, to prove to him you killed them?"

"If he presses, sure," Sam said, "but we need damning evidence to put him and Lara away. Those bodies might come in handy."

"What if he just kills you as soon as you show up? Or plans a sting to finish framing you?"

"He's not done with us yet. He wants information on other vampires so he can keep stealing from them."

"Sam," Ed called softly, making Sam finally realize that while he and his friends had taken up the sofa, Ed stood off to the side.

And Sam did not like his expression.

"It may still come down to killing them. If that happens and all the evidence against me is too much, I'll have to run. I've done it before."

"What?" Sam pushed to his feet and went to him. "Run? Without me?"

"I don't want to, but I might have to."

"You can't. This could just as easily get pinned on me. We don't know what Black has planned if things go south. The only way to beat out potential evidence against us is by making sure the evidence against them is solid. You can't kill them."

"After everything they've done to you…," Ed bit out, eyes flashing yellow in anger.

"I know," Sam said, grabbing Ed by the back of the neck to pull him close, "but we can make this work. Black will still pay. Trust me, it'll be worse sending a cop to prison."

Ed laughed weakly but relaxed against him. "I suppose you're right."

"I am. And you are not running, even if the worst happens. Not without me. Promise me you won't."

He hesitated a few too many anxious heartbeats before he whispered, "I promise."

"*God*, you two are unbearable," Mim groaned, causing Sam to laugh. "Either get a room or get to work, because no one is ready to face Black yet."

They weren't, and the next few hours were filled with more of the same—research, eating when they thought of it, and trying to make sure they hadn't missed anything important before they messaged Black to meet.

As the day wore on, Sam thought he'd asked Gerry a thousand times for the same update.

"What about proof that Black is Cheroneau?"

"I'm sorry, Sam, I just don't know. I can't find anything. He couldn't have done this for so long, especially transferring to different precincts, if he wasn't good at covering his tracks. I don't think I can find what you need in time."

"It's getting late," Mim noted.

"And I just heard Daniel's car," Ed said from the patio archway, having opened the doors again to let in the cool air as the sun set. "He must be home. Black will be expecting us soon."

"Daniel…," Sam repeated, and then leaped to his feet. "We have Daniel! I forgot about Daniel! We can use Daniel!"

"What are you talking about?" Ed frowned.

"You mean the cop?" Mim questioned.

"Yes! It's a risk, but I think I have an idea."

"What?" Gerry asked.

"I'm going to go confess."

ED COULD hardly believe they were at the Neu-Ryans, and Sam was confessing to Daniel… that he'd found Shaw's body in his hotel room.

He lied a little too, tweaking the timing for when Black was there, and saying that Black was the one who'd cleaned up the body afterward. Then he admitted that Black was Cheroneau and explained that he'd been too afraid to come forward, until Cheroneau was in Ed's house that morning and threatened them when Daniel stepped outside.

It was mostly the truth, which Sam confessed wholeheartedly, and Ed could tell that while Daniel was skeptical, sitting with them in his living room, he wasn't dismissive.

"I knew Cheroneau was bad news," Marie said from the doorway.

She'd taken the kids upstairs to bed but had obviously snuck back down.

"Sorry," she said when Daniel shot her a sharp look.

He sighed like he wasn't surprised, but it was clear he didn't know how to handle the situation.

"I know this sounds crazy," Sam said, "but I need very little from you to prove that Cheroneau is trying to frame us."

Since there was no hiding anything from Marie anymore, she came in and took one of the chairs as Daniel paused to digest everything.

"You're saying that my partner has been framing you for murder for weeks, months almost, threatening you, all to get Ed's money? Yeah, it sounds crazy. But you have my attention. What do you need to prove your case?"

Sam explained, and Ed was truly impressed by the final plan. If everything went well, they'd have Black for sure, Lara too, but Daniel had to agree to let them handle things on their own until they called him.

He did, gave Sam what he asked for, promised he'd be ready for their call, and they went back to the house.

All Sam had to do then was send Black the message that the Cramers were dead, which Ed read over his shoulder.

It's done. We're at the Cramers' hideout in the warehouse district. You can come to us.

After all, Ed could get them there in minutes.

Fine, but no tricks.

Wouldn't dream of it.

"Mim, Gerry," Sam said, "you stay here."

"Um, no," Mim protested. "We're—"

"Staying here," Sam said more firmly. "I need you to take care of their car. You might not be used to dumping bodies, but we've all dumped cars before."

That was an interesting tidbit to learn, but Ed supposed carjacking was a fairly common act for a thief.

"We can join after," Gerry said, surprising Ed, since he didn't seem the type to be up for a fight.

"No," Sam affirmed. "There are too many unknowns. I'll call you when it's over. Ed and I will be fine."

Ed wished he could be as certain. He didn't worry for his own safety, but Sam was still weak, still recovering from the blood loss last night, much as he tried not to show it. If anything went wrong....

"Ready?" Sam turned to him.

Ed wanted this over with so he could look at Sam and thoughtfully decide what was best for their future without the weight of being surrounded by enemies.

"Yes," he said. "I'm ready."

SAM WASN'T sure if *he* was ready, but there was nothing left to do but enact the final stage of the plan.

Ed brought Sam and the bodies to the warehouse well before Lara and Black arrived. There was no sign of anyone else, least of all the young man from before, and they didn't try to hide the bodies since they'd already implied the kills had happened there. They merely sprawled them out, made the place look like a fight had occurred with a few overturned chairs and clutter, and waited.

As Sam had hoped, Lara and Black arrived together.

"You took your time," Sam said, standing close beside Ed.

Lara was dressed simply compared to her father's nice suit and trench coat, and while she always looked pretty and put together, there was an air of exasperation about her, like she hadn't gotten the best of sleep lately—just like the Cramers.

Being questioned for murder probably hadn't sat well with her.

"We're not idiots," Black said, and as they drew closer, Sam saw the resemblance between them now, mostly in the twists of their smiles. "We walked around the back first to make sure you didn't have an ambush planned."

"Couldn't help but notice that dear sweet Gerry and your other friend weren't at their hotel today," Lara said. "You understand our concern."

"They're not here," Sam answered easily, since it was true. "It's just us. Just you. And *them*." He indicated the bodies.

"Nicely done." Black acknowledged the act as if genuinely impressed. "Joint effort, maybe? It finally really is just us, but I don't want you trying anything stupid, so let's make a little exchange before we continue.

"You come over here—" He motioned Sam toward him. "—and Lara will go by Mr. Simons. You know, just to keep things friendly."

Sam didn't like that, but it did seem fair if Lara was swapping with him.

Ed didn't like it either, given his knitted brow and wary glance, but Sam nodded anyway.

"As long as we move at the same time," he said.

Sam gave a goodwill gesture by stepping forward first, and Lara followed, each of them moving slowly but in time until they crossed paths without incident and had switched positions.

"Good boy," Black said. "You really can take direction, can't you?"

Ed's fists clenched in Sam's defense, but Sam refrained from doing the same and crossed his arms instead.

"We know what you want. Why you killed all those people to frame Ed, everyone who worked on his house, Shaw, and who knows how many others."

"Do you now?"

"Money. More of it. You think Ed can give you names and addresses of others like him to be your next victims. That's why you haven't tried to kill us yet."

The expression on Black's face didn't change, other than a slight raise of his brow and a subtle nod. "Smart, makes sense, and up until you two, Mr. *Goldman*, that would have been the right answer. But we've squirreled away plenty of funds from our past victims. We don't need any more names or addresses. It's time to end this."

End it? "Then what do you want?"

"We'll get there. First, we need to even the playing field."

"What—"

"Ah!" A cry from Ed startled Sam to look back at him, where he'd fallen to one knee with a crossbow bolt the length of someone's forearm sticking through his left thigh.

Not someone's.

Lara's.

She grinned as she lifted her sleeve to reveal a hidden device strapped to her arm, enough of a surprise to bring Ed down, but a wound like that couldn't possibly—

The lights in the warehouse went out, and in their place came glaring blue, intense and painful to look at. But however painful it seemed to Sam at first, the lights were only an annoyance. To Ed, who started panting, his body falling farther forward rather than recovering and ripping the bolt free, those lights were agonizing.

"UV," Black said, nonchalant and smug. "The sun you can withstand for a time, but direct UV works quicker. And hurts more, doesn't it?"

Sam jerked as if to run to Ed, but Lara raised her arm at him, threatening that she had another bolt ready. He couldn't see through the blue haze around them if Ed's skin was already turning red, but his mewling gasps made that old joke about imploding seem far less funny.

"We never would have agreed to meet somewhere we hadn't already secured. How do you think we survived this long taking out others like Simons?

"Now...." Black coaxed Sam closer, even though they were already only a foot apart.

Sam didn't want to give him the satisfaction of moving, so all he did was stand firm.

And then flinched when a bang echoed around the warehouse and the worst pain he'd ever felt spread throughout his stomach.

He gasped, barely able to believe it as he looked below his crossed arms to see the blood beginning to pool, and then looked up at Black and saw the gun he'd had hidden in his jacket. They were the idiots....

"Sam!" Ed roared, but Black stepped forward and brought the gun less than an inch from Sam's temple, keeping it there even as Sam too staggered to his knees.

"Ah, ah, ah," Black warned Ed. "At this range and in your state, you can't beat a bullet to the head. Had to catch you by surprise, I'm afraid, but all this is necessary to make sure you're agreeable.

"See, I thought framing you would be enough, but this is better incentive, because you're all soft on Sammy here, so I know you'll want to save him. Don't worry, stomach shots take a long time to kill someone. He'll survive if you cooperate quick enough."

"What do you want?" Ed demanded, a wild force of fury even in his hunched position, though the pain was so awful for Sam, he could hardly focus on him.

Black's voice came dimly but still audible as he said, "You're going to turn me and my daughter into one of you."

CHAPTER 11

MAYBE, IF Ed hadn't fed from Sam the night before, the sudden blood loss from the bullet wound wouldn't so immediately have him seeing stars. He'd eaten, had almost twenty-four hours to recover, but it wasn't enough, not when he was going from one life-threatening event to another.

He should have guessed the Blacks would want immortality more than money. Right now, he did too.

Sam had to stay conscious. No matter what happened, he couldn't let himself pass out.

Or he might not wake up.

"You're insane," Ed growled across the space separating them, his face changed now so that his eyes glowed bright and fierce, and his fangs glinted in the blue light.

Lara didn't look concerned.

And neither did Black.

"I'm not denying that," he said with a grin, the gun still aimed barely an inch from Sam's temple, "but be that as it may, you're going to obey my request or Sam is going to die. Tick *tock*." He fingered the trigger.

"There isn't time!" Ed lamented, finally tearing the bolt free but nearly collapsing afterward, the UV light clearly slowing his ability to heal.

Sam kept his left hand on his own bleeding wound but was quick to press the right to his chest before sliding it down to join the other.

"I've never sired anyone. I could kill your daughter by accident."

"Then you better be especially careful, because if I worry for her safety for even a second…." Black tapped the side of Sam's head with the gun.

Sam swayed. He needed to lie down. The room was spinning, and it hurt so badly, but he kept up on his knees. The only anchor he found was Ed, who looked twice as far away.

Sam had to get Black on his level. They could still do this.

"Turn her. Now."

"Don't...." Sam croaked, clutching Black's pant leg and pulling on his trench coat weakly.

Black kicked him away, and Sam sprawled out on the floor, but Black never left enough space between him and the gun for Ed to try intervening. That meant that as he leaned over Sam, his trench coat swayed beside him.

"Don't do it, Eddie," Sam said, clutching and pulling at Black but eventually crumpling. "Don't listen to him... please."

"He'll listen," Black said, "unless he wants to watch you die and slowly burn himself."

No. They had him. They just needed to call Daniel!

"I...." Ed was going to cave. It was clear in his voice, even though his face remained fierce, that Black was right; Ed could be better manipulated by using Sam than any plot to frame him. "I'll try. But please... at least help Sam stop the bleeding."

"Eddie, no...." Sam pressed both hands more tightly to his stomach, but the rush of pain made his vision erupt with fireworks. They didn't need to give in. There was no coming back from that if they did. They had no guarantees Black would bow out once it was over, and if he and Lara were vampires too, they'd never be able to bring them to justice.

"I'll help once you've finished with Lara. Not before," Black said.

No. Ed couldn't give these bastards immortality! Not them.

But dimly from where Sam lay on his back, he could see Ed stagger to his feet. Lara removed her jacket, showing that she had three additional bolts readied on her arm, and tilted her head to let her hair fall to the side.

"St-stop...." Sam tried one last time, seeing the hazy figure of Ed lean closer to her neck....

"Wow, am I glad you said, 'get rid of the car' and not the guns."

Sam snapped his attention toward Mim at the entrance, recognizing her voice more than able to see her, but he was certain that the taller blob beside her was Gerry, and they both had arms raised, aiming what must have been Brock and Celia's guns.

MIM AND Gerry were there, aiming the Cramers' guns at the Blacks— Mim at Lara and Gerry at her father.

"Sam!" Gerry cried, taking in the scene.

Because Sam wasn't simply down, he was shot, and already weak as he bled out onto the floor.

Ed made to lunge at Lara, but Black yelled a warning, "Stop!"

In the instant that Ed hesitated, afraid of Black's finger on the trigger with the muzzle so close to Sam's head, Lara aimed her bolts at Mim. It was the worst kind of standoff, with Ed weakened and utterly unable to offer aid.

"Where did you come from?" Lara spat. "Hiding somewhere we couldn't see?"

"Just arrived," Mim said. "Might have speeded a little to get here."

"You didn't dump the Cramers' car?" Sam sputtered.

"We did. Then we borrowed Ed's. Now—" Mim stalked forward without a single tremor in her arm. "—I think we've got you outnumbered. So, drop the weapons."

"You'd have to get off some pretty lucky shots," Black said, remaining too close to Sam for Ed to make any move against him, "and Gerry doesn't look that steady. *You* drop the weapons, and we'll continue where we left off."

"Lara." Gerry kept his aim on Black, but his eyes went to her. "Please. You think you need to do this because he's your dad, but you don't. It's not worth all this. Didn't what we shared mean anything to you?"

Ed couldn't see Lara's expression, but he doubted it held more than pity.

"You're sweet," she said, maybe even sincere about that much, "but you're not worth more than living forever."

"Your w-wife...." Sam gasped from the floor, speaking over Gerry's heartbroken silence. He looked so pale to Ed now, even in the blue light, eyes heavy-lidded, the hands on his stomach barely able to stem the bleeding. "Do you think... she'd want this?"

"You just know everything, don't you?" Black gave a derisive chuckle. "My wife died because the human body is weak, and if she'd had a way out of that, she would have taken it, and she'd want me to take it too. I spent twenty years looking for a way my daughter and I could escape the same fate. Imagine my surprise when I discovered vampires were an option.

"I'm sure others attempted to hunt them over the millennia, just like in the movies, and I'm sure most of those idiots ended up dead, because they were hunting monsters. We're hunting opportunity."

"Then why not force the hand of the first vampire you defeated?" Ed asked, thinking of all those he'd tried to contact but couldn't reach.

"We were going to, and then we found out there were more of you. Why take one fortune while we still had the advantage of daylight, when we could have twenty."

"Lara." Gerry kept ignoring Black. "Please."

"Enough talking!" Black barked. "Turn her. Now."

"You won't shoot," Mim said with more confidence than Ed felt. "Sam's your only bargaining chip."

"You sure? Because I guarantee you, if you give me no other choice, I am going to end this by making you all suffer." Sam's head lolled, and Black pressed the muzzle to his forehead to lift it back up. "Starting with him. Or maybe someone else. Shoot Gerry so they know we're serious."

Lara startled at the order. Ed saw it in the tension that gripped her shoulders, but still, she shifted her aim to Gerry, and hopeless fool that he was, he lowered his gun.

"I love you," he said.

To his credit, her arm sagged as if she *almost* would have dropped it.

"That's a shame," she said.

And fired.

Ed flinched. He never flinched, but he also never stood idly by. He didn't dare move to anyone's defense, though, not when Black held Sam hostage, and not when he feared that one burst of speed was all he had left.

Mim wasn't as toothless. A toss of her gun and a mad dash forward and she caught Lara by the wrist in time to shift her aim from Gerry's chest to his shoulder. Gerry grunted at the impact of the bolt and staggered back.

Watching the ensuing struggle between equally diminutive but powerful women, Ed cast a wary glance at Black, who stood at the ready but kept his aim on Sam.

Every inch one of the women gave up, they soon reclaimed, back and forth, and back and forth again, but in the end, one had to prove stronger.

Mim wrapped her hand around Lara's wrist to wrench her arm up and point the remaining two bolts at Lara's head. "*Now*," she said loudly, tugging her counterpart against her, "I'm going to count to three, because I'm guessing you care more about your daughter than killing Sam. Although you did just tell her to shoot her boyfriend."

She spared a peek at Gerry. Despite his grimace, the wound looked superficial.

"One." She carried through on her threat. "Two—"

"Stop!" Black bellowed, making an unthinking lurch forward.

Which was all the opening Ed needed.

Summoning what strength he had left, he bolted forward and everything around him slowed. He saw the moment when Black realized the folly of his mistake, trying to whip the gun back on Sam, but Ed was faster and seized Black's arm to move it safely away just as it went off, the bullet missing Sam to strike the floor.

The most satisfying rush of blood hit Ed's tongue when he sank his fangs into Black's throat.

"Don't!" Sam cried. "You can't… kill him, Eddie. We got him… we got what we need. *Call Daniel.*"

Black was a useless doll in Ed's arms, held securely with no chance at escape. Ed wanted to drain him. He wanted it to hurt. He wanted Black to suffer like he'd tried to make them suffer. And the blood felt so good, countering the pain of the wound in his thigh and the UV lights still burning above him.

Looking back at the others, Ed saw that Mim had snapped the remaining bolts and thrown Lara to the ground, while Gerry shuffled over, holding his shoulder, and Lara stared on in dread at Ed drinking from her father.

"Please," Sam said again, so pale, so weak, but still thinking of the plan. "Call Daniel. Then… you can… stay with me. *Please….*"

Ed tore his fangs from Black's throat, making sure to break the skin to hide the punctures. He threw Black down, kicking the fallen gun out of reach, and rummaged quickly through Black's pockets. A small device with only a single switch proved all it took to disarm the trap they'd sprung, and the overhead lights returned to blessed yellow.

Feeling instant relief, furthered by the fresh blood coursing through him, Ed dropped beside Sam. "Get your gun on Black *now*," he ordered Gerry, who instantly if clumsily obeyed, "and call the detective." He tossed his phone at Mim, figuring she'd be more likely to catch it, and she did. Then he gathered Sam close to assess the damage.

Sam's shirt and hands were covered in blood, and so much had soaked into the floor.

The smell of it made Ed dizzy.

"Y-you don't... l-look too crispy," Sam stammered. His skin felt clammy and cold. "Y-you're gonna... s-save me, right?"

"Of course." Ed started to lift him.

"Y-you'll... change me...? You'll save me?"

"Sam...."

"You have to. It's the only... w-way. Please...."

After everything they'd been through, Ed had never seen Sam look so scared.

"Don't let me die."

"I won't," Ed said, stroking Sam's face as he held him closer. "No matter what. I promise."

Sam gave a crooked, weak smile, and then his eyes closed.

THE LAST thing Sam remembered was his eyes closing.

He figured he'd wake up and everything would feel better. There'd be no pain. He'd feel whole and strong as a vampire, and he and Ed could be together always.

But when he finally opened his eyes again, everything hurt.

It was too bright. He thought maybe because the sun was glaring at him now that he was changed, but when he looked around and his surroundings began to take shape, he wasn't outside. He wasn't in the warehouse. He wasn't back at Ed's.

He was in a hospital room.

"Mr. Sam!"

Only then did Sam notice the others with him. The twins, Marie and Daniel, Mim, Gerry with his shoulder bandaged, and—there—Ed, standing apart from the others in the corner.

The twins tried to rush Sam's bed, but Marie held them back.

"Remember what we said," she cautioned. "The nurse only allowed you two in here if you promised to be gentle with Sam. Just say hi. No pouncing."

This was clearly a foreign concept to them, but they listened, walking up more slowly to Sam's bedside.

"We're glad you're awake, Mr. Sam," Dawn said.

"Does it hurt lots?" Joey asked.

Sam was still coming to full consciousness, and he could tell from the IV attached to him that it probably hurt a lot more than he was feeling, so he said, "It does… but I'm pretty tough. I'll be okay. Right?" He looked at the others, Ed last, who was still holding back, like he thought Sam would be angry with him.

He was surprised, truly amazed that he'd survived without the supernatural help he expected, but it was hard to be angry.

"You're going to be fine. The nurse could tell you were going to wake up soon," Daniel said, "so she let the kids come in, but we'll get them out of your hair. We just wanted to be here after you woke up from surgery."

Surgery? No wonder everything hurt.

"You're a hero, Sam. You and Ed went way above and beyond as civilians to bring Cheroneau in—I mean *Black*. I can't believe we almost lost you over that psycho."

"You got everything you needed?" Sam asked.

"Oh yeah. You started the recording on that wire I gave you at the perfect time. We got Black's whole confession. Though it cut out after he shot you. The last thing he said seemed really weird. Something about… Ed making him and his daughter 'like him.' Do you have any idea what he was talking about?"

Even shot and in so much pain, Sam had been sure to press against the wire to turn it off before any actual talk of vampires could be recorded. "No idea. He was definitely off his rocker."

"No denying that," Daniel said. "When I got to the warehouse with backup, Ed had already left with you for the hospital. Black tried to spin things against you and your friends, but Ed had left the recording for me. And besides, once we patted Black down, we found a knife in his trench coat that was clearly the murder weapon used on Brock Cramer, and maybe his wife.

"He tried denying it was his, but he basically fell apart from there. Once he realized we had his confession on tape, he owned up to the rest. His daughter too. You did our job for us." Daniel gently squeezed Sam's shoulder. "Ever think of changing careers?"

Sam would have laughed if he wasn't so sore. "I'm happy where I am, thanks."

It was daylight, he saw through a slit in the curtains. Sam had no idea how long he'd been asleep recovering from surgery, but definitely all through the night.

"We'll give you some breathing room and let you have time with your friends," Marie said, coming forward to kiss Sam's forehead, very motherly and appreciated, before she ushered the kids outside. "We're glad you're okay, Sam."

"Goodbye, Mr. Sam!" the kids chorused.

Daniel followed with an added, "I'll have to get your official statement eventually, but don't worry about anything. The Blacks can't hurt you anymore."

To think, only a few weeks ago, Sam had been worried about the Cramers.

Mim and Gerry still wore the same clothes from last night and didn't look like they'd gotten any sleep.

"The bodies were already there, and the wire was a really smart plan," Mim recounted, coming in close so she could perch on the side of the bed, while Gerry did the same on the other, "but how did you plant the knife on Black? You were dying!"

Sam thought back to just after he'd been shot, when he got close enough to slip the knife into Black's pocket with some classic misdirection. "Magic," he said with a twirl of his fingers.

Mim and Gerry chuckled.

"Shouldn't you be laid up too?" Sam asked, nodding at Gerry's shoulder.

]Sam's entire middle ached, along with a few various bruises around his body and a general throbbing in his head. Glancing at Ed, still so removed and distant, sitting in the corner, didn't make any of it feel better. "I might need an increase myself," he said, holding eye contact.

"We'll tell the nurse." Mim took the hint, contrary to Gerry's pout at being dismissed. "She'll want to check you over but said we could have a few minutes once you woke up. Why don't you two talk?" She cast Ed a gauging—and possibly threatening—look. "We'll get her."

"You're both okay, though?" Sam asked as they rose from the bed.

"We're not the ones who had surgery," Gerry reminded him.

"I'm sorry you got caught up in this, but I'm glad you showed up when you did and didn't listen to me."

"Please." Mim lightly tapped his shoulder. "You can always count on us to ignore you when you're trying to order us around."

Sam huffed a faint laugh, but his eyes went to Gerry and his weary, although brave, expression. "I am really sorry about Lara."

"I'd hoped she might change her mind, ya know? But I'm glad, with her in jail now, that I don't have any doubts about where we stood. I still got you guys. And I'll always be grateful for that." Gerry turned to look at Ed as he said it, but the answering smile Ed offered held far too much sorrow and guilt.

They left then, leaving nothing between Sam and Ed but space.

Sam wished he wasn't so tired. He could probably sleep for a week, but there were more important things to worry about, even if he had nearly found his way to the river Styx.

"I thought you were going to...." Sam couldn't finish the thought. He'd truly believed he'd wake up like Ed, that circumstance had made his argument for him, and Ed had been left with no choice.

"I know," Ed said quietly, not approaching, even with the others gone, "but I couldn't. After all this, I... I need to move on, Sam, find another city."

"What?" Sam's gut clenched from more than any bullet wound. "But we won. Everything's okay now."

"Too much attention has been brought on me—"

"We have a cop on our side. Daniel loves you. You heard him. We're heroes!"

"Your friends were the heroes. You're a hero. And you were nearly a martyr."

"I love you," Sam said stubbornly, feeling as foolish as it had sounded when Gerry said it to Lara, but that didn't change how he felt.

Ed looked away from him.

"If you need a new city, what about with me and my friends?"

"Sam—"

"Please." Sam could feel tears rising with the flood of bile in his throat. "You can't leave. We never even had our date."

That dropped Ed's guard enough for a smile to crack his face.

"I can give you a preview," Sam said, trying not to sound too desperate. "It wasn't going to be just some rehash of the date that never happened. Let me tell you about it."

Ed hesitated, but with slow steps, he finally moved toward the bed.

"I was going to take you to some of my favorite spots in the city and appeal to your inner geek."

Ed's smile cracked wider.

"There's this great comic shop downtown. I'd let you have one—but only one. I'm still responsible for your finances."

A chuckle escaped Ed. He sat too near the end of the bed, but at least he sat.

"There's a club nearby with great views of the city. They have nothing but cover bands playing '70s rock, like the best playlist on your tricked-out radio. You could bring your camera and take photos, even some of me. Especially of me.

"We'd go back to the house after, and you could take more photos, any way you want me, as naughty as you would never be able to ask for without stuttering."

Ed blushed but chuckled again, and when Sam held out his hand, Ed timidly took it.

"Then we'd go to the roof, where I'd already have the telescope set up, and this time, I'd point out constellations to you, and when I failed miserably, you'd laugh and tell me how wrong I was."

Ed's smile was so beautiful, but sad, like his mind wasn't being changed, and he'd get up any minute and vanish, as soon as Sam stopped talking.

So he didn't stop.

"We'd fool around and make love, and you wouldn't hurt me."

"Sam—"

"I promise—"

"That sounds lovely. Truly, it does. I wish we could have done all that."

"We will," Sam insisted. "The story doesn't end here."

Looking at Sam sorrowfully, Ed pulled his hand away.

"It's written in the stars," Sam rushed on, grasping for anything to keep him. "It was written in the Heavens, the other gods would say, whenever mortals asked about Hades and Persephone and all the ages they'd spent together."

Ed looked back at him with a start.

"'How do they make it work?' the mortals would press. And some gods would answer, 'Because they're both death.' 'Because they're forces of nature.' A few still thought one had tricked the other and that they had nothing in common but lies.

"But the real answers could only come from Hades and Persephone themselves. Hades worried sometimes that the whispers were right, that they were too dissimilar, and that Persephone only stayed out of obligation. So, one day he asked if she'd ever regretted her decision to become his queen.

"And she said, 'No. Not a single moment, even those spent in darkness, because they were with you.'"

Ed's eyes had grown damp, and he heaved a heavy sigh. "I still think *you're* Hades."

Sam laughed. "Me too. But the metaphor worked better the other way."

There was Ed's smile again, almost bright enough to overcome its sorrows, but not quite. "We can't do this forever, Sam."

"We could, though. Forever."

"What if you don't really want that?"

"Don't I get to decide what I want?"

"Not right now." Ed sighed again and slid from the bed. "You need rest. But I won't leave town yet. I promise."

Yet—the best and worst word at once.

Sam was terrified when Ed excused himself from the room that, despite his promise, he'd never return, but he did. He was there almost every day that Sam was in the hospital, only absent when he traveled across the country to see his sire's lawyer, and even then, he returned in record time.

He'd arrive as soon as he could when visiting hours began and stay until they reminded him that it was time to leave. He returned sometimes at night too, sneaking inside, staying in the shadows when the nurses checked on Sam, but he never stayed too late, since he'd say again that Sam needed rest.

Sam did. He'd survived major blood loss, followed by more major blood loss and a gut wound.

The others were there nearly as often—Mim, Gerry, the Neu-Ryans, with and without the twins. Sam appreciated all of them, but it was Ed's presence that relaxed him and kept him calm.

Ed would bring Sam books and comics, read to him from them, read from the newspaper, particularly their horoscopes each day or anything pertaining to the Blacks—the serial killers of Riverside. Ed didn't need to eat or rest, so he never needed to step away, and even though sometimes Sam would drift off while Ed was with him, he was always there when Sam woke up.

Sam spent three weeks, almost a month recovering from surgery. He was lucky to not have any lasting damage to vital organs, but he'd still have to use a cane for a while and would need to take things very slowly.

The day of his release, he told his friends that he just wanted Ed there to bring him home. *Home*, which he didn't need to explain, because they all knew what he meant.

It was daylight when he started to check out, but still, he expected Ed to be there.

When Ed didn't show, he started to panic.

He called him, but there was no answer. He waited half an hour past the time he'd said he was being released, but still, Ed didn't come. Sam almost called the others to check on him, but that felt too much like defeat, made it all feel too real that Ed might have....

Sam couldn't face the thought, so he called a Lyft and had it bring him to Ed's house.

He didn't bother knocking on the paneling of the wrought-iron doors or trying to peer in through the glass. It was always dark inside and impossible to see anyway, so he pushed through the door, knowing it wouldn't be locked, and the stillness of the entryway struck him like a blow.

It was empty.

"No...." Sam dropped his cane as he shuffled inside and whirled around.

There were no tables or radios in the foyer, nothing but the square-shaped sections on the floor where there was no dust because something had been there once, but it was gone now.

Gone.

"No!" Sam let his voice ricochet up to the ceiling. "Eddie! *Eddie!*"

"Why are you yelling?"

Sam spun to face the stairs—where Ed was descending from the second floor.

"Did I lose track of the time? Oh goodness, what did I do with my phone? Am I late?"

"You… you son of a bitch…." Sam's breath hitched, and he threw himself forward the second Ed reached the foyer. "I thought you left."

"Why on earth would you think that?" Ed held him tightly.

"Everything's gone!"

"No, it isn't. I was cleaning. See?" Ed kept one arm around Sam as he led him to the living room, proving that the missing tables and radios were right there past the archway. "I was just looking for the mop."

"The mop's in the kitchen," Sam deadpanned.

"Is it?"

"You were… cleaning?"

"Well," Ed said with a sunny, unfair smile, "I haven't had you here to help me."

"I HAVEN'T had you here to help me," Ed said, pulling Sam back toward him, but before he could gather him in his arms again, Sam pushed him away and smacked him in the chest.

"I thought you were gone!" he bellowed, striking him again and again. "I thought you were gone…." And then he buried his face against Ed's chest like before.

This was entirely Ed's fault for neglecting the time. He'd just wanted the house to be nice for Sam, and the foyer had been last on his list.

"Not without you," he said, petting Sam's head and squeezing him close. "I'm so sorry. I guess I'm still hopeless without you around to take care of me and keep track of my schedule."

"Then you're staying?" Sam sniffled.

"I've had weeks to think about this, about us, and I finally decided." Ed nudged Sam to pull away from him so they could look each other in the eyes. "I'm staying. But I won't turn you. Not right away. I still think you deserve more time as a human to be sure I'm what you want. Then, when enough time has passed, if your mind hasn't changed, we'll see."

"I am never going to change my mind." Sam wrapped his arms around Ed possessively.

"I hope not." Ed brushed his knuckles down Sam's cheek. "But I want you to be sure. I've been alive a long time, and while I've never felt this way about anyone before, it's unfair to let you make such a big decision when you've barely lived. When the time is right, if you still want me forever, then that's what I'll give you."

As Ed started to lean in, Sam surged forward first to meet him, ravenously igniting their first kiss since Sam had been admitted to the hospital. They'd stolen a few small, chaste kisses in greeting and goodbye, but that could never compare to this.

To Sam's lips and tongue and hands clinging.

Ed wrapped him up in his arms tighter and kissed him that much deeper, their bodies molding together flush. Eventually, when they paused for Sam to catch his breath, at last Ed could see that the panic and threat of tears in Sam's eyes had been banished.

"No matter what happens next or where we go, I will always need to feed," he reminded him.

"I know. The Cramers weren't the only scum in this city. A little vigilante justice could be fun."

"I still want us to be careful." And Ed didn't only mean with hunting habits.

"Very careful." Sam paused but only loosened his hold on Ed slightly. "Who did you feed from while I was in the hospital?"

"Do you really want to know?"

"We're partners now. We're in this together. I need to know."

Ed carefully extracted himself from Sam's fervent clinging so he could retrieve the cane from where it had fallen by the door. He led Sam to the sofa in the living room and sat with him, leaning the cane against the coffee table.

"You remember I was gone a few days to see that lawyer about my sire's estate?"

"You killed the *lawyer*?"

"No." Ed wrinkled his nose at the idea. "Lawyer or no, he seemed like a nice enough man. But there were a few unsavory characters sniffing around what remained of my sire's belongings. He had some enemies of his own, it seems. Nothing like Black. I just... helped clean things up."

"Did he leave you anything interesting?"

"A few nostalgic odds and ends. Actually, there's something I'd like you to have," Ed said, rising to retrieve it from the nearby chest with his favorite comic books.

This was something different, though. He'd only tucked it into the chest so he could present it as a gift without Sam finding it first.

"Do you know much Norse mythology?" He handed Sam the tome, quite ancient and beautifully illustrated.

For a moment Sam simply stared at it, and then carefully opened it to page through a few stories. It wasn't in English, but he didn't seem to mind. He ran a hand over a few of the drawings, eventually closing the book and setting it on the coffee table.

"I can read it to you," Ed said, afraid Sam didn't like it after all. "I know the language and—"

Sam flew forward to tackle Ed against the cushions, knocking him back and nearly climbing on top of him. He hissed, since he was in no shape to be so reckless, but simply continued kissing Ed and better situated himself to get his hands on him.

"D-does that mean you like it?" Ed sputtered a laugh amid the assault.

"I love it," Sam said. "I love *you*. I was so terrified you'd run away and left me without saying goodbye."

"I am so sorry for that. I promise I'll never be late for something so important again."

"You better not be," Sam chided, but he was smiling, and he kissed Ed lightly on the lips, hand tugging at Ed's tucked-in shirt to pull it free. "But right now… you're going to make love to me. It's been agony missing you all these weeks."

"M-missing me?" Ed trembled at the implications—and Sam's hand sliding up his stomach. "I saw you every day!"

"Seeing and experiencing are not the same thing."

"Sam, you know how I feel about—"

"We'll be careful. I had another thought about that, actually."

Ed sighed in frustration. He appreciated Sam's active libido— his had certainly never diminished over the centuries, even if he didn't always get an outlet—but the last time they were intimate….

"I think it's just a matter of switching things up," Sam said.

"Switching?"

SWITCHING AFFORDED Sam a lovely view, because Ed had a marvelous backside, and right now it was presented before him as a gorgeous curve, while Ed had his face pressed to the mattress, hips lifted and legs spread for Sam's enjoyment.

Sam took his time running his hands over Ed's ass before he reached for the lube.

"I-I would have been okay if… if this was what you preferred from the beginning," Ed said with a raggedness to his voice, though Sam had barely touched him yet.

"Not preferred. I like both positions. Do you?" Sam asked, rubbing his first wet digit down between Ed's cheeks.

"*Yes*." Ed shuddered. "It had just been so long for me, I… I-I didn't know if you'd… w-want…." He moaned when Sam breached him finally with a slow push inside.

"What I want is you, Eddie. There are no more enemies. We have all the time in the world to explore new ideas and… positions."

"Y-you're sure it's… not too much strain for you?"

"I'll manage."

Sam had wanted to stand with Ed poised on the end of the bed, but he wasn't sure he could hold that position, up on his feet for so long. It was hard enough being slow and careful when he used so many stomach muscles for this, but he'd promised he'd let Ed know if he needed a break.

It just meant he'd have to be extra slow once they got going, and he took his time now. In. Out. In a little deeper. *Out*.

"Y-you really think this will work?" Ed squirmed at another slow curl inside him.

"It's harder for you to bite me in this position."

"B-but if I somehow still hurt you again…."

"You won't." Sam added the tip of a second finger, not surprised that Ed opened easily, ever resilient. His cool skin was marvelous to touch, inside and out.

"You always say that—"

"You *won't*. Believe it, Eddie. Believe in your control. I do." Sam leaned forward to slide his free hand up Ed's back and around to his mouth, seeking his lips to have him suck on his fingers, even though he could already feel fangs.

Ed was careful with the twirl of his tongue and light scrape of teeth. "I won't hurt you," he said, ending with a kiss to Sam's palm.

Sam reclaimed his hand to press it to Ed's lower back, bracing himself as he thrust his fingers deeper and faster inside him.

"S-Sam…." Ed moaned again with a broken cry.

Almost three now; Sam was certain Ed could take it, but he still went slowly, letting the third digit scissor in with the others at a gradual pace.

"I-I'd... forgotten what this felt like." Ed flailed back to grip the wrist of the hand Sam had working inside him. "Please, Sam. Fuck me now. I need to feel your length inside me."

Sam was blindsided every time Ed talked dirty. "As slow and sweet as you fucked me."

Though that had turned out pretty wild, and Sam wasn't sure if he could manage *that* the other way around, but he'd try his best—without the violent ending.

After coating himself with the lube, he pressed gently forward, just a light nudge to let Ed know he was there, before he began to push inside.

A growl rumbled up from Ed, and his hands clawed the sheets. Sam marveled like so many times before that he could reduce this powerful being to whimpers and a loss of control so profound there was an honest risk to his life.

But *no*, no, he didn't believe for a second that Ed would ever go too far. Ed just needed to trust himself the way Sam trusted him.

"You're so good to me, Eddie. So good.... And I will always be good to you."

Sam sheathed himself to the hilt with a puff of contented breath, wrapping one arm around Ed's waist while the other held his shoulder. Every tightening of his stomach muscles made his healing wound ache, but the pace he began was perfect, slow and sweet like he'd promised, until there was no pain at all.

Ed's whimpers rose louder than any growls, and he arched back to meet Sam's thrusts without trying to go faster. Deeper, yes—so deep—but never once did he hurry their pace. He panted and tore at the sheets, and there were a few times when Sam wondered if he might roar and spin around after all, ending this like last time, but it never happened. Ed rocked back with hard slams and let his moans get buried in the bedding, but he always, *always* calmed when it seemed like he might lose himself.

"Are you with me, Eddie?" Sam asked, hastening his pace now. "Is it good for you?"

"Mrrrmm... yesss... but slower, Sam... slow...," he murmured. "I like it when you fuck me slow."

Sam laughed in delirious delight as he complied. He could make this last for as long as possible. He'd known it would only take practice and a few varied positions for Ed to hold the beast at bay. Even at his most terrifying, Ed was always worth trusting, because Sam knew from experience that nothing was as simple as it seemed.

NOTHING WAS as it seemed.

Not Ed.

Not Sam.

Not anything about the two of them together.

Except *this*. Except making love in Ed's bed—that was as it should be, because Ed didn't fear anymore that he'd lose himself.

It wasn't the position—though that helped focus him on something other than the pulse of Sam's blood and how delicious it would taste. Like this, he couldn't bite Sam without dislodging him and flipping them, and it made Ed believe that maybe, the more they "practiced" in any position, the more he'd be able to give himself over to Sam fully without fearing he'd harm him.

The slow slide of Sam's length inside him was so good. Maybe that was part of it too, letting Sam slow him down, when with other vampires, they'd often give in to their powers, their supernatural strength and speed, and break the bed. That wasn't always better. With Sam, Ed could rediscover the sweet side to lovemaking and draw out every moment.

"Still want to go slow?" Sam whispered, pulling back at an agonizing pace.

"Y-yes, but… a little faster now… please…?"

"Maybe I should return the favor."

"What—" Ed cut off with a gasp that dropped into a low moan as Sam bit him at the juncture of his neck and shoulder. Nothing fierce, not enough to break the skin, but that faint sharpness sent a shiver through Ed's body that melted him into the mattress.

Each new thrust of Sam's that pressed deeper and slid inside him that much faster, made a heat build within him that almost—*almost*—made him wish he had something to bite.

Ed shoved a fold of the sheet into his mouth and let himself tear into it.

"I'm there, Eddie… right there…."

Ed was too, and Sam knew it, reaching around to grasp him firm and stroke, stroke, *stroke*, faster and tighter, until—*fuck*—Ed was done, beating Sam by several seconds with an all-over quiver. After they were both panting and still, he spat the sheet from his mouth and could barely imagine moving.

It was Sam, slipping away smoothly and returning to clean Ed, who eventually rolled him over to lay out on the bed. Ed knew he still wore his vampire face, but Sam looked at him adoringly anyway.

"Hang on, my phone keeps buzzing." Sam offered a short peck to Ed's lips before disappearing off the side of the bed to dig through their clothes.

"Everything all right?" Ed asked, still breathless but able to banish his fangs.

"Mim and Gerry want to make sure you picked me up okay."

"Please don't tell them I failed."

Sam sat, grinning at his screen. He was breathtaking to look at, not at all lessened by bandages or scars. "And risk Mim's reaction? No worries there. I'll tell them we'll be out of bed in a week or so, and then they can come over."

Ed snickered.

"Except I also have a note from the Neu-Ryans, wondering if we want to come over for dinner tonight to celebrate my return."

"Urg…. You know the problem with having friends? I have to share you."

Sam laughed.

"But the amazing thing is…." Ed reached out, and Sam tossed the phone aside to grasp his hand and climbed back onto the bed. "I like that too. Even though it worries me."

"Worries you?"

Pausing to pull Sam close, Ed kissed the side of his head. In a thousand years, he'd never held something so precious to him. "If you want it, someday I'll turn you. But we can't turn everyone in our lives."

"I know," Sam said softly. "You're worried about how hard it will be when we have to leave them, or when they leave us simply because we can't stop time. Well, quit it. Quit focusing on the bad. Think about how wonderful it is to have them in our lives now. That's the part you've forgotten over the years when you thought you had to keep people at a distance. ''Tis better to have loved and lost,'" he quoted with a smirk.

"As long as I never lose you," Ed said, stroking Sam's face and pulling him in for a harder, bruising kiss. "You are very wise for someone so young."

"That's why you hired me. Which we should talk about, because if I'm going to be moving in…." Sam raised his eyebrows but didn't wait for Ed to counter him.

Ed wouldn't have. He couldn't imagine Sam living anywhere else.

"You cleaning is going to become a regular thing."

Ed snorted. "May I make a request, then?"

"I suppose."

"I'd like to replace the photograph over the safe."

"With what?"

It was important to say this next part without a single stutter. "Something scandalous of you that can only ever be hung in the bedroom."

EPILOGUE

BEING A couple with Ed was never a chore.

Not after Sam discovered Ed was a vampire.

Not after they had enemies in their midst.

Not after those enemies were defeated.

And not now, so many years later.

It was high time they moved to a new city. Sam had always thought it would be nice, a change of pace from Riverside, and he did like it, but he wasn't as used to migration as Ed and needed time to adjust.

Walking hand in hand through the city streets beneath a bright full moon helped. So did having an entire evening to themselves.

Of course, Sam should have expected that they'd be interrupted. With the aid of modern technology, they often were, but when his phone buzzed, he still looked to see who it was, while keeping his other hand clasped with Ed's.

"Marie and Daniel are wondering about next weekend. Can you believe the twins are graduating from college already?"

"Certainly not," Ed said. "Contrary to what you might think, time passing quickly does still surprise me. So much can change in twenty years."

"Even your fashion sense," Sam ribbed him.

Ed bumped his shoulder in rebuttal, though he did still break out a bow tie on occasion. "Will Mim and Gerry be there?"

"That's the plan. It's been a while since we were all together." Mim and Gerry had eventually gotten to know the Neu-Ryans too. It was inevitable after they all sat vigil at Sam's bedside.

"You know," Ed said, pulling Sam closer against him, "eventually they might start to notice—"

"You robbing the cradle there, pops?" a foreign voice said.

Sam froze and felt Ed tense beside him. It was still strange and a little funny that these days people were talking to *Sam* when they said that.

"Wallet and any other valuables, now," their "attacker" demanded, faceless except for the sneer beneath his hood as he crept from the shadows, carrying no remorse in his voice or slack in the hold on his gun. "Better hurry. I've killed for less with fags like you."

Sam smiled. He did so like when they made it easy.

Ed asked him sometimes if he wished he'd turned him while he was younger. But honestly, Sam liked the hint of silver in his hair, and he liked even more how much Ed liked it.

"I suppose I am robbing the cradle a little," Ed said, making the mugger frown in confusion, "but age has never been an issue for us. Would you like this one?" He tilted his head at Sam.

"I can start, but you know I prefer it when we share."

"Aren't you afraid of my darkness, dear?" Ed said with a smile.

"No," Sam answered in kind. "You haven't seen mine yet."

"*Hey*," the mugger called, since they ignored him to share a kiss.

Sam let himself enjoy the press of Ed's lips, and then he turned, freeing his eyes to glow and his fangs to extend, as he sprang—

"The *fuck?*"

—to sink his teeth into his prey's neck and drink.

AMANDA MEUWISSEN is a bisexual author, with a primary focus on M/M romance, and works in marketing for the software company Outsell. She has a Bachelor of Arts in a personally designed Creative Writing major from St. Olaf College, and is an avid consumer of fiction through film, prose, and video games. As author of the paranormal romance trilogy *The Incubus Saga* and several other titles, including many with Dreamspinner Press, Amanda regularly attends local comic conventions for fun and to meet with fans, where she will often be seen in costume as one of her favorite fictional characters. She lives in Minneapolis, Minnesota, with her husband, John, and their cat, Helga, and can be found at www.amandameuwissen.com.

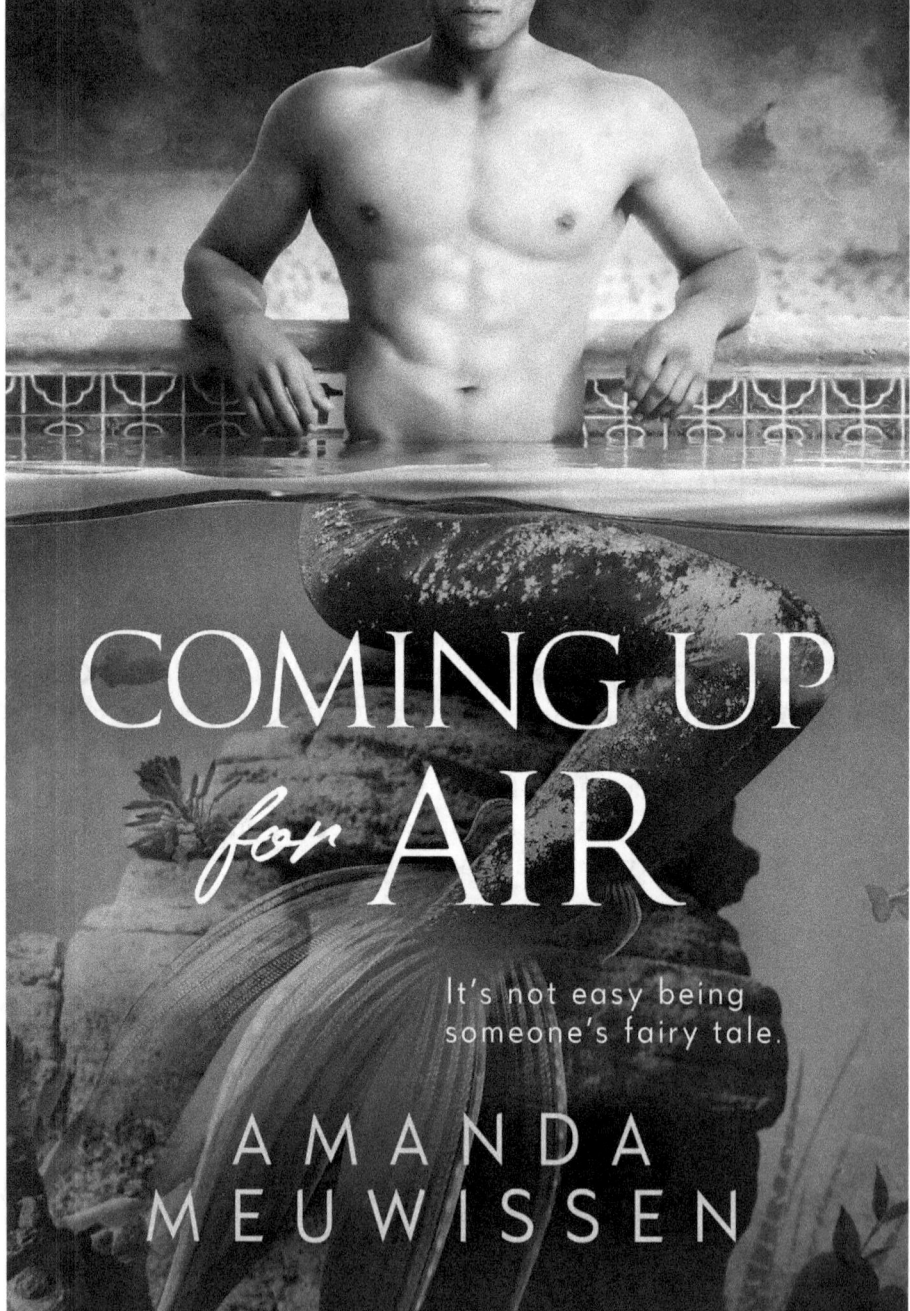

COMING UP for AIR

It's not easy being
someone's fairy tale.

AMANDA
MEUWISSEN

It's not easy being someone's fairy tale.

Leigh Hurley is making a name for himself among thieves and criminals, even if it isn't the life he would've chosen. He shouldn't have screwed over the Moretti brothers, though. It landed him in the river with weights on his feet. But somehow he's escaped certain death. The last thing he remembers before waking on the riverbank is a beautiful face and a soft kiss.

Then, Tolomeo turns up naked at Leigh's apartment.

Tolly comes from a race of killers—merfolk who drown humans for fun. But Tolly is different, and when he sees a human in trouble, he offers a kiss, granting the man the ability to breathe underwater… and himself the ability to walk on land, at least until the next full moon. The ancient laws state that if he is given a vow of love by the one he kissed, he will be able to keep his legs. If not, he will be put to death when he returns to the water.

But love is not something Leigh offers easily… and Tolly has a secret of his own.

www.dreampsinnerpress.com

DREAMSPUN
DESIRES

INTERPRETIVE
HEARTS

Amanda Meuwissen

Love is easy once you learn the steps.

Love is easy once you learn the steps.

In the competitive world of dance, Teddy was a flawless performer and hardass choreographer who students feared and admired in equal measure. But hip surgery ended the glamour and drama, and now Teddy is recovering at his beach house, lost and listless.

Until he meets Finn, his neighbor, who is too perfect, gorgeous, and kind to exist—but very ill timed. In a seaside town as small as theirs, they can't avoid each other, especially since Finn is also Teddy's new physical therapist. But Teddy isn't the man he used to be, and though Finn flirts shamelessly with him, Teddy can't believe a has-been dancer is worthy of someone so young and full of life.

Finn's sunny smile is also hiding heartache. Pursuing Teddy challenges both his professionalism and his self-preservation, but if he can convince Teddy to trust him, maybe they both can heal.

www.dreamspinnerpress.com

A MODEL ESCORT

Amanda Meuwissen

What's the value of love?

What's the value of love?

Shy data scientist Owen Quinn is brilliant at predictive models but clueless at romance. Fortunately, a new career allows him to start over hundreds of miles from the ex he would rather forget. But the opportunity might go to waste since this isn't the kind of problem he knows how to solve. The truth is, he's terrible at making the first move and wishes a connection didn't have to revolve around sex.

Cal Mercer works for the Nick of Time Escort Service. He's picky about his clients and has never accepted a regular who is looking for companionship over sex—but can the right client change his mind? And can real feelings develop while money is changing hands? Owen and Cal might get to the root of their true feelings... if their pasts don't interfere.

www.dreamspinnerpress.com